Dancers in the Dark

IN THE DARKNESS OF HER SKIN, SHE FOUND LIGHT

EJAZ AHAMED

Vitasta

Published by
Renu Kaul Verma
Vitasta Publishing Pvt Ltd
2/15, Ansari Road, Daryaganj
New Delhi - 110 002
info@vitastapublishing.com

ISBN: 978-81-960413-6-6

First Edition 2023
MRP ₹ 450

Edited by Shailaja Nair
Typeset by Somesh Kumar Mishra
Printed at Chaman Enterprises, New Delhi

To

those who are seen and not heard,
to those heard and not seen,
and to those who feel invisible.
To my darling baby Cookie
and to Mummy.

CONTENTS

Chapter 1

That summer, a sense of fervour gripped the village of Kilipur and its residents. It wasn't the heat or the lack of rain. It wasn't the pockmarked main road or the crumbling bus stop which people knew would be fixed when the next election campaign came around, only to be undone by the next monsoon. It was the news that the villagers wished for with every fibre of their being – that this year's annual festival would be graced by *Talaivar* (leader), not just a film star but a superstar. Reincarnation of god himself. The people named him Talaivar because he never broke a promise – at least not in his movies.

The pothole-ridden roads were filled and restored way before the usual time. The local members of the Legislative Assembly had to think of something else to fix to gain votes. Maybe repairing the crumbling bus-stops or fixing the bubbling sewage in the storm drains during the rainy season that eventually found its way into the main water supply. When it did, the pungent odour fought for airspace with the smell of cracked mustard seeds and sizzling curry leaves from the nearby eateries.

The morning of the festival, a cloud of dust enveloped the village in a murky brown haze through which the morning sunshine struggled through. The sweepers wielded their brooms briskly, conjuring up eddies of dust along the side of the road. New saplings were planted in the median. Garbage was loaded onto a cart and dumped behind a wall, well hidden from the main road. Rats rejoiced at not having to travel far for scraps. Rubble from the perpetually under-construction buildings were removed. Streetlights were fixed, garlands of light were strung around the poles and trees that lined both sides of the main road. Beggars were evicted from their usual spots and promised meals for the entire day if they stayed out of sight.

Talaivar's posters lined the main road, greeting every passing vehicle with his hands pressed together. A cocky grin accentuated his black sunglasses. With a cigar in one hand, he blew rings of smoke into the air. He was ready with his signature strut, prepared to walk into the lives of ordinary citizens to provide a rags-to-riches hope that if he could do it, so could they.

Children daydreamed more than usual at school that day. They all wanted to catch a glimpse of the star. Even the cane-wielding teachers could not bring them back to reality. Realising that teaching the students anything today was like whispering knowledge to the dead, the principal sent them home early. The students hurried home with the school satchels whipping against their bums, doing what the teachers couldn't: watch *Talaivar's* movies at home. For the entire week, TV channels broadcast only *Talaivar's* movies. After all, it was his 50th birthday.

Away from the village's hectic preparations to welcome the film star, in a dusty corner electronics shop called Sekar's Electric Repair, where dead appliances came to get a new though short lease of life, two siblings tried to turn on an old TV. They tried moving the antenna. They removed and inserted the wires several times. They even tried hitting it on the side in a bid to get it to flicker back to life.

'I told you not to do that. It's not your father's TV,' Sekar, the shop-owner, yelled at Karthi. 'Tap gently! Like this.' He gave a noiseless tap against his workbench.

'If you had done your job properly, the TV wouldn't need these extra slaps and hits to turn on,' Karthi said, pointing to the broken TVs and VCRs stacked on top of each other, gathering dust.

'Sekar, you deserve this, you idiot! Sekar, you so deserve being talked to like that by a 10-year-old boy.' Sekar grumbled to himself while soldering circuit boards.

'Look, it's coming on!' Kalki screamed at her brother, Karthi. 'Stop moving the TV.' The TV crackled with images for a moment before the white noise engulfed it. 'Do whatever you did before,' she added.

Karthi slapped the TV once more, making sure that Sekar was hidden behind the welding fumes.

'That's it!' Kalki sat down in front of the TV along with her brother.

On the screen, *Talaivar* tossed a cigarette in the air and caught it between his lips before lighting it with a revolver and blowing a circle of smoke towards the camera. He would flip his sunglasses a complete 180 degrees at lightning speed before slowly putting them on as inspirational music soared in the background. The flip of the hair with his hands was enough to make the audience's jaws drop. And that iconic gait that could stop a nation in its tracks.

Karthi got up to mimic *Talaivar*. 'Look, Kalki,' he said as he walked up and down, flipping an imaginary cigarette, and ending with an ostentatious guffaw.

'Let me try,' Kalki said, jumping up. She waited for the song to start. 'You be *Talaivar*, and I will be the fair-skinned heroine,' she said.

'What a sight!' A voice said from behind, Kalki. 'Darkie wants to be a movie star.'

'She won't even be selected to clean toilets in the movie hall,' another voice said with a laugh.

'Don't you two have any other job to do, Dung Roller and Pissy Skirt?' Karthi retorted, angry at them sneering at his sister.

'At least I didn't piss every night and day and roll in cow's shit when I was young.' Kalki stood up and stuck out her tongue at the two girls. Both let out an audible gasp, pretending to be scared of Kalki's face.

'Mock all you want. We don't do those things anymore,' said Dung Roller, whose real name was Gauri.

'That's right. I haven't pissed in my bed for four years now. I am 7 years old. But your dark skin is forever. You are stuck with it. You won't be able to get rid of it ever,' Pissy skirt said.

A broken VCR landed in front of the girls, flicking tiny pebbles towards them.

'Get the hell out of here,' Karthi said with a scowl, dusting his palms. The girls ran away and disappeared out of sight.

'Oye boy, how dare you throw my things?' Sekar said, abandoning his soldering iron. 'Is this your father's shop? I could have you both arrested for that.'

'Let us see who gets arrested first, me for throwing a useless VCR or you for cheating your customers,' Karthi retorted. 'I know that you deliberately damage the electrical goods further to charge more money for repairs.'

'Sekar, you idiot,' the shopkeeper said to himself. 'I warned you not to let him near the shop and watch TV. See, now he knows your secret. Well, it's not a secret anymore, is it.' Sekar quietly went back to soldering the same circuit board of a TV for the tenth time this week.

'We still have some time before the main event begins. Do you want to watch more songs?' Karthi asked his sister.

'Is it true that I can never get rid of this dark skin?' Kalki asked in a sad voice. 'You said that as I grow older my dark skin will become lighter. She scratched her arm leaving dusty runnels down her skin.

'STOP THAT!' Karthi yelled, pulling at her hands. 'Scratching yourself won't help. You are only seven. You still have a lot of time. Just give it a few more years.'

Kalki's lower lip trembled as she looked at the colour of her skin.

'Come on,' Karthi said, grabbing his sister's hand. 'Let us go to the festival. Enough of watching *Talaivar* on this broken TV." Karthi spoke loud enough for Sekar to hear. The shopkeeper shot an angry look at Karthi. 'We might be able to catch a glimpse of him if we go early and stand at the front.'

Kalki's eyes, full of self-hate, glared at the difference in her brother's skin colour and hers as they walked towards the festival. His skin was cinnamon brown. Kalki's skin was the hue of black pepper. 'You were born with the same skin colour as your brother's,' her mother had reassured her. But no one could explain what caused her skin to darken. So dark that it was almost purple, like the colour of brinjal. It had darkened slowly, gradually. When she was born, there was a dark spot in the centre of her belly. Then, dark spots started to pop up on her skin, distant and separate. Then they began to merge, slowly spreading across her little body. It eclipsed her cinnamon-brown skin, taking over cell by cell. All that was left of her former skin colour was a flame-shaped spot on her chest, just below the neck – a brown spectre that forever strangled her for the rest of her life.

People came up with various theories to justify what they saw as Kalki's affliction. They feasted on the topic like maggots on rotten flesh. Some said that the Goddess Kali had touched her. Others attributed it to the devil. For fear of swift retribution, the god-fearing ones bought Kalki flowers, fruits and gifts and hoped for favours in return. Baby Kalki cooed and sucked on her toes and ignored them, merely giving a toothless grin. People quickly changed colour when none of their prayers was answered. Then they maintained that the devil had indeed cursed her.

The burden of Kalki's dark skin was not hers alone to bear. Kalki's mother, Yashoda, tried to atone for whatever sin she could have committed in her past lives. Eating bland food was a non-issue, as their abject poverty kept their food simple and plain. Every Saturday and Sunday, after a dip in the river nearby, she would complete a perambulation of the temple rolling herself on the ground, still clad in her wet saree. As she belonged to a low caste, that was as close as she was allowed to god. When even that did not work, she gave up and stopped pleading with god, the same god she was prohibited from getting close to.

For Karthi, his sister's dark skin was a problem that gnawed away at his mind like a rabid rodent. His nose would actually tingle as the words of the village grandmother, Aaya, stung him like acid rain.

She was called the village grandmother not only because she was old but because she had advice for everyone and on everything. Everyone confided in her. She was the keeper of secrets, carrying 90 years of narratives. Her mind was like a cupboard, each shelf holding the villagers' secrets. Unsatisfied husbands with jaded wives. Infatuated teenage boys with flirty maidens. Curious children with white lies. Ailing ones with placebos. Aaya would listen to them all, seated outside her empty laterite hut, grinding areca nuts in a mortar with a pestle.

'Avoid the sun at all costs,' she said, her mouth full with areca nut, while Karthi and Kalki stared at her, mesmerised by the gory mastication process. The old woman's rotten, grungy teeth tore through the betel leaves and areca nuts, a reddish-brown fluid escaping from a corner of her mouth. Her tongue would efficiently shovel it back in before it could drip.

Her advice to avoid the sun struck Karthi like a flash of lightning striking a lone tree in a barren field. He realised that he was responsible for his sister's affliction.

It was the middle of summer, the hottest one in recent times. The mango trees wilted. The bougainvillea was reduced to dry ashes. Hungry bees retired to their hives, not finding much nectar and even eyeing the glistening eggs of their deflated corpulent queen bee. The whole Indian subcontinent was experiencing severe drought. Harvests failed. The usually lush paddy fields had nothing by cracked mud criss-crossed with ugly fissures. Insects tried to feed on dried husk, juiceless stalks, and ghastly roots. People walked for miles, scouring the land for a drop of water.

'You look after your sister, okay? Remember, don't

take her outside,' Yashoda said, placing her daughter, clad in just a loincloth, in her son's arms. 'It will be a while before I return. I don't know how far I will need to go before I will be able to find water.' She thought that maybe she might dig through the dry lakebed. Or the sewage. The black water should become clear after boiling on a wood-fire, she thought.

'Take care of your sister,' Yashoda said and left, balancing a yellow plastic pot on her head and holding a red one under each arm. The sweat made her blue blouse appear black.

Karthi watched as his mother's silhouette disappeared into the sizzling heat. The hut was like an oven. Karthi opened the door and sought relief under the neem tree outside. He spotted some boys playing with marbles in the shade of the banyan tree across the road. The temptation to join them was too much. Better to move around and get some air, he thought. He placed his baby sister in the shade under the neem tree and ran to join the boys.

It was noon. The sun reached its apex. The neem tree gathered its frilly black skirt of shadow on the ground and tucked it around itself. Kalki lay there in the searing sun, her limbs flailing and grinning at the clear blue sky.

A shrill cry broke Karthi's concentration just as he was about to win at marbles. He rushed to his sister, who was crying out in pain. Her skin had turned scaly and a deep brown. She was as hot as a pot of cooked rice when he picked her up. She smelt of burnt flesh. The sun gloated and hissed through hot winds.

He quickly brought her into the hut, removed her loincloth and fanned her furiously with his trembling hands after sprinkling on her a smidge of water that he was able to scrape from a broken pot. Karthi thought she was going to die. His sweat fell on Kalki like rain. His heart hammered in his chest. Kalki stopped crying eventually and fell asleep, taking short, rapid breaths as though she could not get enough air.

As weeks passed, faint black spots started to appear on Kalki's skin. When her mother noticed her daughter's skin darkening, she was worried and Karthi's heart was filled with guilt. It became his secret, a prickly one. Every time someone called her darkie, a bubble of pain would swell inside him. The guilt ate through his mind. He pictured black wriggling, squelching creatures burrowing deep in his head. He called them worms of guilt. They created an overwhelming itch in his brain, deep in the base of his skull. He tried to convince himself that he wasn't responsible for his sister's dark skin, but with no other viable alternative cause, he still blamed himself.

As Karthi and Kalki made their way to the festival, they joined the crowds going this way and that way. A government-owned electric generator chugged away loudly, lighting up the main streets, emitting white clouds that enveloped the people. Stores nearby had their power lines hooked to the generator for the day to save on their electricity bills.

A temporary stage had been set up and on it stood *Talaivar's* cardboard cut-outs in dramatic poses, looking over the entire village through his dark glasses. Rows of cushioned chairs were on the stage, while a sea of plastic chairs had been placed for the audience. In the front row stood a throne-like chair with red velvet cushions and gold detailing. It was being constantly cleaned by a man. The stage setup was sponsored by the Royal Loyal Fanclub Society of Talaivar. Gopinath, the head of the fan club, had sold all his wife's gold jewellery and also used his life's savings to pay for it. 'You bought it all with my money,' he said to his wife. She couldn't argue with that logic. It might be Gopinath's only chance to see *Talaivar* in the flesh, so he hoped that a gilded stage would be an incentive for him to stop and greet his loyal fans.

Yesterday's ragpickers had become peddlers today, selling *Talaivar* merchandise – masks of *Talaivar's* face with holes for eyes; peanuts, sugar candy and sunglasses branded with *Talaivar*.

Everyone was dressed in his or her best clothes. Men wore stiff plaid or white shirts and starched lungies that rustled when they moved. Women shone in their silk sarees and wore white jasmine flowers in their hair. Mini carousels and the ferris-wheel, creaking and with flaking paint, stood in the middle of the road, blocking traffic. Men powered the rides, deftly pushing the carousel round and round and climbing up the side of the ferris-wheel. The man powering the ferris-wheel looked like a human spider in the middle of a wooden cobweb. Giggling children and queasy adults queued up to ride the carousel and the ferris-wheel.

'Will *Talaivar* pass through here?' Kalki wanted to know, looking at the empty road cordoned off on either side with a makeshift wooden fence. Police officers brandished their batons at wayward pedestrians who were too lazy to go the long way around. When that didn't work, they would dart towards the people, only to be brought up short by their slipping pants, betrayed by the belts that held up their rotund bellies.

'I think so,' Karthi said, looking around at the dense crowd fighting for the best seats. 'Maybe it's over there.' Karthi pointed to a knot of people craning their necks for a glimpse of the arena.

They pushed through the crowd. A nimble man dressed in crisp black trousers and a white shirt was shouting, 'Are you ready to be rich? Are you ready to be rich?' His black tie with blue swirls was being whipped across his chest as he moved around, waving his finger at the mesmerised crowd. His well-oiled hair shone like an inky lake under a full moon.

'This is a once-in-a-lifetime opportunity. I guarantee you have never heard of such a thing in your life. Even the big government banks don't offer such high returns. Our company, Shakti Investments, has travelled far and wide across the length and breadth of India with this golden opportunity to create wealth for people like you. Lakhs of people have signed up already and they are now sleeping in peace with no worries about tomorrow. They don't have to worry whether they will pay their debts off in this lifetime. They are sleeping soundly and living in peace, knowing that they will have more than enough money to marry off their daughters in time. I stand here not as a businessman but as your friend, to guide you to make the right decision.

'Why should your money sit around and do nothing? You all agree that money stuffed under the mattress, inside a coffee container, or your grandmother's waist pouch won't grow, right?'

The crowd nodded in agreement.

'Then why do you keep on doing the same thing? Expecting things to change without doing anything is just plain stupidity. Do something different today. Do something for your future. Your kids will thank you.' The man stopped to take a deep breath. He took out a few folded sheets from his brown leather bag with gold buckles, held it up high in the air so that they caught the evening sunlight.

'This is your ticket out of poverty. This piece of paper is going to change your life for the better. If you sign up today and invest a minimum of Rs 1,000 at 12% for five years, we will give you another Rs 500 as a bonus. But mind you, this is only valid for today.' He studied the crowd. Most of them were standing as stiff and still as dead trees. Their eyes started to wander as they searched for a sight of *Talaivar*. He knew he had to do something quickly to regain their attention.

'Let us see if any men here have the balls to do this?' He slapped the sheets against his palm. 'Is there any man here who will take this step to help his family?' He had hoped his words would lead the wives to urge their husbands to do what is best for the family.

A bald man, with just some greying hair on the side like a frozen waterfall, stepped out. He wore gold square glasses that sat skewed on his broad nose. His shirt was stretched tight over his paunch. In fact, his belly stepped forward before him. He raised his hand and said that he would sign up. Faces turned towards him and a collective wave of murmur broke out among the crowd.

'Now here is a man,' the man said. 'Come forward, sir. You have chosen the right path. You will see for yourself how your life will change dramatically. You won't have to worry about a thing from now on. Let your money do the hard work for you. A worry-free life awaits you, my friend.'

Suddenly, there was a stir in the crowd. Then a ripple. An outcry erupted as the crowd moved in towards the centre of the arena, eager to grab their ticket out of poverty.

'Anna, anna,' Karthi called out to a man who was old enough to be his father. 'What is this all about?' Karthi tugged at the man's sweat-soaked shirt.

'Looks like this man can grow your money,' the man said.

'How?' Karthi asked.

The man shrugged his shoulders. 'Why don't you ask him and find out?'

'I don't have any money,' Karthi said.

'Well, that's too bad,' the man said as he joined the crowd heading towards a worry-free life.

'This is all grown-up stuff. Let's get back to the festival and find us a spot before the parade starts,' Karthi said to his sister.

The wooden fence along the road groaned as people pushed against it, scrambling to get the best view. A few scuffles broke out as people argued who was here first. Karthi and Kalki tried to break through the crowd of irritated people but were pushed back quite violently.

Suddenly, the bickering was replaced by cheers and piercing whistles. A musical horn from a distant vehicle could be heard. The crowd's excitement grew as the retinue of cars drove past. On the other side, Gopinath galvanised a group of people on the flashy stage to break into a chant that rose like a thundering wave. 'Long live *Talaivar*! Long live *Talaivar*!' the people shouted. Karthi and Kalki darted towards the stage and joined a group of kids their age who had no hope of reaching the front of the crowd.

'What are you doing here, darkie?' Gauri asked, grabbing her skirt and twirling it around. 'See, my father bought this for me so that I can look pretty when I meet *Talaivar*.'

'Same as you. I want to see *Talaivar* up close, dung-roller,' Kalki replied, mesmerised by the golden silk dots on Gauri's green skirt.

'Are you blind or what? Have you seen yourself? You think he will want to see your dark, ugly face?'

Luckily, Kalki didn't hear a word Gauri said because of the commotion. But Karthi heard every single word.

'Have you looked in the mirror?' Karthi snapped at Gauri. 'You are talking like you are as fair as Queen Elizabeth.' Gauri put out her tongue at him and turned towards the parade.

Talaivar was a far cry from what everyone expected. He didn't have the bouncy hair that he would run his fingers through in the movies. In fact, in the sunshine you could see bald patches on his head. His face was haggard, not youthful as seen on the screen. And he was not wearing his trademark dark glasses. His eyes looked out through spectacles that were as clear as Mahatma Gandhi's.

No one seemed to care or notice, however. Star-truck, the restless, shrieking crowd thronged the stage only to be stopped by the roadblocks, mental and physical. The cries from the audience were thunderous.

Gopinath welcomed *Talaivar* onto the stage and began to ply him with floral garlands that soon engulfed his face. Jasmine. Marigold. Rose. He fell to the floor and prostrated himself in front of *Talaivar*, sobbing loudly. Nobody could tell if the tears were from happiness at meeting *Talaivar* or from sadness at the loss of his life's savings for a moment with his hero.

Talaivar removed the garlands, stripped off the flowers and threw them at the crowd. Like water-starved soil, his fans stretched out their arms to catch the petals. At least one crushed petal touched by their god. Gopinath led *Talaivar* towards the microphone and begged him to say a few words. He waved his hands and gestured to the people to calm down. A hush fell on the crowd.

'Brothers and sister,' *Talaivar* started to speak. He talked about his humble beginnings as an auto-rickshaw driver, how he was lucky to be the only driver to pass by when a film director's car broke down. He was not supposed to take the turn, but something from above told him to take that path. He talked of how the director paid attention to his unique quirks, how he was asked to be the hero in the next movie, and why everything happens for a reason, when a wrong turn became the right turn. He said that everyone present at the festival had yet to unlock their true potential and become a star, how luck has a way of creeping up on you and changing your life for the better. The crowd drank every word and envisioned themselves giving a speech like this sometime in their lives, when they would talk about how they overcame their trials and tribulations. Maybe it would happen. In some parallel universe perhaps.

Deafening applause erupted as he ended his speech. Gopinath announced that *Talaivar* would meet a few lucky children who were the future of this village and eventually this country.

Karthi and Kalki, along with the other kids, were suddenly corralled to the side of the stage with stairs going up.

'Where are we going?' Kalki asked.

'Just hold onto my hand,' Karthi said.

The children finally reached the stage and were asked to form a queue. Kalki spotted Gauri jumping in excitement. She wrapped herself around *Talaivar's* leg, hoping to be picked up by him. A peal of laughter broke from the audience. Talaivar tried to pry himself from her grip. He kissed her on the head and tried to fend her off. She ran back and wrapped herself around his leg again.

'Who allowed her to come to the stage?' Gopinath asked, yanking Kalki out of the queue. Kalki screamed, but it was drowned in the laughter of the audience following Gauri's antics. She was still refusing to leave the stage. 'Let go. It hurts,' Kalki screamed again.

'Who asked you to come here, you filthy darkie? Spoiling the entire function with your deathly presence,' Gopinath said, twisting Kalki's ear.

'Stop hurting my sister,' Karthi said, as he tried to stop Gopinath.

Talaivar turned towards the commotion after prying Gauri off. He grabbed Gopinath's hand as he was about to slap Karthi. The audience let out a collective gasp.

'How dare you? They are just kids,' *Talaivar* said, glaring at Gopinath, who threw himself on the ground, begging for forgiveness.

Talaivar ignored Gopinath and picked Kalki up, wiping her tears. 'I am here now. Don't cry, my angel.'

The stage lights glinted in Kalki's tears and the rumbling in the audience distracted her from realising that she was in the arms of the great *Talaivar* himself. Once she realised that *Talaivar's* face was next to hers, her crying stopped. Somewhere in the crowd, Gauri's face crumbled.

'Is there anything you want, child?' *Talaivar* asked.

'How do I become an actress so that I can star with you?' Kalki asked. *Talaivar* let out a hearty laugh. He tried to tell Kalki something, but the other kids in the queue pushed forward, eager to be held by him.

The crowd was promised a special screening of the latest *Talaivar* movie at the school playground the next day.

Later that night, the villagers hoped for something serendipitous to happen that would change their fortune. The auto-rickshaw driver took more wrong turns than necessary while facing a volley of curses from his passenger, accusing him of running up the meter deliberately. A dosa master flipped and tossed dosas in the air before serving them to his customers. A sweeper danced with her broom as she swept the day's madness away.

Karthi and Kalki walked back home, full of thoughts about *Talaivar*. There was a full moon that shone down on the village still basking in the afterglow of the festivities. Kalki could still feel *Talaivar*'s arms around her. She wondered what he would have said if he hadn't been interrupted by the other children.

'Maybe he was trying to tell me that my skin needed to be lighter?' she said to her brother.

Karthi looked at her as the worms of guilt began to hollow out a cavity in his head. 'Maybe,' he replied. 'We need to hurry back home before Amma gets back. She will kill me if she finds out you were out today. Remember, this is our secret.'

Chapter 2

Kalki ran her fingers over the flame-shaped mark on her chest, hoping in some miraculous way to activate the lighter shade of brown to spread all over her body. She tapped on the mark like a button, sometimes rapidly, with her eyes closed. She counted till 49 because she didn't know what came after that. And when she opened her eyes, she hoped that one day she would find her skin had lightened.

When the villagers said she was cursed and when children taunted her, calling her darkie, she felt as though she would implode. She didn't know how to make it go away. She would stare at the cracked mirror that hung on the wall, wishing that she could magically become fairer. Once, it hurt her to the point that she scratched her arms until she started bleeding. It was as though she wanted to bleed the dark colour out. It worked, sort of, but it also scarred her. Pale ridges crisscrossed her limbs as the wounds healed. It became a permanent reminder that the dark skin was here to stay. Whenever she was taunted, she looked at the epidermal cobwebs as the phantom pain overtook her desire to turn fair.

She whispered a prayer almost every night. With her eyes tightly squeezed till she saw flashing spots she would pray: I ask you, my God. Whoever is up there, turn my skin to my natural colour, the one I was born with. I won't pester you anymore if it happens. Please fulfil my only wish. The colour I was born with was what you gave me initially. I am just asking for it back. I promise I won't do anything that might make you mad. I won't do bad things. I won't call other kids names even though they call me names. I won't bother you again with any other wishes and demands. Please, God, please. You don't have to make me fair-skinned. I want to be a regular brown-skinned-girl like everyone else. PLEASE give back what once was mine.

'God is too busy with those upper caste people to pay attention to us,' Yashoda said, snapping her fingers in front of Kalki's face to yank her out of her prayer stance.

'Why are we any different? Do we need to pray to another God, then?' Karthi asked.

'Maybe there is no god for us,' Yashoda said, stoking the flames of her clay stove by blowing air on to it through a pipe.

'Why was I born this dark, Amma?' Kalki asked in a soft voice so that only her mother could hear.

Yashoda looked at her daughter. The white of Kalki's

eyes occupied so little space. She struggled to make a distinction between the pupil and the skin. Her eyes were hollow. A vast emptiness, all concentrated in the eye socket. The sombre stare from her daughter's eyes made her wish she could retreat in time and change things so she didn't have to be born dark. Or not be born at all.

The skies were sullen on the night when Kalki was born. Wolves howled in the distance. Stray dogs nearby joined the distant choir. Bats fluttered from electricity poles and hung themselves upside down as their day began, feasting on unsuspecting gnats and mosquitoes.

Yashoda sprawled on the ground of her home with her legs wide apart, her pelvic cavity wide open for three elderly ladies to inspect the process of childbirth. She screamed in agony and dug in her fingers, scratching the stone floor. The wolves outside howled in tandem, sniffing the air suffused with the scent of struggle. As Yashoda let out one final scream, a shrill cry erupted from between her legs. Propping herself on her arms, she craned her neck to see the life that had emerged from her, only to collapse at the throbbing pain inside her head. The cry from the baby only exacerbated it. Three pairs of wrinkled arms worked in tandem, wiping and wrapping the new-born baby, cleaning it of blood and placental discharge, and massaging Yashoda's arms and legs.

When Yashoda regained consciousness, one of the old midwives leaned over the bed and handed her a mewling bundle. Wrapped in a turmeric-coloured sari, Yashoda peered and saw a wrinkled brown thing squirming. Two feet poked out of the cloth bundle, kicking the air. Her head was covered with thin black hair that was still damp. Her eyes were no more than two slits, tightly shut. Her tiny fists were clenched and she had a slight smile on her face.

'It's a girl!' one of the midwives whispered. The other two mumbled among themselves, prophesying the life the baby girl could expect to live. 'How is it different from faeces?' one of them said. 'Except she had to bear unfathomable pain to create this one,' the other said. Yashoda caught their woeful exchange and the disapproving click their tongues made.

'There is something on her skin. You ought to take a look at it,' a midwife said.

Yashoda pushed her matted hair away from her face to see the bundle better and unwrapped her gift of life.

She saw an irregular patch of darkness on her baby daughter's brown belly. As though she was born before god could uniformly colour her brown, or was it the other way round? Did he want to dye her all black?

'It could be a birthmark, but I haven't seen anything like this before,' the midwife said, running her fingers over the mark. 'And I have helped birth more than a thousand babies in this village.'

'The devil has touched that child; that is the mark of the devil,' another midwife chimed in.

'Not now,' the older midwife said, slapping the hand of the other and adding, 'Not here,' as an afterthought. She let out a weak smile at Yashoda.

'We will go and get you some food. You had better start feeding the baby,' she said.

The midwives left her hut, but Yashoda could sense them hovering outside and whispering. She started to feed the baby. The soft suckling of her baby intensified. Even though her spirit was spent, she tried to shut down the other senses and divert all her energy to her ears.

'Only the Lord knows who the father of the baby is,' a midwife said.

'Why do you have to say such evil things in front of her. Poor thing was raped, and she just gave birth to the child. She doesn't need to hear these things right now.'

'Sooner or later, she will hear them. The whole village will be talking about it. First, her drunkard husband dies. Then she gets raped. Then she gives birth to a girl. And the girl has a weird looking spot on her body. Don't tell me that is not the mark of the devil. She should have just come home straight after work instead of roaming the streets at night.'

'Nice one,' one midwife said with a disgusted snort. 'Yashoda didn't want to be raped. Blame the man who did it.'

'Why the man? Who asked her to wander around like a loose chicken? If a chicken is lost, won't someone catch it and make a meal out of it?'

'And you call yourself a woman. The biggest enemy of a woman in this country is not a man but a woman herself,' another midwife said.

'Why are you scolding me? She is the one who gave birth to that wretched thing. I am telling you the child is cursed. I have never seen a mark like that before.'

Yashoda didn't know how to react to their words or the birth of her daughter. She couldn't decide what was worse, a bastard child or giving birth to a girl child with the alleged devil's touch. Her listless eyes wandered between deep sleep and extreme regret for not taking the straight route home that night nine months ago. Before she drifted off to sleep, vivid flashbacks of that cursed night hit her like ice-cold water. The rhythmic sound of her daughter suckling lulled her to sleep, but the vile memories still tortured her mind.

The pain was only a fleeting spectre teasing the back of her neck when she finished with her job at Perumal's house. But it increased as she made her way back home, carrying some food for herself and her son. The pain from the day's work of washing dishes, sweeping the entire house and the yard, washing clothes and cooking, came back and she fell like a crumbling wall. Since the death of her husband following alcohol abuse, she was forced to take additional work to make ends meet.

She wanted to get home fast. She had been told, like all young women were, to only use the main road which was brightly lit. But she had a blinding headache and so she decided to take a shortcut at the end of the street. The narrow lane was flanked by thatched huts and vacant land. Yashoda's head felt heavier with every step. She walked past curious eyes of men and women. It was a look that meant a lot of things: *Are you lost? This is the first time I have seen you here. You are not part of my daily sights. Are you new to this town? Why are you all alone?* Goats shimmied precariously on ledges. Dogs faithfully guarded the entrances. All were minding their own business. She longed for a cup of tea and a nap to soothe her headache. She pushed through the narrow streets. The headache had become a throbbing pain when she entered the alley blocked by the grotesque trunk of a gulmohur tree.

The attack came from almost nowhere. She screamed but a chapped hand muffled her voice. The sour smell of sweat and alcohol invaded her nostrils, making her nauseous. She was dragged to a dead space littered with gravel and broken branches. She could hear rats scurrying away. Her bag broke open, scattering the contents onto the road. Two parading hens eyed the spilled split lentils like cautious thieves. Five rod-like fingers gripped Yashoda's arm like an iron trap, numbing it instantly.

Resistance only exacerbated the pain. Her eyes, wide open, stared at the beefy silhouette, and her tears poured down her cheeks, like blood from a gash. She tried to push the beast away but to no avail. Her headache made her weak and powerless. She whimpered and the man tried to silence her by suffocating her mouth with his lips. She could feel the air underneath her skirt. The dark profile began to move, hurting her. The pain started to pulsate throughout her body – sudden, abrupt and intense. The air between them was sticky and suffocating. The putrid breath of alcohol from his mouth as he heaved made it worse. She gave up her fight.

The beast lit a beedi, outlining his scruffy face. 'Dessert,' he said. 'After the main course.' He blew smoke into her face. Yashoda gathered her waning strength and gathered her clothes. Her head was still throbbing. The beast sniggered. Yashoda cried like a ruptured dam. The hens feasted on their loot.

'Did you enjoy that?' the beast asked, blowing smoke into the air. A lone streetlamp weakly lighted the alleyway, just enough to show the grizzly silhouette. All she noticed was his hands as he vigorously scratched himself as though he wanted to rip off his skin. As he relieved his itch, Yashoda saw flakes of shadow dust falling off him. Like sawdust billowing out of a carpenter's bench.

'Curse this skin. Can't even smoke a beedi properly after a good fuck,' the man hissed. 'What are you staring at?'

Yashoda said nothing, merely shaking her head.

'YOU WHORE! Stop looking at me like that! Now that I have had my way with you, wait and watch, you too will get whatever skin disease I have, or your baby might. Who knows? You can't do anything about it now, can you?'

His scratching and cursing intensified as he left Yashoda alone with the scavenging hens and a pool of furtive, insidious 300 million male gametes inside her.

For the next nine months, she monitored her skin like punctilious in-laws looking for faults in their new daughter-in-law. Every itch would startle her, and phantom itches teased her. She would sweep her skin with her fingers every night to check for aberrations. Even a slight bump would send shivers down her spine, and the ghost image of the flaking rapist grinning at her. She would ask her son, Karthi, to check for any abnormal growth on her back.

'Something is moving inside you,' Karthi said, not knowing they were just his mother's shoulder bones.

The bastard baby inside started to kick. It was almost time for the baby to come out and seal Yashoda's reputation as the one who was raped because she took the wrong path by walking into the alley.

Yashoda thought she had escaped whatever disease her rapist had been suffering from. But it made its way to her baby. She thought it wouldn't get worse. Maybe it would just stay confined to the mark on her stomach. But Yashoda was wrong yet again. The darkness spread across her daughter's body like spilt ink on a white cloth.

Three days after her birth, a severe drought descended on the village, leaving nary a drop of water. This sealed her daughter's fate as the deliverer of bad luck. Yashoda could hear the cautious midwife beating her chest and saying, 'I told you, didn't I? It was the devil's child indeed. Look what that bastard child has done to us, sucked us completely dry. The only thing that will flow in the village will be the tears of hungry villagers. I curse my hands for helping to birth the devil child.'

The drought could have been just a coincidence. But there were instances when Yashoda couldn't ignore the lines that inextricably connected her cursed daughter to some villager's fate. Kalki slept on the stony bank with a thin sheet over her as Yashoda washed clothes in the river. Four pebbles pinned the sheet down as Kalki flailed around. Yashoda kept an eye on the sheet that rose and fell with Kalki's breathing. That was the only way the villagers would allow Yashoda to bring her baby to the river. We shouldn't be able to see a speck of her skin, they said. One day, a gust of wind dislodged the pebbles. The sheet fluttered away like a loose kite. Before Yashoda could run to Kalki and throw herself over her baby, a dhobi saw her. With the fear of bad luck pecking at his mind, he ended up tearing all the clothes he was supposed to wash that day. Not one was saved. It happened on the second day and the third day, and subsequently, his customers stopped giving him clothes to wash. He cursed Kalki and Yashoda. Ultimately, he became a cobbler at the train station. He narrated his tragic tale to customers as he repaired their shoes.

Another time, a woman wanted to know if Kalki could be the darkest thing one would ever see. She went behind Yashoda's hut and peeked in through the square hole, balancing herself over two earthen pots. Her eyes scanned the room inside, but it was pitch black. Suddenly two white circles glowered at her, and she saw a slight silhouette moving. A shiver gripped her as the whites of Kalki's eyes spooked her, and she lost her grip and fell, cracking the pots. A piece of earthenware pierced her foot, leaving her with a limp. Whenever she was asked what had happened to her, she blamed Kalki for making her disabled. 'Be careful. One look is all it takes, and your life will be as broken as my leg.' She always ended her story with that warning.

Fearing that she had given birth to the devil's spawn, Yashoda ensured that Kalki never left the mud house. She tried to hide her in the shadows.

She went to the local doctor to find out what was wrong with Kalki's skin. It was a long wait in the queue with crying babies. Overactive grandparents prophesied death because of their pain. Impatient parents pestered their sons to make them grandparents so that their grandchildren could massage their backs. The doctor finally examined Kalki's skin only to dismiss it as something supernatural. He said he did not have enough medical expertise to treat her. His skills were limited to treating headaches and fever.

'I give white tablets for headaches and body aches and yellow ones for fever. Does it look like I would know how to diagnose your daughter's skin condition? You would need to go to the city for this,' he said. 'God knows how much that will cost. Maybe Rs 25,000. Who knows? Why didn't you abort the baby when you had the chance?' the doctor asked.

Yashoda didn't have an answer. She left the doctor's clinic even as he picked up a syringe to evict the grime from his toenails and wiped it on his white coat sleeves, leaving a streak of dirt.

'Next!' He shouted. A grinning baby waving her arms

in the air greeted her as Yashoda exited the clinic. 'Hope the injection doesn't hurt my precious baby,' the baby's mother muttered to herself.

Yashoda resorted to home remedies. She smeared turmeric paste all over Kalki's body. As the paste dried, Kalki looked like a dry yellow riverbed, fissures and all. Yashoda would massage coconut oil onto her skin till she became a glistening black pearl. Sometimes, she would scratch the black spots with her fingernails, hoping it would peel off. She even tried to smoke the black spots on her daughter's skin with a burning newspaper. When nothing worked, she fashioned a girdle-like ornament with black thread and beads to ward off evil spirits, till she could save some money and take her to a big doctor in the city.

She picked up any extra work she could find. After her regular housekeeping job at Perumal Amma's house, she knocked on the doors of upper caste households and asked if any sweeping or cleaning was to be done. Some refused with a vigorous shake of their heads before bolting their doors shut.

'As though I am going to let a filthy lower caste cook and clean my perfect Brahmin house. If Perumal does it, she must have been a dirty lower caste in her previous life,' a woman said from behind the locked door.

She is not a true Brahmin, the true Brahmins said.

'She eats non-veg. I could smell it every time I walk past her house,' another woman said, waving her hand energetically in front of their nose.

'What do you expect?' asked another. 'Her son works in the Gulf. Of course, he would bring their ungodly, barbaric habits here.'

Some did agree to give Yashoda a single job. But it would snowball into many chores. She would clean the house, the toilet with water and phenyl, sweep the front yard and the back garden, before being asked to cook for the family by the end of the day. And all this for just Rs 50.

She accepted whatever job came her way. By the time Kalki turned seven, she had saved Rs 10,000. It was neatly folded into a roll and stuffed deep inside the tin of rice. No thief, unless he was hungry, would scrabble in a container of rice for money. At this rate, Kalki would be of marriageable age by the time she had saved up the entire sum of money needed to see the city doctor. Who will marry a girl like Kalki? She feared Kalki would be as lonely as the starless and moonless night sky. Treading a thin line of hope and despair, she continued to work for the rich upper castes.

'Amma! Amma!' Kalki shook her mother and brought her back to the present. 'You didn't answer my question. Why was I born this dark?'

'Because you were born at night,' Yashoda replied.

'So, Karthi was born during the day?'

'No, darling. If he would have been born during the day, he would have been fairer,' Yashoda said.

'Then why couldn't you wait till morning to give birth to me?' Kalki asked, unsatisfied with her mother's response. 'I would have been born with fair skin. Look,' she pointed to the flame-shaped mark on her chest. 'That is my original colour, right?'

'No child in India is born during the day,' Yashoda said.

'Why is that?'

'Because ... because…' Yashoda hesitated, searching for an answer. 'Because babies cannot stand the heat. Now enough with these questions. Guess what's for dinner today.'

In her hand was a bundle wrapped in newspaper. The wet newsprint began to blot. She removed the outer paper, just enough to let out the smell. It smelt of damp paper and yesterday's problems.

'Chicken,' both her children said as they inhaled the scent with eyes closed, envisioning chicken curry.

'Now, both of you get away from the stove and play in that corner,' she said. The children skedaddled to the corner and re-enacted scenes from a movie: Kalki, a beautiful fair-skinned heroine and Karthi, a mischievous, lovable hero.

Yashoda unwrapped the soggy paper bundle, containing the chicken bones. The smell from the paper's ink was strong. It coated the bones of the chicken, along with sparse cartilage flesh. *The rise of bourgeois deepens the divide.* The headline was imprinted on the bone of the drumstick.

Yashoda made some dough and cocked her head back to see where her children were. They were engrossed in movie land. She quickly moulded the dough around the chicken bones, turning them into fully fleshed chicken pieces. She then dropped the pieces into boiling water, added turmeric, coriander, and cumin powder, and hoped the chicken bones would release some of their leftover flavours.

'Dinner's ready,' Yashoda called out as the bulb above her flickered. She asked Karthi to set the bulb straight. He grabbed a long stick and gave the wire a little nudge. The bulb shone brightly for a second, then died. He poked again. The light flooded back again.

Yashoda unfolded the straw mat and spread it on the floor. It snapped and rustled as hungry bums sat down on it. Yashoda scooped balls of rice and filled it with the dough chicken to serve her children.

"I need the big piece… big piece", Kalki demanded as she peered into the pot from which Yashoda scooped the contents. She stripped the leg piece of the doughy chicken, and it came off effortlessly,

She gave a ball of rice to Kalki, who made a small hole in the middle of the rice ball and asked for chicken curry to be poured in.

Yashoda served herself and waited nervously for the kids to take the first bite. As they took the first handful of rice and the chicken, something bubbled up from her stomach and lodged in her throat and almost suffocated her. "How is the chicken?" she croaked, clearing her throat.

They answered with mouths full of dough, chicken

and rice. Grinning mouths, two balls on either side of the cheek, as they munched and chomped with pleasure. The sight of her children enjoying the food made her crave for the substandard chicken, more than hunger itself. Yashoda's throat cleared, and that something plummeted down to her tummy. A child's smile is a dangerous thing. A magical curve that is capable of changing things and feelings. It can turn the make-believe into reality – dough-filled, stripped chicken bones to fleshy leg pieces.

'Did they have a feast today as well?' Karthi asked. 'These chicken pieces are much bigger than the ones you had last week.'

'Yes. One of Gayathri Amma's sons has come from the Gulf,' Yashoda said. She was a maid at Gayathri's house.

'I hope her sons keep going to the Gulf and returning, so we can eat such delicious chicken,' Kalki said, digging into her food.

Chapter 3

Later that night, when their mother was sound asleep, they sneaked out of their hut and headed towards Aaya.

They found Aaya sitting with her back against the wall. Her eyes were sunken as if her eyelids were slowly swallowing them. They were just one gulp away from dropping inside her skull. Her jaw opened as though there was something grim around her, as if she was fighting a silent battle with death and all its creatures.

'Aaya,' Karthi called out. He touched her, fearing the worst.

Aaya sucked in a deep breath of air and shuddered back to life. Her eyelids appeared to expel her eyes out. 'What are you two doing here at this time?'

They told her about *Talaivar* and the festival, the suffocating crowd surrounding a money-growing magician who promised wealth, how Kalki was called on to the stage and how she was almost kicked out. How *Talaivar* saved her and how he wanted her to star in his movies if she was fairer.

'Did he say that?' Aaya asked, covering her mouth with her hands in awe.

'Yes, he did,' Kalki said with a vehement nod. 'Now, if you want me to star next to him, tell me how I can get rid of this dark skin.'

'I am just an old lady, and yet you demand so much from me.'

'You are old as time. If you don't know, who would?'

'Alright, alright,' Aaya said. 'You can try this. Go to the temple on Sundays when the white tourists visit. Ask them for tips on how to whiten one's skin. Maybe they have a cream for it.'

'Why do you think they have fair skin, Aaya?' Kalki asked.

'In their country, the sun just skirts the sky. Since they are also far away from the sun, it makes their country cold. That is the reason they come here to experience our heat. But in this godforsaken country, the sun is at its highest in the sky. Raining down hellfire and browning our skin.'

'You keep blaming the sun,' Kalki said. 'Do you think I am dark because of the sun? But I was never outside my home, especially during the day. That's what Amma said.'

Aaya wanted to say something, but Karthi stood up as he didn't like where the conversation was going. The worms of guilt were already waking up in his mind.

Taking his sister's hand, they both left Aaya's hut.

'Aaya thinks the sun has something to do with my colour,' Kalki said, examining her dark skin.

'If we have any hope of asking the white people in the temple about their cream, we need to talk in their language,' Karthi said, steering the conversation in a different direction. 'They talk like they have pebbles in their mouth.'

'But we don't know a word of English,' Kalki said. 'No, wait, yes, we do. I can say hello and bye-bye.' She waved her hands at Karthi, for both the English words.

'I don't think that is nearly enough,' Karthi said with a sigh.

Ever since Aaya had put the idea in her head that the key to becoming fair was to ask the foreign tourists who frequented the local temple about their skincare routine, the temple bells were all that Kalki heard. She would wake up early every morning to the chiming of the bells, only to feel dejected and fall back to sleep because she didn't speak their language.

Today was different. Today she would talk to them, she decided. Ask them two questions in English. She had been practising the two sentences since last week. Her brain was like a broken tape recorder, in a constant loop, reciting, 'How are you? What is your name?'

She heard them first in a TV advertisement at the vegetable vendor's shop at the corner. A sleepy new student dragged herself to the class with a big yawn, clutching at her mother's saree. The teacher, with a broad smile, asked in English, 'How are you? What is your name?' Groggy eyes met the teacher's bright eyes. She then advised the mother to feed her daughter an Ayurveda health supplement which would give her more energy. The mother fed her daughter two teaspoons of the mixture. The ad then cut to the following day, with the student running to the class with a beaming smile and a tired mother trailing behind. The ad ended with the teacher joking that even the mother should try the tonic if she wanted to keep up with her daughter's new-found energy. And they laughed before the ad faded. It was the first time Kalki had heard English on a local channel.

'When will this ad come again?' Kalki asked the vendor, who was lazily scratching his armpit. He shrugged. He rolled his eyes in pleasure as the itch subsided. He grabbed a handful of lady's finger with cruddy and smelly fingers and weighed it for the next customer.

It was 4 p.m. Kalki made a mental note of it and came the next day to watch it again. This time the vendor was scratching his back.

'Hey, you can't just come in here to watch the TV and not buy anything. I am not the cinema. You hear me?' The itchy vendor started to pick at his nose. He retched loudly and wiped his hands on his lungi. His white singlet stretched over this rotund body, and there was a sweaty patch where the swell of his belly began. He got up with great difficulty, like an elephant waking from a long night's sleep and reached for the TV in the corner of the shop. He stood there with his hands on the knob, threatening to turn it off.

'Just five minutes, Anna. I will leave as soon as I see the advertisement again,' Kalki pleaded.

The ad came on again. The new student was still sleepy. The teacher was still enthusiastic. *How are you? What is your name?* Kalki repeated after her, 'How ah you? Vat iz yoor nem?'

Sometimes she mixed up the words. *How iz yoor nem? What ah you?* When she said it right, she shut her eyes and repeated the corrected phrase incessantly, trying to burn it in her brain as though she feared the words hop out of her head like a rabbit. She even asked her brother to wake her in the middle of the night so see if she could say it even when she was sleepy.

'Do you know English words?' Karthi asked, poking his sister to wake her from sleep.

'How ah you? Vaaaat...,' Kalki yawned. 'Vat iz yoor nem?'

Her fingers twitched to the tune of the bells. Her ears pricked up. The ancient Vedic hymns pried open her eyes. With rheumy eyes, she saw her mother sleeping next to her. Her eyes were firmly shut with furrowed brows, as though she did not want any sleep to escape. Next to her mother, Karthi lay, splayed like a starfish on the ocean floor.

The table fan droned near their feet, doling out stuffy air equally to all of them. The oppressive air stung Kalki's watery eyes. Then, it tried to lift her mother's sari tucked between her legs and roll up her brother's shirt. His shirt flapped open to reveal an undulating ribbed chest and a sunken tummy. His mouth was open, sucking in the air and savouring it in his sleep. His eyelids moved as though dreams played on them and drops of sweat glistened on his forehead.

Kalki got up and tiptoed to her brother's side. She gently shook his hand and tried to wake him up. He inhaled deeply through his mouth and woke up with a start, as he crossed from dreams to reality.

'Today is the day,' Kalki said softly.

'Just five minutes more,' Karthi said in a slurred voice as he fell back on his pillow in hopes of finding the ending to his dream. He continued to run from something or someone. He reached the end of the road, a cliff overlooking a vast ocean. The breeze brought some relief and soothed him as he panted. There was no one behind him. He was safe. Suddenly something grabbed his mouth. It came from the ground and pulled him towards the ocean. He then fell into a deep abyss and woke up, gasping for air. Kalki's hands were over his mouth.

'You were snoring,' Kalki mouthed as she looked towards her sleeping mother.

'Why are you up so early?' Karthi asked.

'Don't you remember? It is the day the tourists are supposed to come,' Kalki said.

'Oh yes, I remember. That is what Prakash Anna said. It might not be true, however,' Karthi said.

'But you promised we would check it out. We won't

know if we stay at home,' Kalki raised her voice. Karthi shushed her promptly. Both checked if their mother had woken up and tiptoed towards the corrugated iron door.

They stood by the door and waited for the right moment to open it. The table fan provided them with an opportunity. The breeze from the fan enveloped their mother, and the soft humming filled her ears, blocking out the scurrying footsteps of her children as they opened the cranky metal front door and made their way out. Her eyelids remained closed, squeezing in every drop of sleep she could get.

The morning sun took its time to rise. The clouds hinted at rain, but the wind chased them away to make way for the sun. Smoky-black crows and mynahs crooned intermittently from their hiding spot in the rustling trees. The sound of the milkman's cycle bell opened every door. Swinging temple bells gave way to prayers. Smoke from the *agarbattis* (incense sticks), floated to the heavens. The beggars tried to bring some life to their hands that had turned numb from resting their lice-ridden heads. Tea shops punctuated the streets. Deft hands poured frothing tea into hundreds of glasses. Women, old and young, strung jasmine and marigold into flowery serpents and hawked them to the pedestrians, coaxing them to buy some. The tranquillity of the night dissolved into daylight, slowly at first and then in a flash. Autorickshaws created an unholy racket, buses creaked on rusty axles and wheels, and bullock carts billowed, all jostling with each other on the main road.

The sun's rays unravelled last night's shade from the temple's façade. From top to bottom, the temple appeared bronze in the orange glow of the morning light. The glow emanating from the granite structure spread throughout the city and soon enveloped it. Citizens nestled against its ancient warmth as they carried on with their day's chores.

Sunday worshippers and regular worshippers alike, carrying coconuts and jasmine, stepped through the ornate, imposing *gopuram* under the ubiquitous stony gaze of the divine guardians. Inside, the temple grounds were damp from last night's rain. The pitter-patter of naked feet was accentuated by the sound of anklets clasped around the ankles of women clad in crisp silk saris. Men walked beside their wives, their hands clasped behind them and daydreams weighing down their heads. Children, dressed in their Sunday best, ran around in circles, occasionally bumping into each other, falling down, only to jump back up, rub the sore spot with an 'ooh' and an 'ahh' and resume their running. Karthi and Kalki scrambled up a high wall at the back of the temple and made themselves comfortable, their feet dangling on either side of the wall. Within seconds, their flat bony bottoms were sore from the roughness of the wall.

'Do you think they will come today?' Kalki asked, shifting her legs and letting them dangle on one side of the wall.

'I believe so,' Karthi answered, squinting at the stretch of main road by the side of the temple, looking for a yellow van.

'Why do you say that?' Kalki asked.

'Look over there,' Karthi said, pointing at the other end of the wall where a troop of monkeys had begun to gather. The pack leader took the highest position on top of a spire at the corner, which gave him a commanding view of the people entering the temple. Baby monkeys rode piggyback on their mothers, clutching on their mothers' hair for balance, unaware that their mothers shifted their centre of gravity as the baby monkeys pulled out their hair. A few young ones tested their skill by sprinting across to the adjacent wall, only to be checked by the piercing gaze of the leader. They looked into his eyes and understood. They remained at the high fence, dashing back and forth, hiding from the temple-goers.

'The monkeys are here every day,' Kalki said. 'What is so special about today?'

'The babies. They don't bring their babies out unless they know they can get more food.'

'But how do they know?' Kalki asked.

Karthi shrugged. 'They just do. The last time when they came to see the temple, the monkeys brought their babies with them. I don't…,' Karthi stopped as he sensed someone approaching from behind. 'Oh no…Pandi and Hari are here as well.'

'Who invited you guys?' Karthi asked his friends.

'It is not your father's temple,' Hari retorted as he dusted his palms.

'Yes, it is not your father's temple,' Pandi chimed in. He stood on the wall and stretched out his arms, back arching backwards, unleashing a putrid smell from his armpits.

'You could have at least washed before coming to the temple. You are going to scare the tourists away,' Kalki said, covering her nose.

'You shut up, darkie,' Hari said, defending Pandi. 'Let us just hope that your black face doesn't scare them away.'

'So, what are you two doing here,' Karthi asked.

'We have our reasons,' Hari said. 'Why are you here?'

'Just to see the monkeys,' Karthi said.

'I thought we were going to ask the white tourists about their whitening….,' Kalki's words fizzled out as Karthi cast her a look, warning her to stop talking.

'Oh,' Hari said, cottoning on. 'Darkie wants to ask the white people how to become fair.' He laughed out loudly.

'Of all the places in the temple you had to choose to come and sit next to us,' Karthi said.

'There it is, there it is,' Pandi yelled, pointing at a yellow van that was making its way to the temple.

'Be quiet, you idiot. People will see us,' Hari yanked at Pandi's shorts, pulling him down to sit on the wall. The worn-out string that held his shorts slackened and Pandi quickly grabbed at his sliding shorts and sat down.

The traffic on the main road was heavy. The yellow van moved carefully, taking its time to find an opening to enter the street that led to the temple. The driver switched on the left indicator. The oncoming traffic ignored it. Finally, the van inched away from the main road and wobbled towards the temple.

'See, what did I tell you?' Karthi said to Kalki. 'Somehow, the monkeys know.' Kalki gave a wide smile. The children jumped off the wall and scuttled towards the entrance of the temple.

'Ladies and gentlemen,' the driver said in English to his passengers as he parked the van. 'This is the famous Brihadeeshwara temple. We go inside now.'

Armed with cameras and binoculars, an orderly group of foreign tourists emerged from the air-conditioned van. Wearing sunglasses and wide-brimmed hats, they took out hand-held fans and began to fan themselves vigorously. The driver quickly ushered them to the shade of the temple entrance, away from the blistering heat. 'Give way, move aside,' the driver shouted to the locals as he guided the tourists inside. The people promptly stepped aside. A not-so-distant inherited reflex action from colonial times making them respond instantly. They instinctively bowed and briefly brought their feet together in attention as they scurried into the temple, hugging the wall, like rats hiding from light.

A local bus screeched to a halt. Passengers swarmed out of the bus, shoving and pushing one another. As soon as their eyes met the eyes of the foreigners, their frantic jostling stopped abruptly, as though a modicum of civility was transmitted through eye contact. They gawked at the tourists, forgetting their purpose.

Kalki watched the tourists enchanted, as though she was at a magic show. She admired their crisp linen tops and ironed denim jeans, shorts and skirts. Their bags were chockful with foreign things. Their milky fair hands were covered with golden spots. Their light-coloured hair was curly, wavy and silky. They examined the temple walls, running their fingers over the sculptures.

'Come on, let's get closer,' Karthi said. They inched their way towards the tourists. With palms smeared with spit, they finger-combed their hair. Pandi tightened the drawstring of his shorts. Kalki straightened her blouse and dusted her skirt. She showed herself to her brother and he nodded in approval.

'Where do you think you are going?' the tourist guide, Mohan, asked.

'Look, who's talking! Is the temple your father's property,' Hari snapped.

'Yes, is it your father's property,' Pandi echoed.

'Looks like you are the sidekick,' Mohan said with a sneer.

'Answer the question, fool,' Hari said.

'We just want to look at the white People up close, that is all,' Karthi said, glancing over his shoulder to see if they were still there.

'You say that now but once you get close to them, you will touch them. You want to talk to foreigners. Where will it stop?' Mohan said, standing in their way, his arms crossed over his chest. 'Listen, these people have come after such a long time. I have a family to feed. I don't want you lot ruining things for me. Now scram!'

'How else can we get close to the white people if you

don't allow us?' Kalki cut in.

'If you go near them with that black face of yours, they will take the next flight out of India,' Mohan said.

'The monkeys are allowed inside, but we humans are not,' Kalki said to her brother.

'That is because the monkeys are avatars of Hanuman, one of the gods,' Karthi said, trying to find reason in Mohan's stern words.

'And you are the real monkey. A super black one,' Hari said with a laugh that was echoed by Pandi. Kalki hid behind her brother.

'Enough!' Mohan shouted with a flushed face. 'First of all, you are not supposed to be here. Should I tell the priest about you people? That a bunch of cretinous lower-caste grubs are prowling in his temple? You are aware you are not allowed to enter the temple, right? Now off you go. Get out of here, you filthy animals.'

Karthi and Kalki were used to rejection and derision. Like a noose through the nose of an ox, it guided their life. Towards derelict schools. To the end of queues. To the sewers. To the graveyards. Out of the Constitution. Like the dust that fell from the feet of Brahma.

The tourists entered the temple complex like scared, reluctant sheep. Their shepherd, Mohan, made massive welcoming gestures, which somewhat assuaged their fear. He threw a dirty look at the children, who stood outside with their backs against the wall, which meant, '*Look what you are doing to them, you are scaring them.*'

The tourists moved towards Mohan. Cautious and

light-footed. They were worried that they might do the wrong thing by walking too fast or talking too loudly, as though that would wake the ancient gods from deep slumber and curse them for generations to come.

'Who knows what kind of black magic is at play here,' one of them said. The others nodded in agreement.

Kalki marvelled at their fair skin. Some were pinkish white, some were reddish white. She was blackish black. She wondered how they were so fair. Was it because of something they ate? Or drank? Did they eat only white foods?

'No afraid. Come here. Come here,' Mohan called out to the tourists. 'Relaxing. No worrying. First, remove shoes here.'

Mohan turned to the tourists who were ready for a lesson on the Great Chola Empire. Despite his instructions, one of them inadvertently stepped into the temple ground with footwear. A flurry of apologies erupted from her mouth. Mohan kow-towed, untied her laces, and helped her remove them, saying itsokmadam all the time.

'Photo?' one of them asked Mohan, pointing to the temple and his camera.

'Saar, do vaatever you vaant saar. This your temple,' Mohan said ingratiatingly, his hands folded.

The look of approval on Mohan's face gave the tourists more confidence and they shuffled in. The flashes from their cameras lit the space like a galaxy of stars.

'Don't forget your sunscreen. If anyone didn't apply

before, do so now before we step into the courtyard,' one of the tourists said, interrupting the photography session.

Kalki saw some of them let their bags fall off their shoulders. They plonked on the floor. They began to reach in with their fair hands, scrabbling for something. 'I got it,' one of them said as she fished out a blue bottle from her bag. Others extended their hands, reaching for the blue bottle. The lady with the blue bottle squirted some white paste onto the pleading hands of the men and women. They all slathered the white cream on their exposed skin.

'Look, Anna,' Kalki yanked at Karthi's shirt. 'I think that's how they stay so fair.'

'How?'

'With the cream from the blue bottle.'

'You are right.'

'But how can we get it from them?'

'We can just ask for it,' Kalki said confidently. The temple elephant was at the gate, blessing visitors in exchange for coins. The elephant would receive the notes and whisk it up to its mahout, who greedily snatched it up. The trunk, on its way down, would gently tap on the faithful's bowed head. The amused tourists gathered around the elephant to receive a blessing.

'Let me try giving him a dollar coin. Let's see if he does anything different,' one of them said, bursting into at laughing and depositing the dollar coin into the trunk. As though the elephant would convert the dollar into rupees and bestow an equivalent amount of blessing. The elephant flung the dollar coin to the ground and extended its trunk towards the curious tourist for the right form of money. The tourists roared with laughter at this. The local temple-goers stopped to stare at the laughing white people, wondering at their merriment. Later, they prayed for the ability to laugh out loudly like the white people, who seemed to have no worries at all.

The elephant rocked back and forth, its tail swatting flies off its back, waiting for the next note. The mahout sighed ruefully, sad at missing out on the dollar coin and regretting that he had trained his elephant too well.

The children waited till the tourists disappeared behind a volley of camera flashes. Their shoes were arranged against the wall as though on display. The women's shoes had bows, ribbons and stones. Some had high heels. The men's shoes were shiny, polished and pure white, as though they had somewhere important to go after the tour. Maybe everything they do is important, Kalki thought.

She picked up a red shoe with a bow. It felt cold. And dry. She brought it close to her nose. It smelled sweet, like a bunch of exotic flowers. She pictured the shoe walking on foreign roads, on chilly streets, on neat footpaths. Footpaths so clean that you can eat off it. She put the shoe on even though it was big for her feet. She pictured herself wearing the red shoes and strutting down the street. A lump of burning coal streaking across the white roads.

'Put it down, Kalki,' Karthi warned. 'They might see us.'

Kalki was whisked out of her daydream by the din of locals entering the temple. She spotted something behind a shoe. It was a pink headband. Strands of golden hair were caught in it. She quickly picked it up and tucked it under her top.

'I told you bringing her was a bad idea. She is a bad omen. A dark omen,' Hari blasted Karthi. 'We could have gotten close to the white people. We could have squeezed something from them.'

'Enough!' Karthi barked. 'It is not her fault. Mohan told us all off. He didn't give you any special permission to join the tour group.'

The blame-game went on for a while. With no one available to blame for their failed odyssey, they put an end to their bickering. Succumbing to the pangs of hunger they were all experiencing, they dashed towards the food hall. The smell of rice cakes, crackling mustard seeds and chutney invaded their nostrils. They inhaled the wafting aroma and hurried towards it.

When they reached the food hall, the aromas died. All they could get was the smell of soggy banana leaves, masticated vegetable skins and satisfied burps.

'Again, it's because of darkie,' Hari complained.

'A judgement will fall upon you,' squawked Narayan, a former priest turned crazy beggar. His right eye bulged as he spoke, while his left eye remained shut and swollen with pus oozing out. He was the only beggar allowed to enter the temple premises. Five years ago, after finishing his evening rituals, he tripped on the stairs and banged his head on the temple floor. There was no bruise, just a minor bump. Taking this as a sign from God, the priest decided to spend even more time in the temple. Day by day, his prayers grew longer, as did the bump on his head. Eventually, it settled on his occipital lobe. The last thing he remembered seeing before everything turned fuzzy was the blue sky and a billowy white figure of Ganesh. Eventually, his prayers stopped, but he made the temple his home. He still wore the same orange lungi, which had turned moss green with time and the sacred thread that had turned black, probably because it had absorbed all the sins around him.

Narayan let out a peal of hysterical laughter that bounced off the ancient walls. Heads turned, and Narayan's story was repeated by tired lips again and again to fresh nosy ears.

'He was never a priest, just an ordinary beggar who got lucky to be inside the temple begging,' the villagers said. 'Maybe he killed someone in his past life, or he could have eaten meat. He used to steal people's offerings, and sometimes I did see him stick his hand into the donation box.'

The stories got wilder over time and maybe some were even untrue.

Narayan scratched his head. Thick matted hair stuck out from under his ragged turban. He brought out a small drum, a *damaru*. Flies buzzed around him. Some adamant ones didn't budge even with the vigorous shaking of the drum. Along with it, his head shook, and the stubborn flies took off to find quieter abodes.

'Judgment will soon come...' Narayan said once again.

'What judgement?' Kalki asked.

'Soon, the Cheris will be wiped out from the face of earth.' He meant the untouchables, the lower castes.

'Ignore him. He's a mad man,' Karthi muttered.

'You cannot escape the judgement of God,' Narayan screamed. 'Only those who atone will be spared.' His eyes slid back into his head, revealing the whites of his eyes, which were now yellow.

'Excuse us. We've got to go. Our mother is waiting outside.' Karthi grabbed Kalki's hand. To his surprise, she resisted.

'I'm willing to atone,' Kalki said firmly.

'Are you out of your mind?' Karthi shrieked.

'Hari said I was a bad omen.'

'The girl is ugly but wise,' Narayan said. 'Follow me.'

He asked them to enter the empty dining hall littered with folded banana leaves. Flies and rats scavenged on the morsels left behind. A group of men had started to clean the floor from one corner, placing the banana leaves into a wicker basket.

'Come on now. Take off your clothes,' Narayan instructed the children, playing the *damaru*.

'How is that going to help?' Hari asked.

Narayan brought his face closer to Hari's. 'You dare question the priest? Do you know what this is?' He took a small bottle out of his robe, filled with white fluid.

Hari shook his head. His body trembled as his eyes remained fixed on Narayan's amber, tenuous teeth, secreting cruddy saliva.

'This is the soul of every child who disobeyed me. All of them are inside this bottle.' Narayan took a swig from the bottle. Some of the milky fluid escaped his mouth and coursed through his grimy beard. The rancid smell of the liquid made the children nauseous. 'Do you want to be inside the bottle now?' He played the *damaru* and the sound echoed through the hall.

Scared and exchanging quizzical looks, the children disrobed, covering their genitals with their hands. Kalki placed the scrunchy under her clothes.

'Good children,' Narayan said, stroking their backs. 'Now roll over the plantain leaves till you are soaked in the leftovers of the Brahmins. Your sins will be washed away. No longer will you be a lower caste. Elevate yourself.' The sound of the *damaru* created a portentous ambience.

'Roll, roll, roll,' he intoned. Kalki rolled diligently, making sure every scrap of leftover food stuck to her naked skin. Morsels of rice and vegetable peels latched onto her body. Occasionally, after a few rolls, there were some uneaten sweets. Kalki gobbled the laddu or the jalebi as she rolled. She even took a wad of dal and scrubbed it on her face.

By the end of it, the children weren't naked anymore. They were clad in what was once the season's best produce, the masticated remnants of it anyway. The *damaru* continued to sound, accompanied by Narayan's cackles.

'How do we know if it worked?' Pandi asked Narayan scraping the dried food off his hands.

'I think it is already working,' Kalki beamed and looked at Hari, who usually wouldn't hesitate to call her names. Now he did not even bother. Hari did not look at her but at the blue sky streaked with wisps of clouds.

'Again, the girl proves to be wise,' Narayan said, continuing to play the *damaru*.

'I have another request,' Kalki said.

'Ask at once or forever be tainted with regret,' Narayan said.

'How can I become fair?' Kalki asked, thinking about the woman in the poster.

'Attainable, but will take time,' Narayan said.

'How?'

'What is your favourite fruit?'

'Mangoes,' Kalki replied.

'A lower caste member has the luxury of tasting the king of fruits?' Narayan's eyes widened.

'She is lying,' Hari said.

'I am not. I tasted it once. Someone threw the seed in the bin without sucking the juice out of it.'

'And being the dirty little thing you are, you fished it from the trash,' Pandi said, wincing in disgust.

'Eat mangoes till the darkness in your skin melts away,' the looney priest's silhouette vanished, and the sound of his *damaru* with him, sealing his propositions.

The cleaners in the food hall stopped to laugh at their plight. 'See, this why they are from the lower caste. They will believe anything. Tell them that the sky will fall and they will run into their holes.'

Naked, embarrassed and covered in the smell of curry, they dashed off with their clothes.

As they dressed themselves, a slap landed on Kalki's back. She screamed in pain and tears welled up in her eyes.

'You bitch,' Mohan yelled. 'Where is it? Where is it, bitch?'

'Stop it, stop beating her,' Karthi said, head-butting Mohan, throwing him off balance. Mohan fell, his shoes flying off his feet. Pandi and Hari bolted off and hid behind a tree.

Kalki sobbed, wiping her runny nose with her cruddy arms. She quickly dressed and picked up the headband, squeezing it tightly in the one hand. Suddenly she smelled exotic flowers and stopped crying at once. The tourists were marching towards her. One of them was limping. She had on only one red shoe with a bow. She winced with every step. Kalki felt desperately sorry for her.

'Where is it?' Mohan stood up, dusting himself. 'Where is the shoe?'

'What shoe?' Karthi asked with a scowl as he put his arms around his sobbing sister.

'The red one. Look at Madam's feet,' Mohan said, pointing to the white woman's naked foot.

'We didn't take it,' Karthi said.

'Don't you dare lie to me? I saw the two of you playing with the shoe.'

'I said we didn't take it. Does it look like we have it?' Karthi yelled.

Scared that Mohan might find the headband, she hid her hand behind her.

'What is that? What are you hiding in your hand then?' Mohan grabbed her hand and prised it open. The scrunchy fell out.

'What is this?' he barked. 'If you stole this, you must have stolen the shoe too. You better tell me, or else I will call the police. You know what they do to a bunch of untouchables like you, especially if you have committed a crime.'

Karthi's eyes welled up, and tears streamed down his cheek They landed on his sister's face. Seeing her brother's tears made Kalki cry even more. A trickle-down effect. They were tears of shame, hopelessness and utter devastation.

'There, there. It is okay. Don't cry,' someone spoke in English.

The white lady with one shoe, made her way towards Kalki. She stretched her arm to console Kalki, but her arms quickly contracted as though a scorpion stung her.

At that moment, Kalki realised that white people could change colour like a chameleon. Her face was red when she felt sorry for Kalki. A soft pink when her arms were reaching out for Kalki. Then she turned deep green upon seeing Kalki slathered in pieces of curry leaves and dried up bits of yellow pulses.

'She is sick,' the white woman said, throwing up at the sight of Kalki.

'Look what you did. Get away from here,' Mohan said, before rushing to the aid of the breathless woman.

Kalki took one last glance at the ailing woman. She looked at Kalki and began to vomit again. A pool of yellow bilious vomit flowed onto the temple grounds.

Soon, Hari and Pandi joined them. Eight naked feet scuttled away in silence. Hari didn't have anything to say. He felt sorry for Kalki. No insults. No dark skin jokes.

'How do we know if it worked?' Pandi asked, oblivious to everyone's current feelings. He was scraping the dried food off his hands. 'Did we ascend to the upper caste?'

Karthi took his sister's hand and drew her away from Hari and Pandi. They made their way back home.

Pandi was still wondering if the ritual had worked or not. On their way back to the slum, Pandi got his answer. A man from the upper caste scolded him for being the first thing he saw when he lit the lamp in his house.

The children's minds were clouded by all that had happened. They were distracted but the dependable landmarks guided them back home. The street bulb that flickered day and night. The rancid smell of open sewage. The raspy barks of pariah dogs. The doppler effect of the voice of the vegetable seller reverberating as he pedalled his cart loaded with scrawny vegetables.

They knew they were almost home, but loud screeches stopped them in their tracks. Ahead of them, the same group of monkeys from the temple were fighting, toppling each other and baring their fangs, followed by demonic hisses.

'I think they have the white woman's shoe,' Kalki said, after getting a glimpse of something red being thrown around among the brown furry upheaval.

Karthi gathered some stones lying around and pelted them to scare them away. He charged towards the one who had the red shoe shouting at the shoe-loving primate. It proved difficult for the monkey to carry the shoe and dodge the stones. So, it dropped the shoe and raced up a tree. Seeing a window of opportunity, another monkey tried to grab the shoe but changed its mind when Karthi threatened it with a handful of rocks. It snarled at him and joined its siblings on the tree.

The shoe was wet with monkey slobber and had holes in them. The flowery scent was gone, replaced by a primal monkey smell.

'Should we take it back?' Kalki asked. In her eyes, it was still a perfectly desirable shoe, faults and all.

'Keep it. I don't think the woman would want it anyway now. What do you say? Shall we go to the mango orchard tomorrow and gather some mangoes and see if it turns your skin white or not?' Karthi asked.

Kalki smiled. She slipped on the red shoe and hobbled back home, holding her brother's hand. The red shoe hung from her black foot like burning coal.

Chapter 4

Four pairs of eyes squinted at the clear evening sky. With hands cupping their eyes, forming finger telescopes, Karthi, Kalki, Hari and Pandi scanned the sky for a hint of black to streak downwards towards them. Kalki stayed in the shadow of the Golmohur tree because Aaya had told her to stay away from the sun. Now that Narayan had told Kalki to eat mangoes to shed her dark skin colour, it had become their new obsession.

They couldn't steal from the fruit and vegetable vendors. Their flitting eyes caught any movements behind them as they served their customers thanks to the ample training the monkeys have given them. There was no escaping the vigilant eyes of the cart vendors. They could try the fruit sellers in the bazaar. Maybe the crowd would provide ample cover, they thought. Their hopes were dashed when they noticed that the piles of shining vegetables and fruits sat on high tables out of their reach.

They had to think of something else. 'Subramaniam's mango orchard,' Karthi said.

'But how,' Kalki muttered. She pointed out that there was barbed wire on top of the wall all around. Nobody could get in, not even the nimble monkeys. She remembered watching the monkeys try to get inside the compound to get at the juicy mangoes. The older monkeys tried to grab the wire and pry them open. The little fellows squeezed through the wires but emerged with bloody wounds. She could hear the shrieks of the baby monkeys as their mothers untangled them with care. One unlucky monkey was caught so firmly that the other pack members watched on helplessly as it writhed around, flapping its body, which made its injures worse. The next day the monkey died.

Subramaniam decided not to remove the monkey's mangled body. 'Let it be a gruesome reminder to whoever tries to come to my property to steal my mangoes,' he said.

But Karthi's plan didn't involve scaling walls and jumping through wires. It didn't require breaking locks or digging holes.

'If everything goes according to plan, Subramaniam will allow us voluntarily into his mango orchard. All we need is a bat and a ball. For that, we need Pandi and Hari as he has a ball,' Karthi said.

Kalki didn't want to include Pandi and Hari in the plan because she didn't want them to make fun of her dark skin. But Karthi said they didn't have a choice. 'Hari is the only one with a ball, and we need the ball for the plan to work. And wherever Hari goes, Pandi follows.'

It was just another usual morning for Hari the day he found the ball. He was on his way to relieve himself. He didn't go where everyone went. Behind the thorny brambles, on the railway tracks. Armed with a net on a stick and his rectangular wooden panel, he would go to the sewer canal. With the panel positioned across the canal, Hari would hang his bottom over the edge to defecate while he used his net to catch whatever caught his fancy as it passed downstream on its way to the sea. He had managed to gather a neat collection of things. A broken toy car without the chassis. A plastic watch that didn't fit him. A dented frying pan which he gave to his mother. A holey shoe. Hair clips. A pencil box and an empty perfume bottle full of sewage water.

One day, the tennis ball bobbed along the sluggish stream towards Hari. The bright neon green of the ball suggested that it was brand new. As he reached his net to pick it up, the ball ducked into the water, coming out entirely black and past him. Hari quickly jumped into the stream to grab it, not wanting to let something unbroken, completely intact, pass him by. Smeared in crusty black sewage, Hari emerged from the canal, victorious, like a drowned rat with a prized meal.

The boys were near the orchard, hitting the ball with a wooden slat. 'Where did it go?' asked Hari, wiping the sweat off his forehead. A little bit of salty sweat trickled into his eye, stinging him.

'I told you to hit in that direction,' Karthi said, pointing to the wall. 'The ball would have landed inside Subramaniam's compound.'

'I did hit in that direction,' Pandi asserted. 'Now it is somewhere up in the air. God knows where it went.' He flung his bat to a side.

'Shut up,' Hari screamed. 'I went through shit to get that ball. Suppose it doesn't come down. I will drown you where I found that ball,' he threatened.

Only Kalki's eyes had followed the arc of the ball. She didn't alert the boys lest she lose track of its downward trajectory. She heard a soft rustle in a bush nearby.

'There it is, there it is,' screamed Kalki, jumping deliriously with a hand over her fat belly, which was part of their plan. 'It dropped behind that bush.'

The three boys rushed towards the bush and started to look for the tennis ball. Its original green colour had turned to a putrid yellow, a result of its adventures in the sewer.

'See, if it wasn't for my sister, we would be wasting time hunting for the ball,' Karthi said, smiling at Kalki proudly. Kalki's face brimmed with satisfaction, and she looked toward Hari for approval.

'Finally, darkie proves herself to be useful,' Hari said and got ready to throw the ball. 'I think a fat belly suits you, just like it suits Subramaniam.' Hari laughed and elbowed Pandi to laugh with him. Pandi snorted and let out a supportive laugh.

'You know the reason for her fat belly,' Karthi defended his sister.

'Doesn't mean I can't laugh at it. Look at her.'

'If you don't stop laughing, I will scream.' Kalki opened her mouth to scream but Karthi's hand flashed out and covered her lips. 'It is ok. Don't worry about them. You are here to play the most important role,' he said.

'Why is this my part? Why can't I bat or throw the ball?' Kalki asked.

'Because I don't trust these fools to do your part,' Karthi said.

'Is it trust or something else?' Hari looked at Karthi. 'You better get me some mangoes from the orchard. That is why I am allowing you to use my ball.'

'Come on now, Hari. Enough,' Karthi said, trying to change the topic. 'Throw the ball straight. Don't think you are some big bowler. We are not here to play. We are pretending to play.'

The sweat cooled their faces. Everyone took their premeditated positions. Pandi was to bat and hit the ball into Subramaniam's compound. Karthi crouched, not too far away, to field the ball while looking out for snoopy neighbours. His job was to catch the first glint of suspicion in their eyes or the way they arched their eyebrows or the craning of the neck from side to side. His eyes scanned their faces for any gesture that would alert nosy neighbours, who would question their presence in this alley, right next to a mango orchard near Subramaniam's house. A man walked past them, with one arm tucked behind his back and the other holding a neem twig, brushing his teeth. He paused to peek into the alley. A raucous yell erupted from Pandi. 'I am ready, start the game. Throw the ball, Hari. Let us play.' The man shrugged and walked away, vigorously chewing on the twig between his teeth.

The ball flew from Hari's hand and whistled as it tore through the wind. Pandi steadied his bat and firmly planted his bare feet apart on the uneven earth, glancing at the rugged mammoth wall and plotting the intended trajectory. Karthi scanned the road for any suspicious onlookers. There were none.

The ball bounced off Pandi's bat and followed its promised trajectory, up and above the gigantic wall, past the zenith of the mango tree inside the compound. Everyone's auditory senses heightened. They tried to catch the sound of the ball falling somewhere on the other side of the wall. A staccato of rustles confirmed that the ball had indeed landed on the ground, signalling the start of Kalki's role in the operation.

'Don't screw it up, darkie,' Hari said, waving his finger at her.

Kalki stuck her tongue out at him and walked away. The boys scuttled into a concrete bin with holes. They watched Kalki from their vantage point.

Kalki made sure her fake bulging belly was secure and shuffled towards the imposing black and gold metal gate. It looked menacing. The steel felt hot as she clamped her hands around it and climbed up to reach the bell. She rang it twice and heard it ringing inside. She could see the house through the gate. It had multiple roofs, like three pairs of upside-down boats stacked together and floating in the sky. She searched for the ball in the mango orchard adjacent to it. She spotted it nuzzling among the fallen leaves. A pair of squirrels darted back and forth, from the ball to the tree and back again, studying the motionless intruder. A lorry thundered down the road behind Kalki. Then a burly figure walked down the path towards the gate.

'WHAT ARE YOU DOING HERE, SCUM?' He thundered at Kalki scaring her into falling from the gate. She fell on her back, scraping her elbows on the stony path. Crimson streaks of blood marred her arms. She got up and brushed the dust off her skirt.

Subramaniam's imposing figure eclipsed the sunshine. He wore a white *vesti* with a shimmering yellow border. His hairy right leg poked out of it, reminding Kalki of a log swarming with ants. He had no shirt on. He had two gold chains that circled his hairy chest. A thick green belt was wrapped around his wide waist as though it held his enormous body together. His silhouette, with writhing hair, pulsated with every breath he took.

'WHAT ARE YOU DOING HERE?' He shouted, emphasising each word.

'Who is it?' someone called out from the house, behind Subramaniam.

'Nothing, dear. I will take care of it.' Subramaniam replied as though to the house.

Kalki shook like a leaf. Her hands reached for her

paunch and clasped it tightly. 'Ball, ball,' she stuttered, pointing to the ground beyond the gate.

Subramaniam grunted and studied her dark skin. His face twisted, and his ample moustache, with bouncy curls at the end, fluttered. At first, he thought the low caste girl must have fallen into a pile of cow dung while playing, because no one could be this ugly and dark. He bellowed to sniff the air to make sure but couldn't smell any cow dung. But when his eyes got used to her, he realised that her skin, the dark hue, was all her. Then his eyes travelled to her unusual, swollen tummy. It bulged as though she was pregnant. Her slender body, brittle arms and legs did not justify the enormous bulge that ran from her upper chest to her lower abdomen. *She is carrying something,* Subramaniam thought. *A disease. Kwashiorkor. Indeed, given her low caste and her protein-deficient diet. How many adversities must a person struggle with?* he thought. He exhaled loudly through his mouth before he felt a tingle of empathy. *Not my problem,* he thought to himself and shrugged.

Subramaniam swung open the gate till it creaked to a halt. Another bulge erupted from Kalki's throat and travelled to her tummy, where it stayed as Subramaniam grunted at her, his flaring nostrils occasionally blocking his vision.

'I already warned you dirty kids not come to our side. Don't test my leniency. Go on now. Pick up the ball and nothing else. Leave this area at once. If you don't leave in five minutes, you will face my wrath.' He waddled outside with his arms on his waist, to check if there was someone else. The eyes inside the rubbish container closed briefly to be one with the bin.

Kalki ducked under his arms, holding her belly and raced towards the ball and scooped it up before Subramaniam had a chance to see the ball. Subramaniam flinched as Kalki walked next to him and hopped back in case he caught her skin disease. A wave of bitter anger spread through Karthi as he watched his sister being treated like an untouchable person. But he knew that without Kalki this plan would not have worked. If it had been one of the boys, Subramaniam would have chased them away before they could even open their mouths. He took his chance with Kalki and used her as a dark pawn.

'I think it is on the tree,' Kalki said, pointing up. Subramaniam flicked his hand, which meant she could go up the tree.

Kalki started to climb the tree, looking like an enlarged toad. The squirrels flitted in front of her. They squeaked incessantly, either cheering her on or wishing that she would slip and fall. In no time, she had hoisted herself onto a nearby branch, laden with mangoes. Making sure Subramaniam wasn't watching her, she unbuttoned her shirt and let balls of crumpled newspaper tumble. Yesterday's breaking news became today's aborted paper foetus. There was no more bulging tummy, just a dark sunken valley.

'Did you find the ball yet?' Subramaniam yelled from below.

Kalki shivered and showed two fingers indicating she need a couple of minutes.

'Who are you talking to,' the voice from house yelled again.

'Don't worry, dear. Everything is fine,' Subramaniam replied. 'Find the ball fast,' he told Kalki.

The mangoes hung in groups. Triplets. Quintuplets. The top ones were green and the bottom ones reflected the colours of the setting sun. Kalki's mouth watered as she allowed the smell of mangoes to travel to her nose. She quickly plucked four plump mangoes, wrapped them in paper, and stuffed them inside her shirt. She made her way down. She held the ball in her right hand, making sure it was visible to Subramaniam.

'Here it is. I found it,' Kalki waved her hand with the ball. Her left hand cradled her mango belly.

'Wait a minute,' Subramaniam's rough puffy hands stopped her. One of his bushy eyebrows raised, he eyed her tummy. Before he could utter a word, Kalki pre-empted him. 'I will go now. I got the ball.'

'How did you get the ...?' Subramaniam asked, patting his own paunch.

Kalki sucked her lips in and started to grind her teeth. 'Uhm...Uhm...'

'When did your stomach start bulging? What happened to your skin? It is so dark. I have never seen anyone with such dark skin.' Subramaniam was mildly curious.

Kalki didn't know what to say. Suddenly something

moved inside her shirt. The mango kicked and wanted to come out. She tried to adjust it, but it was too late. She wasn't quick enough. One mango fell and rolled towards Subramaniam's foot like a lost puppy returning to its rightful owner. Subramaniam's curiosity was quelled, and the eyes in the bin bulged.

'RUN!' Karthi shot out of the bin and screamed.

Subramaniam splayed his body like a threatening grizzly bear, so Kalki had nowhere to run. Spooked, Kalki ran to the other side of the orchard, past the big mango trees. Subramaniam thundered towards her. 'Don't go there!'

Kalki reached a garden at the back with rows of saplings. Like little droopy umbrellas, they shivered at the slight hint of wind. With nowhere to go and Subramaniam gaining on her, she zipped to the wall at the back, crushing a few anorexic green umbrellas on her way, and started to climb them, but it was too high.

'What the hell is going on here?' the voice from the house growled one last time, and out of the back door came a stumpy woman on a wheelchair. She had a large red *bindi* on her forehead, which matched her furious red eyes. Her silk sari was stiff, and it made tsk-tsk sounds as it touched the wheels of her wheelchair, like a stumpy watermelon on wheels.

'Look at what she has done. You idiot! You broke my precious baby mango saplings.' The woman howled in anger and banged her chest with her tiny hands. 'What kind of a man are you? Can't you stop a small girl?'

'Don't worry, dear. You go inside. I will take care of it,' Subramaniam tried to pacify her. 'It is not good for your heart to be this angry, my dear.'

Kalki, making use of Subramaniam's distraction, made a dash towards him, trampling on some more saplings. She ducked past him and ran out.

'Listen,' the woman called to Subramaniam. 'She is escaping, you silly man. She is getting away, and she destroyed more of my babies.' She continued to pummel her bountiful chest and rotated her wheelchair wildly.

Outside, the boys were waiting for Kalki with bated breath.

'Did you get the mangoes?' Pandi asked. 'How many?'

'Did you get my ball?' Hari asked.

'Is that important?' Karthi barked. 'We need to get away from here. He is coming for us!'

Subramaniam emerged, waving his big bulky hands wildly. 'Come here, you little shit. Wait and see what I will do to you lot once I have got my hands on you.' The chains around his neck slammed against his chest.

'Let us meet at the train station. Now run in different directions,' Karthi said, grabbing his sister's hand

They ran past sun-dried houses, past angry wives and drunk husbands, jumped over fences, pushed through a herd of cows, scared the chickens and ducks, knocked over clay pots, rubbed off the white *kolams* at the entrances of houses, before grabbing a low branch and climbing up a massive banyan tree. Panting and tired, they searched for Subramaniam. In the distance, a bent brown blob was gasping for air. Every inhalation and expiration of the man sounded like a bull's bellow. Rearranging his gold chains and readjusting his lungi over his humongous waist, Subramaniam roared and punched the air above him. 'I know what you look like, darkie. I will catch you.'

As soon as he disappeared, they made their way to the train station and saw Pandi and Hari, who demanded their share of mangoes and the ball.

'Bloody darkie, you really are cursed, aren't you?' Hari said, snatching the mango and the ball.

'We all played our part properly without any trouble, but you have to stir shit up,' Pandi said, taking his mango. There was only one left.

'Shut up. Go and enjoy your mangoes.' Karthi said. 'You can have the last one,' he told Kalki.

'But what about you?' Kalki asked.

'It is all for you. Let's see if what the priest at the temple said was true.'

On the railway tracks, Hari, Pandi, Karthi and Kalki sat tearing the flesh of the mangoes. Streaks of dry urine ran in the middle of the train track. The smell of uric acid blended with the scent of mangoes. They tasted mangoes for the first time. It was juicy, sweet, with a dash of prickly sourness. Like dollops of sunrise making its way down their parched throats. The moment was full of squelchy sucking sounds and licking lips, satisfied giggles, and not-so-grumbling tummies. Kalki offered some to her brother, but he declined.

'Check your skin,' Karthi said. 'Maybe it's working.'

Kalki wiped her yellow hands on her skirt and looked at her arms. They were still the same colour. Pitch black. Maybe the flame-shaped mark on my chest is expanding and eating the darkness away, she thought. But it was just the same size. Disappointed, she tried to throw the unfinished mango away, but Karthi stopped her.

'Maybe you have to finish the entire thing. Suck every juice out of it.'

'But it's not working, and there is a big seed inside.'

'I have heard the seed is the best part.'

'Yes. Yes, the seed is the best,' Hari and Pandi agreed in unison, stripping the seed bare of flesh.

Karthi removed the pudgy yellow mush from his sister's hands. He plucked the debris that peppered the mango seed and gave the seed a gentle wipe with his shirt, every so lightly, so the sap stayed put. 'Now, open your mouth.'

Kalki slurped the stringy bits of the seed, some wedging themselves between her teeth. Her face contorted as the sour bit hit her first, then she smiled. And Karthi smiled back at her, glad that she was enjoying the sweetness of the mango as it washed the inside of her mouth.

'Look, darkie. Look. I am turning fair,' Hari and Pandi said in mock shock, showing her their hands and laughing at her. Kalki thought she had eaten the wrong mango and genuinely checked their hands before she realized what was happening. Hari and Pandi started to dance and sing.

'Darkie, darkie, only wants one thing,
That is to be as fair as London's king,
But she is so dark like the night,
And when she smiles, we go affright.'

'They are just a bunch of idiots. Just ignore them,' Karthi said. 'It is because of you that these fools got to taste mangoes for the first time.'

Kalki looked at their yellow crusty lips and could not contain her pride in giving them something unattainable. She smiled with yellow teeth as she watched the boys enjoy the fruits of her labour, as in the distance, a chugging, rapid rattle of the Madras Mail approached them, whistling ominously.

Chapter 5

'Listen! I want the mother of those kids, especially the mother of the black girl, to pay for what her daughter has done,' Subramaniam's wife, Lakshmi, declared, folding her arms across her chest. 'Get rid of Chellamma. I want their mother to be the maid from now on.'

Subramaniam tried to reason with her and said it was only a few saplings. They could surely replace them. Lakshmi's angry eyes pricked his skin, and he didn't discuss the issue any further. He nodded his head and walked away with his hands behind his back, wondering what to do. Subramaniam always did whatever Lakshmi asked for two reasons. One: He was the cause of his wife's disability. Two: He wasn't sure if she knew that he was impotent. If exposed, it would ruin his status as the village leader. People would castrate him with their words and stares. All the goodwill would be questioned and be probably reversed because the judgment of a sterile man is only as good as a woman's. So, he couldn't risk not doing anything she asked.

It was at the level crossing that Lakshmi had become disabled. He wasn't sure if he had any part in it, whether it was deliberate by his subconscious self or if it was just an accident that happened because they were at the wrong place at the wrong time. Or was it the right place at the right time?

Before his marriage, Subramaniam was an eligible, good-looking, rich man, thanks to his inherited orchards and farms. Also, thanks to his formidable figure and daunting voice, he towered over everyone in the area. People turned to him for answers and solutions. Eventually, Subramaniam became the leader of the village. He was present at every congregation, every wedding, every ceremony conducted in the village. Whenever there was a hint of commotion or a flicker of unrest, he moved towards the source, like flies drawn to burning lanterns. His voice reigned supreme. His indomitable body made everyone look up to him. He set up agreements and broke up fights; he doled out advice and patched up families. He threatened wayward young husbands and brought them back in line. He wiped the tears of hopeless wives and straightened their family life. Every solution cemented his position even more. He passed judgments by whipping out his right arm with a pointed index finger and would say, 'This is my final solution.' Power surged through his body, wobbling in the fatty distended flesh of his upper right arm. And everyone listened.

Subramaniam was riding high with his decisive judgement, his index finger, until he got married. The wedding was an extravagant affair, almost like a festival. The local temple was hired for the entire day. People didn't have a god to worship that day. Nothing less for the chief of the village. People poured in from neighbouring villages. Some attended the entire wedding ceremony. Some came for the food with drooping empty tummies after fasting for two days to have more space for all the food. They also brought containers to smuggle out food. Some came for fresh gossip, to find out whose husband lost his job, whose wife was barren, whose child was a half-wit at school.

Almost a year passed after the wedding and Lakshmi had borne no child. And the whispers began. Subramaniam could feel the whispers burning into the back of his neck. There are big secrets in small rumours. He couldn't provide solutions to problems as he did in the past. He could almost hear their thoughts as they wrinkled up their nose and said, 'Can't even produce a child, but here he is telling us what to with our lives.'

'Breathe. Breathe out, ma,' the local doctor said when Subramaniam took his wife to the hospital, pressing the stethoscope on Lakshmi's chest, listening to her ovaries through her heart. He showed her how to breathe. His face puckered up. His eyes widened behind his spectacles, the springy white hair stood up on his head, his body ballooned and then shrank. Her heart drummed in his ears. Tap-tap. Tap-tap. Tap-tap. A language that only he understood. Subramaniam opened his shirt and bared his chest, thinking it was his turn next. 'No, no, sir. I don't need to check your health. You see, traditionally, it is always the women's problem,' the doctor said.

'See, there is nothing I can do,' the doctor said after listening to Lakshmi's heartbeat. 'It is all in His hands.' He looked to the ceiling as though he was expecting an apple to fall into his hands. The doctor's bald head shone like a full moon. 'Go to the temple and place your problems in His hands. He will look after you.' Just like that, he relegated his job to God.

The next day, they joined the queue of devoted worshippers at the temple. A private audience with God. The priest was the conveyor belt. Sporting a hair bun and gold silk fabric tied round his waist, the priest made multiple trips from the mortal realm to the heavenly abode. A human vessel has capricious desires and ephemeral piety. The sandalwood streaks dried on his skin and turned into crumbly yellow cake. He shed them, leaving a trail of gold dust for ants to follow and find their way to God.

'What brings our village chief and his lovely wife to the temple?' The priest asked.

'What else would a newlywed couple ask for?' Subramaniam said with a smirk, nudging his wife's shoulder with his.

'God will deliver everything at the right time,' the priest said, wiggling his ears as he searched for an answer for the pair from the sea of prayer he lived in. He inspected Subramaniam's wife, her breasts, her broad hips through her silk saree as though he had gynaecological eyes, before he cast his eyes on Subramaniam.

Before they could leave, the priest pulled Subramaniam to the side and explained that it couldn't be Lakshmi's fault as he groped the air in front of his chest and shaped them into breasts to indicate her generous endowment. 'Maybe you are infertile. The aura around you seems off,' he said, looking at Subramaniam's nether regions. The prospect of being infertile hung around them like an unanswered prayer. Subramaniam's face trembled with rage, and he tossed the offering plate that the priest held. Coconut, flowers, betel leaves flew through the sky, teased the Gods, and fell before they could grab it. 'These are not my words. The gods whispered your secrets to me,' the priest said.

To be sure and to remove any doubts, he asked his doctor to test him. He felt they would exonerate him from the stigma of infertility. Unfortunately, the tests proved otherwise. After handing him the results, the doctor asked him to imagine what would happen if this news got out and the public came to know about the great Subramaniam was impotent. He then asked Subramaniam to imagine the wonders money could do in suppressing the information and avoiding any leaks. Subramaniam passed a bundle covered in cloth. Rs 50,000 bought the doctor's silence.

At home, Subramaniam sat on the swing suspended

from the high ceiling. His feet acted as propellers as he thought hard. He was scared that the secret might get out somehow. He believed it was already out because Lakshmi went to the hospital without telling him and her attitude had been different since. She shot suspicious glances at him, as though she was medically scanning him. Every time Lakshmi would say *listen* to grab his attention, he felt a knot in his stomach. But he let out a sigh when she merely asked what the time was or what special movie was on TV that night. But the fear and suspicion never left him. Convincing himself that he had enough knots in his body, knots which made him less of a man, he suggested that they go to a fair to celebrate their first wedding anniversary.

On their way back from the festival with a tired Lakshmi sleeping in the backseat, and his mind heavy with thoughts about his virility or lack thereof, he sped through the inky darkness and shot through the railway level-crossing just as it was closing. He made it through as the beam grazed the car. But rear wheels of the car got stuck in the middle of the railway track. He could hear the train coming towards them. He quickly got out to push the car off the tracks, but it wouldn't budge. He didn't know what to do. Should he try to push a little harder and save his wife's life or let the accident happen and loosen the knots within him?

Lakshmi woke up and groggily called out to her husband. 'Listen, what is happening?' She spotted two bright lights hurtling towards her and her husband at the back of the car with his eyes as big as the midnight moon, filled with fear and helplessness.

Lakshmi ended up in a wheelchair having lost control over the lower half of her body. For Subramaniam, this was worse than anything. Now he had to carry the guilt of not having done enough to save Lakshmi. The question whether his wife knew about his infertility began to eat through his mind. He felt he was drowning in guilt, fear, shame and regret.

To appease his guilt, he bought a big house with a mango orchard next to it because she loved mangoes. She would eat a mango after lunch and dinner whenever she could. He hired a maid to look after Lakshmi. He would purchase gifts through the sons of the villagers who worked abroad. They earned a commission each time they helped him buy a gift from abroad. He got her eucalyptus oil from Oman, Tiger Balm from Singapore, gold, perfumes and chocolates from Dubai, and even an O-General AC because nothing but the best would do for his wife. He bought her multiple tubes of face, hand and body creams, all of which promised to make her skin fair and radiant. Lakshmi lined them up on her dressing table. She applied the creams and sprayed the perfumes, but she had nowhere to go. She remained confined to the wheelchair. So, she would find Subramaniam and give him not a moment of peace. She always had a list of things to do for him. Because she couldn't walk, she made him walk till he got fed up and felt what it was like not to be able to walk.

She wanted to sell the unwanted pieces of furniture in the attic. So, she ordered Subramaniam to bring them all downstairs, dust them and clean them up. After he had spent a whole day getting rid of the grime and polishing them, she said that it would be a pity to sell all the teakwood furniture to someone who would not be able to appreciate them. So, she asked him to take them all back upstairs to the attic.

'At least they are clean now,' she said before wheeling herself away.

Subramaniam carried all the furniture upstairs to the attic. He was working well into dawn and slept on the stairs.

Every night, she would order him to massage her legs and feet even though she couldn't feel anything. He didn't know this, but he realised that she didn't have any sensation in her legs when he pushed his fingers hard into her calves. She didn't even wince. He looked forward to massaging her legs after that just so that he could punish her for making him do pointless things. Sometimes, he didn't cut his fingernails so he would leave crescent-shaped marks all over her legs. Sometimes even a bloody crescent.

When Lakshmi heard about the new scheme that could increase your wealth more than what any standard bank could do, she could have sworn she could feel goose-pimples on her numb legs. She ordered Subramaniam to deposit a large sum into the scheme so that she could save enough money to allow her to fly abroad and fix her legs.

She had squirrelled away a small fortune without telling her husband. Despite his mild protests that it could be a fraudulent program and suggestion that he would work even harder to save money the right way, she would not agree. She glowered at him with a fierce intensity that seared his insides. She wanted to strip her husband of everything. His honour and dignity by browbeating him, even his security by making him lose all his money. In the end, it would all be his fault. She had even come up with a defence when he learned that all his money had been swindled away. 'Where is your masculine sense? Did someone strip you of it? I am just a woman. Why would you listen to me and make stupid decisions?' she would say. It was a perfect plan for revenge. She could blame all her misfortunes on him, and the people would only pity a disabled woman who had lost everything. They would ostracise him, and she would inherit the house.

When Subramaniam broke the news to the maid that she had to leave for good, she prostrated herself in front of him and begged for forgiveness. She apologised for taking leftover food home for her family, stealing two dented tumblers and an earthen pot. She said she would return the items but begged him not to kick her out. He didn't budge and asked her to leave before the new maid came.

Kalki lounged against her mother outside their mud hut. Karthi squatted next to her. Yashoda scanned Kalki's scalp for lice. Kalki scratched her head. 'Stop doing that. You are going to disturb my method. I have finished half your hair, and I don't want the lice jumping to the other side,' Yashoda said.

'But it is so itchy,' Kalki complained.

'My head is itching too,' Karthi said. 'I bet I have more lice than you.'

'Amma, find more lice. We have only found 26 till now,' Kalki shook her head, hoping to agitate the lice and make them come out of hiding.

'Subramaniam Sir has asked you to come to his house tomorrow,' said a lanky man who appeared in front of Yashoda suddenly. He lifted his lungi with one leg and tied it around his waist.

Karthi and Kalki looked at each other as soon as he mentioned Subramaniam's name.

'Why?' Yashoda asked, pausing in her hunt or lice on her daughter's head.

The man shrugged. 'That is all I know. You must be at his place before ten.'

'Why does he want me there? I haven't even crossed his street, and the last time I saw him was when … I don't even remember when….' Yashoda didn't even finish her murmur as she turned towards her children. 'Do you two have something to do with this?'

'No…nothing. I don't know what you mean,' Karthi said, looking away.

'Look at me while I am talking to you. Kalki!' Yashoda growled. 'You better tell me before I find out from someone or else. I don't know what I am going to do.'

'She had nothing to with it,' Karthi said. 'It is all my fault.'

'I hope you have a good explanation,' Yashoda said sternly.

Karthi narrated the whole incident about the crazy priest in the temple suggesting that Kalki eat mangoes to lighten her skin, how they couldn't steal any mangoes in the market, the plan to steal mangoes from Subramaniam's orchard, the fake cricket game and Kalki's fake belly, and how Kalki damaged the saplings when she went to fetch the ball, and about a lady in a wheelchair who banged her chest like a monkey.

As Yashoda listened, her eyes widened. 'Why Karthi? Why do you do such silly things? That priest is a madman. Of course, he is going to say stupid things. And you, Kalki,' Yashoda turned to her daughter. 'You must follow him and do everything he asks you to do? How many times have I told you to stay hidden, so no one can blame you for their bad luck?'

'At least he is trying to do something to make me fair, unlike you,' Kalki said in an accusing tone.

Yashoda was silent for a few minutes. Then she said, 'Kalki, you think I don't do anything for you? You think I am not even trying?'

Kalki wished that she could take back her words, but it was too late. She looked at her mother with shameful eyes. She didn't know what to say.

'I am making a big wind for you,' Yashoda said.

'Wind?' Kalki was confused.

Yashoda went inside the mud hut and returned with the tin of rice. From it, she pulled out a roll of cash. A few grains of rice clung on to the roll of money. She unfurled the notes, straightened them out and showed Kalki. A whiff of money and rice smell tickled Kalki's nostrils.

'Right now, the wind is tiny. Soon these notes will become much bigger and create a storm for you that will wash away all the sadness, the humiliation, the ridicule, and the bad luck. You wait and see. Your mother is almost there. The wind is almost full,' Yashoda said, wiping away her tears. 'Also, you are far more precious than you realise.'

'How so?' Kalki asked.

'Because of your dark skin. The deepest darkest well holds the purest water. And did you know why some people go underground where it's pitch dark?'

Kalki shook her head.

'Because that is where all the precious things in the world are hidden. In the dark, so no one can see them. You are precious. Hence you are blessed with dark skin. We are the unlucky ones.'

The flame-shaped mark on Kalki's chest tinkled at Yashoda's words and reached for her heart, spreading a bittersweet warmth throughout her body.

The next day, Yashoda stood in front of Subramaniam's mansion with Karthi and Kalki hiding behind her. Subramaniam sat on a low wicker chair, shaking his legs. She wore her good saree with no holes. It was her wedding saree, blood-red with yellow spots. She wore it because she didn't know what to expect from Subramaniam. After all, who in their heart would allow someone's wedding dress to be ruined. Either she would be admonished or be asked to clean up the mess that her children had made. She thought dressing decently might make Subramaniam take pity on her and just reprimand her. It was a gamble she was willing to take.

'From today, right from this minute, you are working for me,' he said when a cough from behind interrupted him. 'You will be working for my wife,' Subramaniam corrected himself.

'But I already have a job. I work as a maid in Gayathri Amma's house, Ayya (sir),' she said.

'You can forget about working there,' Subramaniam said.

'But Ayya, how can I quit just like that?' Yashoda asked, snapping her fingers. 'She will think badly of me.'

'You think her thinking will change your image? We all know your history. We know what happened before she was born,' Subramaniam said, pointing at Kalki.

Yashoda stood there in silence as the events in the dark alley enveloped her again and the rapist with flaky skin sniggered at her again. Even though everyone lived in their homes and had their own lives, nobody was allowed the luxury of secrets in a village like this. It's always in the open, for everyone to stare at, prod, mock, envy, gaslight, do what they want and as they pleased.

'You will be taking over here. She was our previous maid,' Subramaniam said as he looked at a woman hurrying down the stairs, carrying a cloth bundle. She looked at Yashoda and mouthed, 'Venomous whore' before she dashed towards the main gate.

'Payment?' Yashoda said softly under her breath, raising her hand, asking for imaginary cash.

'What?' Subramaniam thundered. Karthi and Kalki shivered.

Yashoda tried again to broach the subject of wages. 'How much will you pay me, Ayya?'

'What money? Your children come and destroy my beloved saplings, and you thought I will welcome you here to my house with a job and pay you good money? Is that what you think is happening here? Is the word fool written on my forehead? Is it?' Subramaniam asked, thrusting his head towards Yashoda. Karthi and Kalki peered from the side and looked at his forehead. They couldn't find the word fool written on his forehead. A lone bead of sweat traversed the wrinkled terrain before dispersing itself among Subramaniam's bushy eyebrows.

'But...but...how will we survive with no money?' Yashoda asked.

'You should have thought about that before letting your little devils loose and allowing them to damage other people's property.'

Yashoda's face was drained of all blood. Her mouth was open, and she started to breathe heavily through her mouth as though the world had run out of air. Her hands trembled. A wave of panic rose inside her. Yashoda dragged her children from behind her and slapped them as hard as she could. Slap! Slaps on their faces. She pinched them and kicked them on the shin. One pair of hands and legs for each kid. At the end of the Yashoda's punitive dance, both Karthi and Kalki were a blubbering mess, begging their mother to stop beating them. Yashoda stopped because she couldn't breathe. She watched her children as they rubbed their arms and legs to soother the pain from the beating. Seeing her children suffer because of her, she collapsed in tears herself. 'Please forgive your mother. Please. I don't know what came over me,' she said.

'Enough, enough,' Subramaniam said, looking back to check if his wife was around. 'I will see what I can do. You will get some money. Come on now. Stop crying and clean yourself up.'

Yashoda dusted herself and her children before wiping their faces with the end of her sari. They looked at her as if to say but this is your wedding saree. Yashoda smiled at them and allowed them to blow their noses on her saree. Karthi and Kalki gradually stopped crying. Like a sputtering car engine giving up.

'I will come tomorrow morning then, Ayya,' Yashoda said. As she was about to leave, a voice came from inside the mansion, making Subramaniam get up from his wicker chair. He stumbled, and the chair fell on its side.

'Why tomorrow? You can start today itself,' Lakshmi said as she propelled herself towards Yashoda and stopped at the stairs. She looked at Subramaniam, who promptly backed away and stood behind her wheelchair. 'There is so much to do, and here you are trying to slip away just like your darkie daughter did after uprooting my precious plants.'

'But… but…,' Yashoda began.

'No buts. Just get inside the house, and I will show you what needs to be done.' Lakshmi beckoned Yashoda into the house. 'Leave the rats outside. Do you think I am going to wheel myself now that you are here? Grab the handles and let's go,' Lakshmi said.

Yashoda clutched the cold steel handles as she pushed Lakshmi around the house. Lakshmi gave directions and Yashoda steered. She showed Yashoda the kitchen. 'I should be able to see my reflection in the aluminium plates. That's how clean they should be,' she said.

In the living room, Yashoda was supposed to clean the floors with phenyl till they shimmered. The curtains were to be dusted till not a speck remained. 'I will be checking the curtains against the sunlight,' Lakshmi warned. The teak furniture dotted around the house had to be wiped thoroughly to make them shine like brand new. All clothes had to be washed by hand. The whites needed to be whiter than before and crisp when dry. With every instruction, Yashoda could feel the cold steel of the wheelchair binding her to the whims and demands of Lakshmi. Like a prisoner tied to the cold steel bars of a prison.

When they reached the bathroom, Lakshmi didn't talk about what needed to be done. She chose to talk about Yashoda's children.

'You know what makes me think that this world is an unfair place?' she asked.

Yashoda shook her head.

'When a dirty low-caste woman like you can have

kids, and I can't.' Lakshmi ground her teeth. 'Look at your saree! How come you were able to afford a lovely saree like that?'

'It's my wedding saree.'

'Oh, you filthy things had a wedding? Anyway, I want the tiles of my bathroom sparkling clean. I want you to show me how you clean.'

Yashoda looked around the bathroom for a rag to clean the tiles with.

'What are you searching for? There are no rags here. Use your saree. What is the difference?' Lakshmi said, with a nasty smile.

Yashoda scrunched up her saree and tried to mumble a plea.

'Do it,' Lakshmi bellowed.

Yashoda dipped the ends of the saree in a bucket and wiped the sticky bathroom floor. Smells of mould, the morning's ablutions and old soap hit her nostrils.

'Clean, clean properly,' Lakshmi said. 'Now you know how I felt when your dirty dark child killed my precious mango plants.'

Karthi and Kalki, exhausted from crying, were fast asleep on the stairs when Yashoda came out. When their mother woke them up, they were startled, not conscious as to what day it was or where they were. Lakshmi told Yashoda to bring her kids tomorrow as well as they could be helpful around the house. They can reach tiny spaces, she said.

The mother clad in a saree drenched in toilet smells

and her two groggy kids walked home like ghosts in search of their resting place. Yashoda only realised after she had dried her face with her saree that she had made a mistake. She became nauseous. Karthi and Kalki rubbed their mother's back in unison.

Karthi stopped rubbing his mother's back when he heard the familiar sound of a peddler. 'Are you ready to be rich? Are you ready to be rich?' Karthi spotted the same man with the same black tie with blue swirls he saw at *Talaivar's* festival. Karthi began to walk towards the sound, only to be stopped by his mother. Karthi tried to explain what that man was trying to do with money, but he knew he was not succeeding.

'That man can make our money grow, Amma,' Karthi tried again.

'Don't be foolish. Nobody can do that,' Yashoda said, wiping her mouth. They reached home, had some of yesterday's gruel and slept early that night.

Karthi woke up to the sound of his mother's sobs.

'I don't know what I am going to do,' Yashoda said. Karthi crawled to the wall in the dark and pressed his ear against it. 'I will have to work at their place for free till she is satisfied. I don't know when that time will come around.'

'Don't worry, Yashoda. It is not like that she-devil will make you work forever,' another voice spoke. Karthi knew it belonged to Sumathi, their neighbour. 'Mark my words. She will only carry on with this act for a few days. Otherwise, go to the police.'

'You have no idea what she is capable of. Besides, she is the wife of the village leader. Whose side will be the police be on?'

'That's true,' Sumathi said with a sigh.

'If she doesn't release me soon or not give me money, I won't have money for us, let alone Kalki's operation.'

Karthi's ears perked up.

'I feel like I am responsible for her dark skin. The local doctor said there is a cure in the big city, but it will cost money. Without any pay, I won't be able to save that kind of money.'

Yashoda's sobs were muffled. It seemed she was crying into Sumathi's shoulder.

'Try to find out when she will release you from the debt. Till then don't worry about it. I have my daughter's wedding engagement in a couple of days. Come and help me. That will be a good distraction for your mind. Everything will be alright in time. You will see.'

Karthi was relieved, sad, and confused at the same time. First, he was relieved to hear that his mother had a hand in darkening Kalki's skin. Is that why she said she was making a wind for Kalki this morning to make her fair? But that feeling didn't last long, and confusion dispelled relief. If only she had spoken a bit more about it, he thought. But it could be a general feeling that all mothers in the world have, that they are responsible for everything their child was, is and will ever be. Till he could find out the truth, it would be his burden to carry. Then sadness took over and drenched him like the monsoon rain. He looked at his sleeping sister in guilty silence. It was his fault that she turned out to be that way. It was also his fault that he blocked his mother from creating the wind for Kalki. If it hadn't been for his stupid idea about stealing mangoes, his mother would have somehow cured Kalki. Only one thing mattered now. He had to turn his sister's skin fair somehow. Until then, the worms of guilt frolicked rent-free inside his head. That night, they got out of his head and swirled around his forehead. He could feel their wet skin slithering away. The pain constricted his head, and he remained half-awake as the worms of guilt refused to let him sleep.

Chapter 6

From the outside, the houses on the more backward side of the village were not different from each other. They stuck together, competing for territory, only to be divided by a dingy narrow lane which allowed for some breathing space. It sprawled in all directions, claiming as little space as possible to house fretful souls, enough to create stories, hopeful and tragic. Nothing in between.

The insides of the houses didn't reflect the dull exterior that was covered in a sheet of beige and dust. The people made it so. Even though poverty was the common thread that connected them, their stories and desires set them apart. Some just wanted to get through the day and found comfort in the tedium of their lowly monotonous schedule. Some looked at the white planes in the sky and dreamt of going to the Gulf. Some dreamt of transcending caste lines and getting a job that wasn't menial. Some dreamt of marrying those who didn't have menial jobs. Some dreamt of forbidden love, while some just wanted a man to say yes to them for marriage. For Priya, this would be the third chance to impress a man.

It was Priya's girl-seeing day, where the prospective groom would visit her family to judge everything, from the clothes she was wearing to the involuntary twitch when she played with her hands. The house contained the impending ceremony, tightly holding it withing its moss-covered roof and chipped walls. It succeeded in keeping the secret. There was no feast for prying eyes. They moved along, on to the next vulnerable house, looking for something to talk about. Priya didn't want to jinx this, so she asked her family to keep a tight lid on it till it was time. The first man had rejected her and quickly dashed out of the house without giving a reason. The second, a mute bricklayer, also dismissed her with a vigorous shake of his head, but didn't give a reason. Since there was no reason, people made one up. The usual suspects reared their heads: maybe she is too dark, too frail, doesn't have childbearing hips, her hair is too thin.

For the third, and hopefully, the last time, the house was made more attractive than usual in the hope of turning strangers into relatives. Big sacks containing old clothes were woken from their slumbers. Priya's mother, Sumathi, rummaged for something new to wear for everyone. Something that had not been worn for a long time. Something that was not torn. She found her old red sari, which still retained its original colour. The only thing from her marriage that didn't change. Sumathi's mind wandered back over the years to her engagement day, when her mother had packed the saree. The musty smell invaded her nostrils and heaved her out of the past and into the present. Now it was her turn to give away her daughter.

The smell from the incense hung low. The smell of sandalwood and burnt matchstick mixed and spread. The reddest apple, the firmest orange, the juiciest mango, the stoutest banana was carefully handpicked at dawn from the market before it went on display for the public. They were laid on a shiny aluminium tray that could pass for silver at a fleeting glance. Sumathi wiped and wiped till the aluminium shone. A bundle of betel leaves was kept in the centre in the hope of an auspicious beginning, along with mounds of Cadbury Eclairs with their jaded wrappers, collected over the years, given by the vegetable merchants as change, when they ran out of coins. The house was ready to welcome strangers. To welcome inspectors. Judge, jury and executioner. To welcome Priya's future in-laws.

Priya arched her back and gazed into the mirror, with a pink border resting on the mud wall. She had cracked the top half of the mirror when she flung it away, when the second man refused her. This time she didn't want to be rejected. So, she considered all the rumours in case there might be some truth in them. She fattened herself a bit by sleeping and eating a bit more. She applied coconut oil to her hair to make it shinier. And she stayed at home during the day and avoided the sun. During the night, she would sneak in as a cleaner at wedding halls and into the bride's rooms and steal leftover face creams and talcum powder to whiten her skin. She left no stone unturned.

'What does that do?' Kalki asked, resting her head on her knuckles, with her mouth open.

Priya eyeballed Kalki and continued to meticulously roll the paper-thin tube of face cream from the bottom to the top to extract the last remnants of whatever was left inside it. Her face contorted with every push. The cream reared its white head before diving back inside.

'What does that do?' Kalki asked again, tapping the mouth of the tube, pointing to the object of her interest, in case Priya hadn't heard her the first time.

'Don't touch it,' Priya said. 'There is not much left.'

'What does it do?' Kalki ignored Priya's concern and was relentless in her curiosity.

'It turns dark skin fair,' Priya said, rubbing the smidge of cream onto her cheeks in rapid circular motion.

'Like the fair woman pictured on the tube,' Kalki asked, looking at the now-creased face of a smiling, fair woman. Behind her was the same woman but with a smaller face and dark skin looking glumly away. Does the fairness cream also teach you to smile, or was she smiling because she was fair, Kalki wondered.

'Yes. Exactly like her,' Priya said.

'Can I have some?' Kalki extended her arms.

Believing that she had sucked out every useable drop out, she dabbed the tube's mouth on Kalki's skin, leaving behind crumbling white circles on her skin that looked like a series of disintegrating white moons strewn across a pitch-black night, somewhere on a distant planet where darkness engenders beauty.

Kalki smelled her hand. A fruity scent tickled her nostrils. She brushed the flaking moons onto her cheeks and rubbed her cheeks furiously as though she was scrubbing dirty cloth. Priya stopped her by grabbing her hands and showed how to rub gently. Kalki massaged the remaining faded white streaks first clockwise and then anti-clockwise, pushing the cream into her dark epithelial cells. The area of the cheek with absorbed the cream was damp and cool. The fruity scent faded. Her cheeks twitched a little. Maybe it's working already, she thought. With closed eyes, Kalki imagined an army of little white people forcing their way through her dark skin and turning her white from the inside. She pictured them washing with their magic soap, scrubbing and wiping the darkness away and finally making her fair. She spoke to them with her mind voice. She directed them to the flame-shaped mark on her neck and asked them to dip their paintbrushes into the wheatish flame pool if they ran out of fair paint.

She waited and waited for the tingling sensation to fade. Her eyes were firmly shut. She wanted to touch her cheek, but she refrained in case she tainted the skin and disturbed or angered the busy little white workers. If this worked, all she had to do was somehow buy a fresh tube of the same cream and apply it all over her body.

'Am I fairer, now?' Kalki asked Priya, presenting her cheeks, one at a time.

'Not so soon, silly.' Kalki looked at Priya's fingers and made sure that no cream was robbed from her cheeks. She swiped Priya's fingers for any trace of cream and put it back where it belonged. Priya playfully pinched Kalki's cheeks. Little white people inside her cheeks cheered.

'You should use it regularly. Look how fair the skin on my face is compared to my hands,' Priya said, placing her hand next to her face. 'Can you see?'

'Not that much of a difference!' Kalki said, her eyes darting back and forth between Priya's hands and face.

'Why aren't you applying the cream on your hands and legs?' Kalki asked.

'The face will do. I don't think the man will be staring at my legs and hands. I will use my saree to cover my hands and legs.'

'I think you should eat mangoes. The priest at the temple said so.' She whispered into Priya's ear, afraid that someone else might steal her secret.

'You got your mother into trouble by stealing some mangoes,' Priya said with a smirk.

'As if it will work with cream alone,' Kalki snapped back petulantly.

'What a big mouth you have,' Priya pinched her cheeks again, this time a little harder.

Kalki screamed and checked Priya's fingers for traces of the cream.

'Leave the little one alone,' Priya's mother, Sumathi, shouted and marched towards them with a bunch of sarees in her hand.

'Well, I was trying to not be dark like....,' Priya stopped, and her eyes locked with Kalki's, who waited like a deer in the jungle, about to be pounced on. But it didn't happen. She was safe.

'I am not doing anything to her,' Priya said.

'Don't you have better things to do than pick a fight with the kid?' Sumathi said, dropping the pile of sarees. 'Here you go. Wear this. This is a wedding saree. It still looks new. Maybe it will bring you luck this time.'

'So, you are saying that I am unlucky,' Priya said, extinguishing any optimism her mother was about to impart. 'If you were so lucky, why did you give birth to such an unlucky girl like me who can't be married off?'

'Maybe if you can curtail your tongue a little bit, the men wouldn't have said no.'

'So, it's my fault?'

'No, no, no. Nothing is your fault. Everything is my fault because I gave birth to you and your three baby sisters. Is it such a big wish to wear your mother's wedding saree? I am only trying to help you. If you get married, will I benefit from it or you? Don't you have a bit of concern for your sisters and their future?'

Priya's senses were all devoted to making her eyes pop. She ignored her mother's drivel. She applied mascara with shaking hands, several times till they were the darkest thing on her face, darker than her pupils. Creating a sharp contrast so that her brown skin wouldn't look so brown but light enough to make her seem almost fair-skinned.

Sumathi gave a long sigh and begged Priya to try

on the saree. After much hesitation and a series of tsk-tsks, Priya got up, collected all her beauty products and disappeared into the room. She came out quickly and grabbed her mother's saree, and went back inside.

'It is not I who is getting married,' Priya's mother said, bursting into tears. She dropped her face into her palms. 'Who will marry her if she gets rejected again?' Sumathi wiped her tears and said, 'Arranging this third proposal was like squeezing blood from a stone. After this, they will think she is cursed and what will happen to my other daughters? We will be shunned. Branded as the cursed family. It is worse than being untouchables.'

Kalki didn't know what to do. She watched Sumathi crying. Sumathi grew uncomfortable since there was no one around to assuage her grief. So, she stopped crying and went in to prepare the house to welcome the groom's family.

Priya was ready. Her hair was oiled and braided. Her mother's imitation jewellery adorned her neck and face. A bundle of jasmines strung together adorned her hair, the scent mixing with the aroma of coconut oil. Her mother's saree was brought back to life by ironing it with a small copper pot filled with hot water. Priya looked at herself in the mirror. It was the third time she was dressed up like this. But this time, despair weighed in and weakened her even more.

In the distance, children's voices become louder, followed by the blaring horn of an Ambassador car. Kalki and Karthi were among them, trailing behind the vehicle, shouting despite the dust that belched out from the back tires. With one hand on the steering wheel and the other striking the door, the driver yelled at the boisterous following. '"Out of the way, you monkeys! I will ram you down. Out! Out!'

Priya's parents waited outside, along with their other daughters. They must be serious about this proposal, Sumathi thought, coming in a white Ambassador car. A smile rose on her lips. Eight people burst out of the white Ambassador car. Women in shimmering sarees and men in stiff cotton pants and shirts.

Trays full of fruits and sweets were spread on the ground. It overshadowed the measly single tray offered by Priya's family. Priya's father, Mohan, pushed his tray towards theirs so nobody could tell the difference. But it was too late. The mother of the boy picked up on it and grunted. The boy's family gathered on one side. The girl's family on the other. Karthi and Kalki made themselves comfortable at the back as though they were about to watch a movie. Kalki stood up so she could see better despite her mother yanking her down. She stood and waited for the show to begin.

'Don't think we belong to some other caste,' the boy's father said. 'Just because we came in an Ambassador car and are wearing nice dresses. We are the same as you. Once an untouchable, always an untouchable.' The group giggled. Untouchables that managed to become slightly touchable.

'We have just one son. If we don't do these things for

him, who else will we do it for,' he continued, pointing at his son. The boy sat in the middle, with his head down, his hair drenched in oil, and twiddled his thumbs.

'He can't stop fiddling with his fingers,' his mother said. 'He works at the Xerox shop, printing paper. All day, he pushes the buttons on the Xerox machine, from day till night, and he carries that habit home too.'

'Just like a kompyutrr enchineer,' Sumathi said, brimming with happiness. She meant computer engineer.

'You can say that,' the boy's father said. 'Honestly, who would know the difference?'

As the chit-chat died and everyone ran out of things to talk about, Mohan took the opportunity to speak. 'I think the boy is getting restless and is waiting to see the girl.' He indicated to his wife to bring Priya in. With that, everyone's eyes shifted towards the doorway covered with hoary curtains.

By now, Kalki had moved to the front, like a slow-moving ant. Soft anklet sounds slowly permeated the room and broke the anticipation of all the guests. Priya entered the room with her head down, eyes glued to the tumblers of filtered coffee she carried on a tray. They took the coffee and murmured something to the person sitting next to them. Kalki's eyes were glued to Priya's saree. The saree covered her hands and legs and didn't show an inch of her body. Priya's feet were orange from the henna application.

The boy had his eyes fixed on her anklets as Priya walked around with the coffee tray. Finally, it was his turn to take the coffee. He reached for his coffee, and from the corner of his eye he caught her looking at the lone tumbler. Priya quickly bowed and touched his parents' feet. The saree slipped and exposed Priya's back under the blouse. Kalki caught the man looking at her back and flinch. Dread spread within her. Something was about to happen. Something bad. She wanted to reach out and cover Priya's back, but what was seen cannot be unseen.

Meanwhile, the man whispered to his mother that Priya had a big ugly scar on her back. The mother whispered back that she might have a disease. Their mind was made up. All Kalki heard was sibilant whispers with the word ugly poking out during the muted conversations.

The man stopped fidgeting with this thumb and looked towards the exit. Mohan and Sumathi looked at the inspecting crowd as they talked among themselves, looking for signs of approval and the absence of condemnation. Finally, the boy's father spoke.

He talked about how the horoscopes of his son and Priya matched perfectly. Even the astrologer had encouraged him to go ahead with the marriage without even seeing the girl. The chatter went on for a while, without a word about the reason they were there at Priya's. It ended when the boy uttered a heavy smacking sound with his lips.

'Oh, look at the time,' his father said, glancing at his watch-less wrist. 'Thank you for everything. My son must rest now. He has pushed buttons all day long. He is a computer engineer, after all.'

'But what about Priya?' Mohan asked.

'We will talk,' the father said. With that, the group disbanded and raced to the Ambassador car. The driver was smoking a beedi, daydreaming. At the sight of his passengers, he doused it and scuttled to the car and started the engine.

Priya emerged from the back and joined her parents and her sisters as they looked at the car vanish round the corner, children following it with raucous cheer, carrying the answer to their quandary and Priya's prospects. Kalki knew the outcome, but she kept it to herself and wished tomorrow would bring a different answer. That Priya wasn't rejected because of her brown skin but because of something else altogether.

Later in the evening, an answer arrived. But it wasn't a direct answer from the boy's side, but an answer which proved to Kalki nothing good awaited her in the future. It was a howl from Priya's mother calling out her name and charging out of the house. 'Priya!' Sumathi cried out. It was the wail of a broken angel.

It was Hari who found Priya's body floating down the sewer as he was relieving himself perched on the plank. Priya floated among other things, with listless eyes, glaring at him. Her body like a starfish spinning languidly as the assiduous currents carried her like every other reject the village spewed out. Scared, Hari quickly pulled up his shorts, ran towards the village, and screamed that a ghost was in the sewer.

The stage was set. The star of the show had more than

enough tragedy to create a buzz. The audience trickled in to get the best seats in the house. Several women gathered around Priya. Sitting cross-legged. Their sad crying faces cradled in the palms of their hands. Men sat on their haunches with their back to the wall, compromising their view for comfort. Their spine stretched and latched to the wall.

Priya's body writhed on the straw mat. They had somehow managed to bring her back to life. She groaned and kept calling for her mother, 'Amma, Amma…it hurts... I cannot take it anymore.'

Priya's head rested in the lap of an old lady. A musty fungal odour emanated from her groins enveloping Priya. She was a healer for the lower castes, administering medicine made from various plants mixed with cow's urine. Surprisingly, the primal concoction cured most ailments. It was blamed on the patient's fate if any illness did not respond to her potions. She was still celebrated. As she aged, her eyesight diminished, and she started to lose her hearing. Incapable of differentiating the roots and bark and unable to hear her patients, she resorted to things found in most kitchens. Milk, ginger, garlic and spices were her medicines.

She administered a pungent dark liquid to Priya.

'Will anyone help her at all?' Sumathi asked, crying and banging her chest. Her loose hair added drama to the scene. By hitting herself, maybe she thought she could alleviate her daughter's pain and suffering. But that didn't happen. Priya still suffered. She had fits of coughing.

Then she vomited. A watery one with shiny flecks of blood cells. The audience sucked in all the air from the room as they inspected her puke.

Sumathi banged her chest even harder as the blood glinted on the ground. Priya's throat clenched and grew veiny as she struggled to breathe.

Gossip took flight outside Priya's house.

'Why would someone try to kill themselves just because the boy said no? If it isn't this boy, there will be others.'

'This was the third one, though.'

'Who can blame her? I would have done the same thing too.'

'Poor thing! She did try a lot, though, to impress this man. I noticed she is fairer than before. If only she were a bit fairer.'

Kalki heard it all and felt hollow within.

'It is not working, Priya... Let us go to the doctor on the other side,' Sumathi pleaded. 'They can't be such heartless bastards as to refuse to treat you…they just can't.' Her wails swallowed her words.

'We don't need to take her to their doctor. I can bring the medicine from the doctor.' Karthi's voice tried to cut through the commotion. No one heeded him. He tried again in a louder voice. The crowd turned towards Karthi.

'You fool, how will the doctor know what's wrong with her without seeing her?' a woman shouted.

'I know what to tell the doctor,' Karthi said. Bloody vomit. Restless limbs. Shortness of breath. He took mental notes and left the house. Kalki followed her brother, pushing against the stagnant, pitying, pitiful crowd.

'How far is the doctor's house?' Kalki asked as she raced to keep up with her brother.

'It is just right there. Follow me,' Karthi said as they started to walk up the dirt path.

'I know the reason why Priya wanted to die,' Kalki said.

'What is it?' Karthi asked, paying only part attention to Kalki, as the search for the doctor's home took all his concentration. He zig-zagged from house to house, reading the plaques outside – silent signs of the wealth, education, caste and status of the inhabitants inside. His mind repeated Priya's symptoms presented on loop. Bloody vomit. Restless limbs. Can't breathe.

Kalki explained how the man had spotted the brown mark on Priya's back. She wasn't meant to show her natural skin colour, but the saree had slipped.

'I saw him look at her skin and wince,' she said.

'No, that's not true.'

'I saw it. Maybe the same thing will happen to me when I am old enough to get married. I, too, will float like Priya in the sewer.'

Karthi stopped dead in his tracks.

'Tell me, brother, will my dark skin kill me too some day?' Kalki asked, tears springing to her eyes.

As the words slipped from Kalki's mouth, the worms of guilt came to life in Karthi's mind.

'You can't get rid of us,' they said. "It is your fault

your sister is as dark as the night. Soon it will be because of you that she will die. You did this.' The worms let out a howling laugh. The wind picked them up and sent chills through his bones.

'I promise you this. I will make you fair even if I have to snatch the moonlight and make the whole world dark to do so.' Kalki blinked back her tears. 'And besides, Priya will be alright. You will see. And you can ask her that question yourself. I am sure it was not because she is dark. It must be something else.' Karthi sincerely hoped the reason was not that which Kalki thought. He now furiously scooted from house to house, searching for the doctor. To save Priya. To save Kalki.

They finally found the doctor's house. The title DR. gleamed in gold, followed by Vel. Karthi unlatched the front gate and banged on the teak door as hard as he could. Lights sprung to life. There was movement inside. A twitch of the curtain. Stealthy footsteps.

'Who is at the door at this hour?' a man's voice growled from inside.

'Sir, someone is sick. Please help,' Karthi said.

The door opened. A perfectly rounded potbelly greeted Karthi and Kalki. Shielded by an off-white vest. There were scattered holes on it like a white sky with brown stars.

'What the hell are you doing here?' Vel asked, yawning. 'Get out of my house, right now.'

'But sir…doctor sir, someone is dying.'

'Who?'

'My neighbour. Bloody vomit and dress. Restless limbs. Short of breath,' Karthi blurted out.

'What?'

'She vomited blood. Her dress is also soaked in blood. She can't breathe properly, and she thrashes her hands like this,' he demonstrated how Priya was writhing on the floor. 'Please, doctor …please…please come.'

'Please,' Kalki added to Karthi's plea.

'You filthy mongrels!' Vel said. 'You not only came to our neighbourhood with your dirty feet, but you also woke me up, and my whole family. You have the audacity to ask me to come to your vile area to touch your kind. NEVER!' He slammed the wooden door on the children. 'Get out before I call the police,' he added from behind the closed door.

Karthi and Kalki returned home alone. In a densely packed hut, a breathless audience watched a swollen Priya. Her mother begged Priya to stay alive. Soon, Priya stopped breathing. An enormous outcry of weeping buried Priya.

Karthi scanned the lifeless body of Priya for a movement, a twitch. He wanted to believe that she was sleeping. Maybe in the morning, when she was better, he could ask her why she did what she did. Then, he saw the worms of guilt greedily feeding on her body and staring at him. *This is going to be your sister's fate, too, if she doesn't become fair and there is nothing you can do about it.*

He grieved for Priya and also grieved for his sister sometime in the future. How does one grieve for things that are yet to happen? You practice by dying a little inside. You teach your heart to skip a beat. Your lungs do not expand so much. You cry. Your gut twists in pain. Till a part of you dies inside and you hold on to it till the time in the future when the natural grieving begins.

Chapter 7

The night's quietness was stubborn, and it didn't want to leave. It settled in, giving company to lonely roads, to the gnats romancing the yellow orbs of streetlights, to the still trees and to the dreaming stray dogs lucky enough to last the night. It stayed as though it was still grieving Priya's death, giving her company a bit longer on her last night on earth.

With their lungies doubled up to their hips and sorrow weighing them down, a few men walked around, smoking beedis. The smoke curled upwards, chasing away the night. The garrulous ones chatted among themselves, with their hands tied behind their backs. About lives lost. About what could have been. What could be and that which cannot be. Talking about possibilities. Their minds shuffling life's deck of cards.

A man dressed in khaki pants and shirt emerged from a cloud of smoke in the adjoining street, a rumbling noise behind him. The fumigation machine in his hand spewed smoke, choking up the road. Confused streetlights flickered as the smoke blocked the emerging, streaming sunlight. Orbiting flies lost consciousness and fell from the heavens. Corpulent lizards, sticking to lamp posts, darted greedy tongues, feasting on the fallen angels, unaware of their own impending death.

Two pairs of groggy legs wobbled as Yashoda woke up Karthi and Kalki. 'Get up, you two. We are almost there,' Yashoda said. Last night's death still weighed on the children's eyelids.

'Ammaaaa!' Yashoda called out to Lakshmi in the silent house. 'Are you in there?' The house swallowed her voice and gave nothing in return. The house breathed with an open front door, its windows shut.

'Amma!' Yashoda called out again. A lone orange light flickered at the end of the hallway. It moaned and groaned. Then came the sound of water rushing into a hole. A silhouette emerged, enveloping the narrow hallway. The shadows gave birth to Lakshmi in a wheelchair. She propelled herself forward with a cotton towel in her hands, constantly dabbing her sweaty forehead. The wheelchair grumbled as she moved her restless bottom. Huffing and panting and fanning herself with her fingers, she wheeled ahead.

'First day of work and already late,' Lakshmi said with anger in her voice. Karthi and Kalki's eyes flew open, chasing away deathly dreams.

'Someone died...,' Yashoda started to speak.

'Huh?'

'A girl committed suicide. That is why I am late.'

'What kind of excuse is that? Are you the girl's mother? You are not in a school. Stop making stupid excuses! And why did you bring your kids?'

'You asked me to bring them.'

'Ok, OK.' Lakshmi conceded and let out a hiss and bent forward, holding onto her stomach.

'What happened, Lakshmi Amma?' Yashoda said, concern in her voice.

'God knows what was there in that wretched food. Since last night, my stomach...," Lakshmi flicked her hands upwards, symbolising the failure of her digestive system. 'I have been having loose motions all night.'

Karthi and Kalki sniggered. They looked at each other and then burst into a delighted laugh. Holding their tummies and looking up at the velvet sky. Yashoda tried to silence them.

'Shut up!' Lakshmi said, effectively arresting all laughter. 'When you shit, you don't shit out sandalwood paste. Yours is as bad as mine. In fact, it will be worse than mine.'

Lakshmi's sweaty face contorted and turned purple. Her hands reached for the belly button as if it was an actual button that could stop the bouts of diarrhoea. She signalled Yashoda to grab the wheelchair and push her to the toilet. Yashoda scuttled down the corridor towards the lit bathroom, pushing a writhing body ready to explode towards the ground.

Karthi and Kalki made their way to the toilet and sat

on their haunches. Sulphuric smell stung their nostrils. They pinched their noses. Kalki gazed at the orange light seeping through the steel bars above the toilet door. It moaned. It called for god's help. Then it let out a satisfying sigh. They heard their mother comfort Lakshmi: 'It's over. It's over. It's all out of you.'

Karthi and Kalki got up as their mother pushed Lakshmi out of the bathroom. Lakshmi searched their faces for any signs of impending laughter as she breathed through her mouth to calm herself. She waved her index finger at them and warned of dire consequences if they ever laughed at her again. She waved Yashoda off to the kitchen and asked her to make strong ginger tea. It should have froth at the top, she warned.

'I need to sleep for a while. You two better not go around looking for trouble,' she snapped at the children.

Yashoda pulled them to her and wrapped her arms around them. 'They will be with me. I promise they won't disturb you.'

Lakshmi studied them like a painting at the museum. 'I have a job for these monkeys. Send them both to my room once you have prepared the tea. After that, start cleaning the house. Dust, sweep and mop everywhere. I will tell you what to cook later.' She licked her lips as she mulled a menu for lunch.

The inside of the house was dark and still. Cockroaches meditated, their antennas probing the secrets of the universe. Ants scurried to their homes with their night's loot. Other than that, the kitchen was quiet.

Pots and pans upturned on the bottom shelf lined with yellow paper. Plates slotted into the steel shelf, arranged accordingly to size. The sink was full of dishes. The leftover cold food – a fried chicken leg buried among the sucked and stripped bones, morsels of rice, chewed-up curry leaves and a handful of beans – stared up at Yashoda. She looked at them as dinner possibilities for later tonight and bundled them into a plastic sheet.

The ginger tea in the stainless-steel glass, housed inside a stainless-steel bowl, bubbled. The air had its share of fun by popping tea bubbles on the surface. Karthi held the glass with a stiff hand and waited outside Lakshmi's room with Kalki.

'You take the tea in to her. I will open the door,' Karthi said, passing the glass to his sister.

'No, you take it,' Kalki said, pushing it away. Some tea spilled into the steel bowl.

'Just go,' Karthi said, opening the door and placing the glass of tea in Kalki's hand. A hot circle localised on Kalki's palm. A bust of chill air streamed through the gap and hit them both, inviting them in. With her eyes planted on the rim of the glass, she inched forward. They felt goosepimples pop up on their arms as the cold air grazed their skin before escaping through the door. The coldness on the skin felt strange and foreign, like piercing needles. It reminded them both of Aaya's words, how the cold weather contributes to fair skin.

The room was alive and breathing. The ceiling fan stirred up a host of smells: disturbed sleep, wet sheets, sweat, fruity talcum powder, and stale banana chips. It was also full of sounds. Lakshmi sat in the middle of the room between a teak bed and a dressing table with a mirror. The ceiling fan creaked above her as she rocked herself in a rocking chair connected to a swing. The bed was half-made. Lakshmi's weight was still on the pillow and the mattress. The blanket curled at the bottom like a shed snakeskin. The mirror was dotted with red *bindis.* Various tubes and tubs of creams guarded the mirror. In the corner of the room, something grumbled, as though it was hurting.

'Aieeeee,' Lakshmi shrieked, stopping the rocking motion. 'Close the door, you idiot. The cold air is getting out of the room.' Kalki quickly placed the swishing tea on the dressing table and closed the door. The cold air ran around to every corner of the hermetically sealed room, looking for an escape route. The prison swelled with cold air till there was no room for warm air. Lakshmi rocked back and forth.

'God only knows how expensive it is to run this thing, and now all the air escaped,' Lakshmi said. 'Why are you here?'

'Tea,' Kalki said, pointing at the tumbler.

'Bring it here,' Lakshmi commanded. 'Bring that too.' Her stubby fingers pointed to something on the dressing table. As Kalki ran her fingers over the things on the dressing table, Lakshmi shook her head. With every tube she pointed to, her shake grew more vehement. 'The one with the pink lid,' she said.

As Kalki walked towards her with the tube of cream, Lakshmi stared at the girl and made a face as though she had just a bit int an overly sour lemon. Kalki was used to these contorted facial expressions by now when people looked at her. She had learned to pretend not to notice. Only when they didn't grimace did she look, and a little flutter of hope would arise within her, but seconds later, when they had a clear look at her face, the fluttering inside her would grind to a halt.

'Tell me one thing,' Lakshmi said. 'Are you really from this country? Is she your sister?' She asked Karthi, and he nodded swiftly.

'Why?' Kalki wanted to know.

'Your skin colour says something else. Have you heard of Africa?'

They both nodded indifferently.

'It's a big country far away from us. It is full of wild animals. I saw that on Discovery Channel. Zebras. Lions. Elephants. The people of that country are so black that they have to wear bright-coloured clothes and jewellery to make them visible to the naked eye at night. You might be one of them. Someone came over from Africa and may have left you here by mistake and forgot all about you.'

Being of a strange dark colour was one thing. But a suggestion that Kalki might not even be from this land or Karthi's sister or Yashoda's daughter was like being shuttled away at cosmic speed to a lone sandy island surrounded by a swirling perpetual dark storm. Kalki shivered. She felt as though she was standing naked on sand as lightning flashed. With her head bowed, she was dragging her feet around in the sand, searching for something. Anything.

Just then a giant hand reached out to her, tearing through the storm and picked her up.

'I am here, sister,' Karthi said, holding on to Kalki's clammy hands.

Kalki gave him a tight smile.

'Why is it so cold here?' Karthi asked, wrapping his arms around him, wanting to draw attention away from Kalki.

'Stupid low-caste kids,' Lakshmi grunted. 'See that thing in the corner. That is what produces the cold air. It is called an air-conditioner. It is also from Dubai.' Lakshmi pointed to a white box in the corner installed in the wall. It had dark lines running vertically. On the left was a flap that moved up and down. Karthi placed his hands on it, and it kissed him with multiple cold lips.

Lakshmi asked Kalki to apply the cream on her foot. 'Use only a tiny bit and massage it well into my feet,' she said. 'Here, let me see.' Kalki squeezed out a dollop of the pinkish cream and held it out. Lakshmi nodded, giving her the green light. She asked Karthi to do the same on her other foot.

'Will this cream turn your skin fair?' Kalki asked.

'How do you know about this?' Lakshmi asked, her eyes closed.

'Priya, my neighbour, uses ...,' Kalki paused as she remembered the events of last night and corrected her tense. 'Used to have a cream like this.'

Lakshmi laughed. 'Impossible. She won't be able to afford this cream. It must be some cheap one. This cream is from Dubai, and it's expensive and will make you fairer. With this air-conditioned room full of cold air and the cream, I will be fairer in no time,' Lakshmi giggled as she looked up at the ceiling.

'How will the cool air make you fair?' Karthi asked.

'Look at your skin and look at mine,' Lakshmi placed her arm alongside Karthi's. There was a difference. Only slight but enough to convince Karthi that he had finally found a way to whiten his sister's skin. 'Isn't it obvious? You roam in the sun, and hence you are darker than me. I have been in this room only for one night, and look at my skin,' Lakshmi smiled proudly. 'Now, be quiet and do your work.' She slurped the tea at one go and settled even deeper into the rocking chair. The wooden frame moaned.

Lakshmi's legs glistened. Even the hair on her leg shone. Kalki watched Lakshmi as she slept, a smile on her lips and probably dreaming fairer dreams. Karthi and Kalki looked at each other and knew what they had to do. They waited till Lakshmi was fast asleep. They massaged her legs a bit more for good measure, and Karthi gently pinched her skin to make sure she wasn't awake. A guttural snore from Lakshmi's open mouth confirmed that she was fast asleep.

The tube read Fair and Gorgeous, the same as Priya's, except this was full of cream and had the image of a woman with a radiant smile. There wasn't a dark spectre of her past self behind. She smiled as though she had no worries in her life. As though she had all the strength in the world to face the hurdles of life. As though she was a goddess.

Armed with the knowledge that the cream made skin fairer and that the cold air accelerates the process, Karthi squeezed the cream onto Kalki's hand. Kalki rubbed the cream all over her body. She smothered her arms, legs, body and her face with the cream. Turning the blackness of the skin into a grey-white. They glanced at Lakshmi. She was still in deep sleep. Silence pervaded the room like an icy tomb.

Soon Kalki transformed into a grey ghost with black hair. She walked towards the air-conditioner with her arms and legs apart as though she was balancing on a tight rope. It beckoned her with its moving flaps. It snarled. As she presented herself in front of the air conditioner, Kalki shivered. Then, it streamed cold air all over her body like a performer in a palace seeking the king's approval. The king approved and breathed forth his magic air all over Kalki, turning the cream into a light crumbly crust.

A swift flick to her ear ended it all. 'Again, you two have started with your antics,' Yashoda whispered angrily. 'How many times do I have to tell you to stay out of trouble?'

Yashoda grabbed her children and tiptoed out of the room. Lakshmi belched a snore. Kalki left behind a trail of white crumbling flakes, an open door through which the air prisoners escaped, while the warden reached the climax in her dreams where she was crowned Miss Fairest of Them All.

Yashoda didn't utter a word as she worked the pump in the backyard. She furiously pumped the green handle. Air hissed out in the beginning. Then a gurgle. Then a splatter of water dropped like a rock onto the pail.

'I just wanted to turn her skin lighter,' Karthi said with hunched shoulders, feeling sorry.

Yashoda glared at Karthi and pumped her anger into the water pump and the pail. It spilled out from the bucket and rushed towards Karthi's feet.

Yashoda spilled the contents of the bucket. Stinging cold water drenched Karthi. "This ought to teach you something. You are next," Yashoda looked at Kalki as she pumped water into the pail.

Crying, Kalki begged her mother not to wash away the cream. That the cream was working its magic, she could feel it. She could sense the army of little white people busy turning her fairer. But her pleas were swallowed by the cranking sound of the water pump, and soon she was wet with cold water too. Two shivering bodies looked at Yashoda. There was a clear puddle at the feet of one. At the feet of the other was a milky pool with little white people drowned in it.

'I think it is time I tell you two about Poochandi,' Yashoda said as she dried them. 'I have held my tongue for so long, believing that you won't make any more mischief, but it's about time you knew. Since you are not scared of me, surely you will fear him.'

'Who is Poochandi?' asked Karthi as his head shook to the beat of Yashoda's drying.

'He has red glowering eyes and a ghostly white face. A head full of matted hair. Some say his hair is made of snakes. Lots of them. They are his eyes. Watching for stray children. Searching for children who don't obey their elders. He carries a bag on his side. Filled with ashes and bones of the children he consumed, the blood of the children makes his eyes red. No one knows where he lives. Some say he lives everywhere. In walls. Inside wells. On trees. He will come at the right moment to kidnap misbehaving kids.' Yashoda pawed her fingers in front of two pairs of frightened, listening eyes.

Yashoda's slithering voice wrapped around Karthi and Kalki as they hugged each other. His fear hugging her and hers hugging him. Their knees wobbled. A rumbling noise from the side of the house erupted. Inside the house, Lakshmi woke up, turning off the air-conditioner. Karthi and Kalki let out a scream, covering their ears. They dived towards their mother, hugging her tightly for safety.

'Please, Amma, tell Poochandi to go away,' Kalki pleaded. 'I will behave.'

'Me too,' Karthi whimpered.

'It is ok now,' Yashoda said with a smile. 'There is no Poochandi now. He is asleep. He will only come when there is no one around you.'

'How do you know that?'

'If he came out when there are others around, wouldn't

he have been caught already?' Yashoda said. 'Besides, you are lucky. He won't steal you.'

'How am I lucky?' Kalki enquired.

'He doesn't steal dark-skinned kids.'

'My skin is useful after all. You should probably stay close to me, Karthi. Otherwise, Poochandi might take you away,' Kalki said, looking at her brother. They all laughed. Kalki thought she had found her secret power. Karthi and Yashoda laughed at her innocence.

Lakshmi watched them through the gap in her bedroom window curtains. It didn't matter that the cold air was escaping. She didn't see three members of the low caste community who owed her a garden of mango saplings worth servitude, but a mother being motherly towards her children. Jealousy ran through her body, pickling her inside. Her heart turned sour like vinegar, and a bitter taste rose in her mouth.

She wondered why happiness did not elude them despite their lowly status. Why were their smiles not small like their class? Why was Yashoda given nothing but at the same time was blessed with children and a reason to smile, whereas Lakshmi had everything but nothing. These thoughts, these questions to which she would never find the answers, caused her to grind her teeth involuntarily. Her hand shot towards her stomach, forming a shield with four gold rings. As though she did not want the thoughts to slide into her infertile womb and make it more barren. They stayed in her eyes, in the grinding of her teeth as she watched Yashoda and her children live in a world of which she was not a part of, socially speaking, and would not be, biologically speaking.

'That's enough, you lot,' Lakshmi called out from the window. Three smiles vanished immediately. 'Giggling and talking will not repay your debt. Get back to work.'

Yashoda nodded.

'Also, send your rats home. I don't want them here anymore. They are distracting.' Lakshmi slammed the window shut.

'Go straight home. Don't wander. Poochandi is watching,' Yashoda warned them and sent them away. It was mid-morning already. The heat was stifling. Trees suffered silently, helplessly, in the airless atmosphere. Everyone cursed the unforgiving sun.

Karthi and Kalki walked cautiously through the streets, looking for glowing red eyes among the people walking past and for anyone with a sack filled with writhing children.

Meanwhile, Kalki jumped from one shadow to another to protect herself from thc sun's wrath. Thc meagre shade of a weather-beaten tree. The slanting cover offered by a bent wall. The pencil-thin black line of the electric poles. Kalki fit within these shadows. Unseen. Perfectly blending like a drop of water in an ocean. Lost. Dissolvable, but separable.

'Aren't we going home?' Kalki asked as she saw her brother peering into alleys. Her eyes were on the ground, making sure no part of her body was touched by sunlight.

She intertwined her legs. She twisted her body. And she had every reason to avoid the sun. A trillion skin cells of them.

'I am just making sure Poochandi is not around.'

'You don't have to worry about him with me around. Didn't you hear what Amma said? He won't be interested in me, so you are safe with me,' Kalki said. She continued to chart her shaded path: One tree. Jump to the next tree. And along a wall, followed by the moving shadow of a wandering cow. She waited till the cow's rotund shape encroached and merged with the wall, creating a shaded route for her. Kalki sprang forward as soon as the cow moved away and landed next to Karthi, under the shadow cast by the transformer box, pushing him onto the street.

'Stop pushing, Kalki!' It was half plea, half an order.

In the next street, an autorickshaw rumbled towards them, kicking up dust. Karthi thought, 'This is it. Poochandi has arrived.' It steered away from them and halted with knife-like precision along an empty wall on the other side. The auto-rickshaw had a yellow top. Two people emerged from it. One, a lanky man with long wet hair that hung like black icicles from all sides, holding a roll of papers, and a small bald boy with an ill-fitted loose tee-shirt, carrying a bucket of gloopy white stuff. Kalki's eyes were fixated on them, wondering if they had any little white people in them, just like in the fairness cream.

The man unfurled the sheets. It rolled out a few meters away from them, revealing the many faces of *Talaivar*. Both Karthi and Kalki's eyes lit up. It was the promotional poster for his new movie. There was *Talaivar* everywhere. A smiling *Talaivar* was looking up at the sky. A serious *Talaivar*, exiting a blue car. A loving *Talaivar*, looking at his fair lover.

The boy then whisked a blade from under his tee shirt and started to slice the sheets to make individual posters. Dipping his hand in the bucket next to him, he smeared the glue on single sheets and handed them to the other man. The man's deft hands plastered the posters on the walls with dexterity. Slice. Dip. Smear. Swoosh. Stick. The rhythm never broke. It was as efficient as the heart pumping blood in the body. Within a few minutes, the tenacious duo had covered almost all the walls on one side.

Karthi and Kalki peeked inside the rickshaw. Rolls of movie posters, arranged on top of each other, sat idly like smuggled passengers.

'There is nothing there that concerns you two. Get your head out of the auto,' the man said rudely, sticking a poster on the wall.

Seeing Kalki, the boy screamed, 'Black ghost, black ghost!' In his fear, he tipped the glue bucket over. He was genuinely frightened, flailing his hands with closed eyes to make her vanish. 'You look like the same ghost I saw in a movie once. Go away! Go away!'

The man hit the boy on the head and yelled at him for spilling the glue. 'She is not a ghost, you idiot. She is just a dark girl. The darkest person I have ever seen.' The man glanced at Kalki. A flicker of anger passed through her eyes. It made the whites of her eyes stand out, and she looked even more frightening. The man felt goosebumps on his arms. The boy shuddered and hid behind the man for protection.

'Can I take one?' Kalki asked, reaching out for one of the posters. The boy shot a don't-touch-it look at her. She retracted her hand in a hurry.

'Instead of staring at us, why don't you help us, darkie?' the man said.

'To do what?' snapped Karthi. 'You couldn't even spare us a poster. Why should we do anything for you?'

'Then go away and don't disturb us,' the boy said, flicking some glue at them. The heat sucked any liquid content out of the droplets on their way to Karthi and Kalki, and they dropped down like dried mucus.

'How about five posters?' Karthi began negotiating.

The man and the boy exchanged looks. There was a lot of scratching of heads with sticky hands. Then the man spoke.

'Alright, you can have two posters and Rs 5 if you finish the other street.'

'Each?'

'Maybe,' the man said, arms akimbo.

Karthi didn't want to push it any further in case the man revoked the deal altogether. He nodded.

'Take one bundle and make sure you cut them individually and paste them neatly.'

Karthi had already picked up a roll. Kalki picked up a half-empty bucket of liquid glue. They were given a quick tutorial on how to stick posters efficiently. Slice. Dip. Smear. Swoosh. Stick.

'We will take care of it,' said Karthi. They hurried to the next street. The opened the roll and started to cut out the posters one by one. A vinegary smell spread in the air from the glue bucket. It was time to slice, dip, smear, swoosh, stick. They went to work with intense concentration as though the success of Talaivar's new movie depended on them. Papercuts flew. Liquid glue flicked around and fell on them like heavy rain. They weren't progressing anywhere near as fast as the other duo. Their rhythm wasn't that of a heart pumping blood but that of a disabled person trying to climb the stairs. The few posters were wonky and saggy.

'You know what, Kalki,' Karthi said with renewed interest. 'This is going to take longer than I thought. You wait here.'

With the posters stretched out on the ground, Karthi picked up the paste bucket and poured it on the posters one by one. He then rubbed the glue evenly on each poster with his feet. By the time he had done, his feet were caked in glue. Holding one end of the posters and Kalki on the other end, they hoisted the soggy posters onto the wall. They pressed it diligently until both reached somewhere in the middle where *Talaivar* looked at them with a sense of appreciation for their ingenuity.

'So fast?' The man could not believe it, searching their hands and peering into the empty bucket. "I will go and check, and you better not have played any silly games."

He quickly dashed over to the other street and saw a smattering of people gathering in front of the posters taking mental notes of when and where the movie will be played. An indication that the posters were working. A group of bleating goats gathered too for a fresh serve of paper lunch. After shooing the goats away, he returned to Karthi and Kalki.

'Where is our money and posters?' Karthi asked.

'Smart kids!' The man smiled, showing his yellow teeth. He handed them a five-rupee coin each. 'Go buy some ice lollies for yourself.' He also gave them three posters.

Four eyes stared at the small thick five-rupee coin staring back at them. Their first income.

Frantic with joy, they jumped on the man, wrapping themselves around his legs like the posters and thanked him. The man shook them off and scolded them for dirtying his beige bell-bottomed pants.

With their five-rupee coin and gluey clothes, they marched home basking under a bubble of accomplishment. An hour had passed. The man and the boy finished their quota for the area. The posters stuck by Karthi and Kalki sagged in the middle. All it took was a yank by a twisty tongued goat to bring the whole strip down. The herd of goats feasted on paper and glue, leaving motley strips of posters on the wall turning *Talaivar's* movies into fresh milk with a hint of glue in the morning or extra dry pellets.

'What if we go back and ask the man if we can do it tomorrow as well?' Kalki asked.

Karthi knew exactly where Kalki was going with that question.

'It doesn't give us enough money to buy the cream,' Karthi waved her suggestion off.

After they reached home, Karthi had an idea as he searched for the rice tin where his mother hid the cash.

'That's not for you. That is for me,' Kalki protested. 'Mother is creating the bank for me.'

'But I know someone who can grow this stack of money quickly.'

'Who?'

'Do you remember the man who was yelling at the crowd at the festival?'

Kalki squinted trying to jog her memory.

'Remember what he said? He said there is no point in money just sitting here. If we give this to him, he will grow it for us, and soon we can buy hundreds of fairness creams. You can even use one tube a day.'

'Really?'

Karthi smiled. 'I promise,' and he started to jump. The worms of guilt raised their heads once again and latched onto his mind, refusing to let go, weighing him down.

Kalki jumped up and down too in excitement. 'Finally, I am going to be fair. To be fair. To be fair. Like the woman on the tube,' she squealed. It was almost as though her dark skin cells shared her optimism and excitement. A trillion hopeful shrieks of excitement enveloped her in a cocoon of optimism.

Chapter 8

Karthi didn't know where the man's office was. The man who promised to grow money beyond everyone's expectations. All he knew was that he wore a tie with blue swirls on it. He had the wad of cash tucked inside his underwear. The children wandered aimlessly down the main road, looking for signs of a crowd of greedy people.

Dusk was falling. Fruit and vegetable vendors pushed their carts around, yelling till their throats hurt, trying to sell the orphaned produce of the day. They hid the scars and dents on the rejects and showed their best side like a bride with hidden secrets. They yodelled with much gusto, waxing eloquent about the quality and freshness of the fruits. The fruits were traded for a princely sum, a befitting dowry for damaged goods. Motorbikes whizzed by carrying more passengers than they were designed for. Men were fit on them like stacked cutlery, tightly pressed from the crotch to bum, and the motorbikes belted down the road, through thin gaps, between vehicles, with the flexibility of a rubber band. Buses raced by, tilting to one side, passengers almost spilling from the doors and windows. And all these vehicles had to negotiate around stubborn cows that refused to move from the road despite furious honking. Bicycles rang their bells continuously, seeking attention. Pedestrians jostled past each other, looking more like a colony of ants than human beings.

In the middle of all the chaos were two disabled beggars changing the flow of the stream of people who went around them, fearing they might catch some illness from the ill-kempt couple. One had a broken leg while the other beggar had no legs at all. The broken limb, the beggar's right leg, was bent like that of a running ostrich. His right hand held the right knee in place, replacing it as the fulcrum, shifting and moving it as he moved. The beggar with no legs was seated on a moving wooden tray with wheels and pushed himself with hands housed in slippers. Both of them were engrossed in a profound ethical discussion on the economics of mendicity.

'It is my turn to beg on this side of the village. What are you doing here today? You were here yesterday,' the beggar with a broken leg said. He took out a crumpled sheet of paper from under his shirt and began to cross-check, as though it contained some divine commandments.

'There are plenty of people here to fool, enough for the both of us,' said the other beggar.

'But they will pity you more. Your fraud is more successful.'

'You should have given a thought to your disability. One bent leg?' He laughed so hard that his legs, which were supposed to be non-existent, almost poked out from under him.

'Laugh all you want. I can expose you by just pushing you off the cart. Do you want all these people to throw stones at you?'

'I can expose you too.'

'You wish! You cannot wake up a person who pretends to be asleep. Your fake disability is sound asleep and it needs to stay that way. My knee is pretending to be broken. There is a difference between us. You better think carefully as to who is more at a disadvantage.'

After careful consideration, the beggar on wheels wheeled himself off. His hands acted like oars. When he was far enough away, he got up and walked off to the other side of the road.

Karthi approached the beggar with the broken leg to ask where the office of the man who promised to double people's money was. If anyone knew where everything was, it would be the beggars. The keepers of records.

'You mean the chit fund office?'

The word chit fund meant nothing to Karthi. He merely shrugged.

'What business do you two children have at the chit fund?'

'We got lost. Our father is there,' Karthi lied.

'Oh, then he must have a lot of money?'

'I don't know about that,' Karthi said.

'And why are you so dark?' the beggar asked Kalki. 'Will you come and beg with me? With a skin like yours, we can get double the alms.'

'We didn't ask you for ways to make money,' Kalki retorted.

'Oh ho, for someone who looks like a wretched thing that even a dog won't piss on, you sure do have a big mouth.'

'Please sir, where is the office?' Karthi asked again, making the beggar feel important. Upon hearing the word sir, he felt like a king.

'It will cost you,' the beggar said, scratching his matted hair. 'How much do you have in your pocket?'

Fearing that the beggar might find the money hidden in his underwear, Karthi quickly but reluctantly pulled out his five-rupee coin. It felt heavier than usual and got heavier and heavier as he extended it to the beggar. The beggar looked at the begging bowl near his naked cruddy feet. Karthi followed his eyes and dropped the coin in it. It landed with a heavy clang, spinning for a while, like a captured animal, looking for a way out, and then it fell silent.

The beggar belted out the directions. 'First, take a left under the yellow tailor's sign, then keep going straight till you reach a teashop on the right and next to it is the chit fund office.'

Karthi grabbed Kalki's hand and ran towards the tailor's shop in case the beggar asked for more money. As they walked down the street searching for the teashop, they saw people walking towards them holding a white sheet. Some looked dazed, looking at the paper intently and then performing calculations on their fingers. Then they gazed up at the sky as though looking for an answer. Others looked at the paper their hands with gratitude, smiling and kissing it.

'Looks like we didn't have to ask the beggar for the directions and lost Rs 5 for no reason whatsoever,' Kalki said, clicking her tongue.

'But he could have found our bundle of money. I had to do it.' Karthi comforted Kalki and himself.

They were greeted by streams of tea being poured from jug to jug by the tea-master who served the frothy tea to his customers. This time Kalki wanted to ask for directions, so Karthi let her. Kalki checked with the tea-master if this was where the money-growing office was.

'Money-growing office? What do you mean?' The tea-master's eyes never left the steam of tea that he juggled between the jugs. Karthi remembered the word chit fund which he had earlier heard from the beggar.

'Where is the chit fund office?' he asked.

'Can't you see a line over there? Don't disturb me. Can't you see I have customers waiting?'

A long queue of tired people stood leaning against the building, running along the length of the wall into the compound and up the stairs. Some sat on their haunches. The people in the queue ordered tea and snacks from the teashop but they did not leave their spot in the queue. Some men carried black bags under their arms, probably with money. The women carried no purses or bags. Their money was probably stashed in their blouses, tucked near their breasts. And they cursed their useless husbands for having to stand in line to make their lives better. Everyone shot suspicious and jealous glances at each other, measuring the size of the bags and breasts to calculate how much money each one was carrying. A few dozed using their hands as a pillow, but they remained alert to footsteps and gossip.

Karthi and Kalki walked to the building and up the stairs. A man yelled at them for cutting the line, but a woman stepped in, scolding the man for his stupidity in assuming that the children were here to deposit money. 'They must be looking for their parents,' she said. Kalki nodded and they were allowed to go inside the office.

A wave of hot and humid air mixed with sweat and high hopes washed over them as they pushed the glass door open. A low ceiling fan droned above. On the wall, portraits of gods watched over the crowd.

A lone man sat behind a glass counter, his eyes fixed at a bundle of papers, busy in a perpetual motion of stamping papers. The room contained rows of interconnected green chairs that creaked if anyone moved. Like an audience in a movie theatre, the people's eyes were fixed on the TV in the corner. It sang and showed selected *Talaivar* songs, boosting hope that difficulties can be overcome. Some people tapped their feet in tune with the songs. Others hissed at them to stop it. A few gathered around the portrait of their favourite god and prayed and thanked for being granted this opportunity to better their lives.

Some were inflamed by *Talaivar's* songs, which warded off despair, and they added more money, more than they could afford, to the deposit. *Talaivar* praised them for taking a chance by singing:

> A chance like this won't ever come again
> You will look back and think differently
> That you could have taken the risk
> And everything in your life could have changed.

The bald man with short grey hair at the sides darted from one person to other, making notes, asking questions, and checking files. Whenever he appeared, the audience diverted their eyes from *Talaivar* and their gaze followed him. *Talaivar* sang loudly for attention, but he was no match for a man who had the magic to double people's money.

The bald man brought Karthi a sense of familiarity and comfort that he was in the right place. When he left, people started to talk among themselves and prodded others.

'Why did he come to you specifically?' one man asked the other. 'What did he ask? Is there a problem?'

'Nothing. He wanted to see if all my documents were in order,' said the man who was blessed and lucky to be questioned by the bald man.

Karthi and Kalki tried to walk towards the room where the bald man had gone in. Before they could take more than a couple of steps, someone noticed Kalki and gasped. Everyone looked at Kalki, feasting on her skin like vultures on carrion.

'Never seen someone with such dark skin before!'

'Poor kid! Everyone must make fun of her, calling her darkie or little phantom.'

'We are done for. That darkie is a black omen.'

'Or maybe her black face will frighten away any misfortune,' someone said, trying to be optimistic.

Then they took few more steps. A flurry of 'Oyes' erupted from the seated audience.

'Do you think that we are idiots sitting here?'

'Look at these two! Walking like they own the place!'

'No, they are acting like they are the descendants of the queen of England,' someone else said.

'Get back in line,' shouted a man with blazing red eyes.

'This isn't a place for children,' a woman said softly, approaching Karthi and Kalki. 'Are you lost, children?'

'No. I think our father is in there,' Kalki said. 'Mother asked us to bring him home soon.'

'Oh, such good kids. Sounds like someone's husband is going to be in a lot of trouble,' the woman said. 'Go and find your father.'

Karthi and Kalki scuttled away into the dark corridor before someone else stopped them. They could hear the woman chiding the people for even thinking that the children were somehow involved in adult's business and about how money had blinded everyone.

They didn't know which door the bald man had gone through. There were four plain beige doors on either side of the wall and one double door at the end with red panels. The plain doors were silent and stoic, giving nothing away and promising nothing. The red door, on the other hand, beckoned and promised them answers.

They could hear a man's voice behind the door as they opened it. He sat behind the table, furiously making notes and counting cash.

'Murthi, looks like we would need to stay for a …,' the man stopped when he saw Karthi and Kalki walk in. 'Who are you two? Murthi!' he yelled.

'This is not a place for children,' he said. He got up from his chair and hurried towards them, shooing them away like unwanted flies. He wore a stiff white shirt and pants and a black-tie with blue swirls.

This was the man from the festival. Karthi reached into his underwear.

'Chee, chee! What are you doing, boy? Could you stop it? Murthi!' the man yelled again.

Karthi took out the bundle of cash and showed it to the man. 'Are you the money-growing man?'

'Son, for that much money, you can call me anything,' the man said, his eyes shining with greed. 'Take a seat.'

Karthi and Kalki sat on the wooden chairs, pushing themselves in till their leg stuck out like discarded steel rods at a construction site.

The man's table was filled with stacks of paper waiting to be picked up and studied. Pens and pencils were scattered around the table like bodies on a battlefield. In the middle of the table, a gold nameplate with the name 'Surya, B.B.A', meaning 'Sun, Bachelor of Business Administration', reflected gold from the ceiling lights.

Surya began to scribble something on a paper. 'So, tell me, how much do you have?'

'Can you really grow our money?' Kalki asked with a wide grin.

'I… Sure.' Kalki's dark-skinned face arrested Surya's thought. She noticed the change, but she was eager for an answer. 'Tell me, did something happen to your skin? You are the darkest person I have ever laid my eyes on,' Surya said.

Karthi opened his mouth to answer, but Surya cut him off.

'It doesn't matter. You can be purple or yellow for all I care. As long as you give me money. How much do you have?' He gazed at the bundle of money.

'I am not sure,' Karthi said, opening the bundle.

'Let me do that for you,' Surya snatched the money, wet his thumb, and sifted through the notes. He counted the cash and went into a trance.

One hundred. Two hundred. Three Hundred. Suddenly he remembered that the money had been stashed in the boy's underwear. He spat out a few times and started counting again. Four hundred. 'Anything can be excused with money,' he said to himself.

Five hundred. Six Hundred. 'Are your parents here?' He looked sideways at the children but quickly turned back to the money.

Karthi shook his head.

Seven hundred. Eight hundred. 'Did your parents send you here with this money?'

Karthi nodded.

Nine hundred. A thousand. 'Where did you get this much money?'

'My mother…,' Karthi started to speak.

Two thousand. Three thousand. 'Oh, I see,' Surya spoke to the money. 'Ten thousand.'

Surya said, 'Look, there is not enough money. You can't deposit so little money and expect it to mature fast.'

Two pairs of eyes stared at him.

'I mean, I can't grow this money. It's not enough.'

'But that's all we have,' Karthi said in a pleading tone.

'No, we have some more,' Kalki said, putting down the five-rupee coin that she earned earlier in the day.

Surya laughed till tears poured down his cheeks. A high laugh that made some papers on the table tremble and scatter and fall on the children.

'You children are something,' Surya said. 'Leave it with me. I will make it grow.' He dragged the five-rupee coin towards himself. 'You can leave now. Murthi! Where is that bastard?'

'How much will the money grow?' Kalki asked.

'Enough.'

'How long will it take?' Karthi asked.

'Long enough.'

'When can we get it back?' Kalki asked.

Surya slammed his hands on his desk. The stationery bounced once, stayed afloat, and crashed landed. Papers fluttered. Receipts of money deposited by hopeful investors flew down. 'You are too young to understand these things. Leave now.'

Karthi and Kalki pushed themselves out of the chair and left. On their way out, they saw Surya giggling as he straightened the notes out and put a rubber band on them before placing it inside a green duffel bag with gold handles.

'On your way out, get a white paper slip from the man behind the counter. Tell him I have sent you and he will give you the paper. Remember, it's a very important paper,' Surya said with a wicked grin that made his nose appear pointy, his teeth long and sharp, and his eyes beady.

Before they headed out, Kalki walked to Surya to try her luck one more time. 'Do you know when my money will grow really big?'

'Come back here in two months,' he said, waving her off.

'Two months!' Kalki exclaimed in a trembling voice. Her mind wandered two months into the future. She would buy all the fairness creams in stock and apply them daily from head to toe till she turned fair. No one would call her darkie anymore. No more disgusted glances. All the frightful flinches will turn into caresses. She wouldn't have to walk in the shadows anymore. She would belong to her brother. Her mother. And most of all, she would belong to herself. To her own skin.

As they were on their way out, Murthi finally arrived, and Surya lambasted him for not heeding his calls.

'Looks like we need to turn the others away and ask them to come tomorrow. We have reached our daily limit for today,' Surya said as they exited the room.

Outside, the room was waiting for something. *Talaivar* was still persuading the audience to be courageous and take a chance. The lone man behind the counter was still stamping papers. People felt their armpits sweating. Some were snoring and drooling. Others were wishing for fortune and planning the future. The gods were watching.

Suddenly, an announcement come over the loudspeaker. 'We have met our quota for today. We won't be accepting any more applications today. Tomorrow will be the last day we will be here. So come tomorrow.'

The crowd stirred. Some woke up from dreams of counting bundles of cash. They didn't know what to do. A few got up and rushed towards the man behind the counter. Curses erupted like firecrackers. There was a lot of pushing and pulling. Shirts got torn. Lungies got ripped off. Women slapped men next to them as their sarees were pulled off in the melee. People crowded at the counter, demanding answers. The man sat there unflinching, feeling safe behind the protective barrier of glass. He shook his hands and head. He had no answers for them.

'How are we going to get the white paper now?' Kalki asked.

'We have to wait till everyone leaves,' Karthi said as they crouched behind a potted plant, away from the chaos.

Then Murthi appeared. Half the crowd peeled away from the window and encircled him. He stood there like a protruding monolith jutting out of the stormy sea as the people swarmed around him.

People begged. Pleaded. Demanded angrily. Some even promised to give more money. 'You can't leave here without taking our money. You are our only hope,' someone said.

'What can I do?' Murthi said. 'This scheme has become very popular. We must set daily limits. Otherwise, we will be working here till midnight. Don't we have families?'

'For the amount of money you are receiving, I would have moved my family here,' someone else said. 'What a fool!'

Murthi stood there with his arms folded, staring into the distance as the clamour swelled. Finally, some people got tired and left. A few remained to check if he would break his pose. They too left as soon as the lights, fans and the TV were turned off.

Surya emerged from his room with his green bag slung over his shoulder. He leaned on one side to offset the weight of the bulging bag.

'Look at today's haul,' Surya said, slapping the rigid bag.

'Who is a fool now? Idiots! Just need to start a fire under their bums. See how it worked. Saying that we will be here for only a week more worked like magic.' Murthi said, looking at the empty waiting hall.

'I bet that even our *Talaivar's* movie doesn't get such a crowd,' the man at the counter said.

'Did anyone ask you, Kumar?' Murthi asked.

'I will unload some money into the truck right now and go to the bank to deposit the rest. Decide which city you want to go to next,' Surya told Murthi.

'Somewhere full of fools,' Murthi said. They all laughed. The gods looked down with a foreboding smile.

Karthi and Kalki didn't know when to come out and ask for the white paper. They stayed behind the potted plant and watched the three men through the leaves. Karthi watched Surya's bag. He could hear the money he gave him inside it, jostling with other people's money for space to grow. Suddenly, his leg slipped and kicked the pot. The plant fell, and two pairs of shocked eyes looked at three pairs of confused eyes.

'What are you two doing here?' Murthi said as he dragged them up, twisting their ears.

'I remember you, darkie,' Surya said as though they were old friends meeting after a very long time. 'Did you get your receipt?'

'Receipt?' Murthi said. 'What would these filthy kids know about this scheme?'

'Don't underestimate them, Murthi. It is because of them,' Surya banged his bag again. The money inside groaned. 'Only the desperate ones take the biggest but stupidest risks.'

'Maybe we should make that our motto, sir,' Kumar chimed in again.

'You idiot, we are trying to entice people, not scare them away. Who hired this guy?' Murthi said, slapping his bald head. 'Anyway, get out of here, you two.'

'But what about the white paper?' asked Karthi.

'Can't you see the office is closed? Come tomorrow,' said Kumar, tossing them outside and locking the door.

Not wanting to give up, they waited outside on the street where a few people still prowled looking at the office, saying something and then walking away.

Moments later, Murthi and Kumar came down carrying a bag each. They looked around before getting into the truck and driving away. Next, a man raced down the stairs as though he was about to trip and fall. He wore a cap and sunglasses, and his head was bent. Karthi spotted the green duffel bag and knew it was Surya. This time the bag looked deflated. His heart sank to his feet, and his toes felt heavy. His money, his mother's money, all gone with nothing to show for it.

They followed Surya, hoping to get the white paper receipt from him. Surya walked down the main street while the children climbed onto the low walls and pursued him. They had an almost aerial view of his movements.

Surya stopped now and then to look around to see if anyone had followed him.

After a while, the children's rubber slippers couldn't give them a grip of the stony walls. So, they shook them off to run faster. They skipped like playful goats to avoid the wall's rough edges.

Surya picked up pace when he was further down the

main road. Karthi jumped off the wall holding his sister's hand, his eyes fixed on Surya's cap. Kalki slipped and landed on her back, but she quickly scrambled to her feet.

Surya was just a few metres away from them. Karthi could almost reach his hand and touch the bag. He could feel his money inside the bag, calling out for him to rescue it before it vanished without any proof. But the crowd in the main road swallowed Surya whole like a greedy river. Just like that, he disappeared.

The sun was about to set, casting a light orange and pink light. Shops like illegal colonisers poached pavements to extend their business and trap more customers. People had to funnel through the gap created by the shop and their extensions like clogged arteries. Karthi and Kalki were pushed into the flow inadvertently, as vendors accosted passers-by with their wares.

As they went wherever the crowd did, Karthi spotted Surya's cap and made a mad dash toward him and yanked his bag. With the pull, he provoked a fast-moving hand that landed flat on his cheek, which produced a sound like a burst tyre. Karthi was thrown aside, and he fell along with his sister into the gutter. His cheek swelled and stung. The hastening crowd stopped for a momentary gasp and continued walking.

'Thief, thief,' Surya yelled and disappeared again.

A group of concerned citizens gathered around and watched. They started to scold the children. Karthi and Kalki picked themselves up from the open gutter coated in chocolate wrappers, banana peels and strings of hair.

The crowd pinched their nose in disgust and disbanded.

Wet and stinky, tired and disheartened, but unwilling to give up, they scoured the street – every lane, doorway and shop – for Surya.

Suddenly, the green bag revealed itself on the opposite side of the road. Surya stood there talking to someone outside a bank before entering it. Wasting no time, they pushed themselves through the crowd. They didn't need to put much effort. The stench emanating from them made people give them a wide berth.

'You have to be ready,' Karthi said. 'First, I will grab the bag when he comes out. Then we are going to run as fast as we can.'

'But to where?'

'I don't know. Just follow me. Promise me you will.'

They waited outside the bank. Catching their breath, gathering their energy for the run of their lives. They stretched their sewage-water-sodden limbs to dry. Within minutes, Karthi looked as though he was halfway through shedding his old grey skin. For Kalki, it didn't make any difference. The dark shade of her skin merged perfectly with the black water.

Karthi's eyes were heavy, but he pinched himself to stay awake. Just then the door swung wide open and out emerged Surya whistling one of *Talaivar's* songs.

'Run!' Karthi screamed as he lunged towards Surya and jerked the bag from his hand.

As Karthi dashed into the unknown with Kalki behind him, he felt victorious. He could put the money back inside his mother's rice tin and everything would return to normal, he told himself. There must be other methods they could try to make Kalki fairer, less risky methods. But his optimism didn't last long. It was sucked into a hole as the bag slapped his back loosely as he ran. It was light, like it only contained air. Where was the money? You fool, why else would one go to a bank?

With Surya still chasing after them, Karthi had no time to stop and check the bag. He ran as fast as his legs could carry him and paused only to check if his sister was still following him.

Their directionless, aimless, clueless sprint led them to the gate of the railway station. Surya was still behind them although he was quite far off now.

Announcements blared to unheeding ears. People went this way and that on the platform, hurrying, ambling, stumbling. There was only one train standing at the station.

'Where are we going now?' Kalki asked.

'If we can cross over to the other side of the train tracks, we can lose him,' Karthi said, standing on his toes searching for Surya among the crowd.

Another announcement cut through the tension like a saw on wood. 'Attention, passengers. Madras Mail will depart in ten minutes. In ten minutes. Please make your way to the train.'

With ten minutes left to cross over to the other side, they hoisted themselves into the train. They heard a familiar voice. Surya was charging towards them. Karthi and Kalki were about to cross over to the other side of the train and jump out when a swift jerk pulled them inside.

The train started to move.

'We have to get off,' Kalki said in a panicky voice.

Karthi searched for an opening on either side. One side was full of people. The other side was blocked by steel pipes that fed water to the train. He waited and waited, but the train picked up speed and steadied itself on the rails, taking them away.

'What have I done?' Karthi said as he collapsed on the ground, holding on to Surya's bag, his body shuddering with his sobs. Kalki joined him and rested her head on his shoulders. She looked out through the open door and saw the deserted railway tracks upon which they had sat eating mangoes not too long ago. Her spectre waved a goodbye. A chill coursed through her body.

The new announcer received a swift slap on his head from the control room in-charge.

'You fool, you were supposed to make the ten-minute announcement ten minutes ago, not at the exact time of the train's departure,' said the station master.

Chapter 9

Rubber bands of various colours.

Bits of torn paper.

Paper clips.

A green rectangular business card.

And a scuttling cockroach.

These were the only occupants of the duffel bag. A robust musty smell like old dusty, discarded cardboard boxes wafted up to Karthi's face, making him and Kalki sneeze. Frightened, the lone cockroach dashed out of the bag and scurried under one of the train's berths.

As Karthi stared into the almost empty bag, it appeared to get deeper and more cavernous. He wanted to fall into it and be lost so that he would never have to answer to his mother for the missing money. And the pesky worms of guilt would stop bothering him.

His head almost sagged into the bag, but Kalki interrupted his fall into oblivion by pulling him back with her words, back into the small area where they sat, sandwiched between the toilet and the train door.

The green business card seemed to call out to Karthi. He picked it up and on the other side was some writing in gold lettering. There was a picture of a man with his hands pressed together on the left-hand side. His eyes were tightly closed as though in deep conversation with a higher power. His moustache was pointy and twisted. He had three white lines and a deep red mark on his forehead that ran from the middle of his eyebrows to this head, like a flame. On the right-hand side of the card was written:

> Shakthi Family Investments, where money is like family
> Company president: Shakthivelu
> Head office: 3025, Old Cantonment Road,
> Vijaya Nagar,
> Chennai 621867

'Maybe we can go to his office and ask him. He looks important,' Kalki suggested.

'Yes, but do you know where Chennai is?'

'Far.'

'Very far. I don't even know where this train is heading to?' Karthi looked around for clues. 'Come on, let's go inside and find a seat.'

As Karthi zipped up the bag and was about to get up, a man came out of the toilet. A whooshing and piercing rattle sound erupted as he closed the toilet door behind.

'Where do you think you two dirty things are going?' he said, frowning at them as though they reminded him of something dirty he had seen in the toilet. 'As if begging on the station is not enough, you people won't leave us alone inside the train too. Can't even travel in peace,' he said as he spat into the washbasin. He pulled the tap's nozzle upwards, and a thin stream of water trickled out. He mocked the Indian Railways management for it. 'The British gave us one thing that is good, and the bloody government can't even take care of it.' He gulped a mouthful of water, gargled, and spat into the basin, raining droplets on Karthi and Kalki. He waved his finger at them, warning them not to come into the compartment.

The train picked up speed, finding its groove in comfortable swaying rhythm. Karthi and Kalki fell into a deep sleep on the floor. Karthi rested his head against the wall of the compartment, using his elbow as a pillow. Kalki slept inside the duffel bag, curled up like a foetus.

A sharp bang woke them up. The unlatched toilet door slammed back and forth in a threatening manner. The stench of dry urine, water and faeces hit them every time the door opened. It made Karthi throw up. But very little came out as the children's stomachs were empty.

The train tooted as though acknowledging their hunger. It reduced its speed and started to wobble a lot more, sparking a commotion among the passengers. Soon, a group of passengers crowded near the door. Karthi and Kalki moved out of the way and cowered near the toilet.

The passengers glanced at them through groggy eyes, not with pity or dislike but just indifference. The man who had admonished them at the start of their journey was at the head of the line of passengers waiting to get off.

Eventually, the train came to a halt and began to hiss as it approached the station. A skirmish broke out at the doorway as exiting and incoming passengers met, neither ready to give way.

Vendors selling tea, coffee, two-day-old vadas and samosas that had been twice-fried, once to cook and the second time to reheat, flocked to the windows, parading their edibles on top of their heads. As the vendors walked past the train door, a hand darted through the grilled opening of the door, like an elephant extending its trunk, and grabbed some food.

Their hunger sated, Karthi and Kalki decided to try their luck and find a place to sit now that the finger-waving man was gone. As they moved from one section to the next, many pairs of probing eyes followed them. Their tattered clothes and dark sweats stains, the sour smell didn't make them desirable passengers.

'Did she fall into a tarpit?'

'Nuisance these people are, yuck!'

'Look at her skin. She is as black as the elephant we saw at the zoo.'

'Can't stand the smell! My brain is going to melt and escape through my nose.'

Karthi found an empty berth with a brown blanket. He draped it over Kalki to solve one problem. The blanket pricked Kalki, but it was better than the prickly eyes of strangers. Karthi placed the duffel bag by his side and opened it again to check if the business card was still there. He saw Shakthivelu still in communion with God.

Opposite was seated an old couple, side-by-side holding bottles of Coke and hearing aids in their ears. As the children approached the seat, the old couple didn't flinch or seem perturbed by their presence. They watched them from behind thick glasses. Karthi quickly sniffed himself to check if the smell had magically disappeared. No, he smelt as putrid as ever. They giggled at them, showing crooked and protruding teeth.

'Where are your parents?' the old man asked.

Karthi and Kalki didn't answer. They merely looked out through the window. Outside, porters hurried by with mounds of bags on their head. A mother carried her baby on her back, as she swept the platform. The dust rose and flew into the train. Passengers clutched their bags tightly as their eyes darted around. A lone man sat on his haunches, surrounded by colourful plastic bags.

'They want to sit by the window. Their parents must be here somewhere,' the old woman said to her husband.

'Why are you covered in a blanket? Are you feeling cold? Strange! It's so hot in here!' the old man asked Kalki, fanning himself with a rolled-up newspaper.

'Let the kids do what they want,' the old woman said indulgently.

The old man grinned and extended a bag of banana chips to the children. 'Take it, dears.'

Karthi nodded his thanks and Kalki stuffed her mouth with the yellow chips.

As the crunching of the banana chips competed with the noise from the platform, a man entered the compartment. He wore a stiff grey safari suit and smelled of coconut oil. His fingers fiddled with the fanny purse strapped at his waist, zipping and unzipping it.

'Look, their father has come,' the old lady said.

'Father? Whose father?' The man looked around in a confused manner. Then he spotted the children. 'No, no, no, you are mistaken. I am not their father. My name is Cheran. Where are you going?'

Cheran sat on Karthi's berth and struck up a conversation with the old couple. They talked about their travel plans. About the condition of the Indian Railway. About the government's lack of competency in sticking to a schedule. About ill-gotten advice and promising investments, which lead them to talk about Shakthi Investments.

Karthi pricked up his ears at the mention of Shakthi Investments. He interrupted their conversation. 'Do you know the way to the office of Shakthivelu?'

'How do you know about Shakthivelu, son?' Cheran asked.

'TICKET! TICKET! TICKET!' A loud voice interrupted them. A man wearing a black suit with a white shirt and red tie came in, carrying a clipboard. On his head, he wore a cap with a golden emblem in the centre. His mouth had a permanent pout like it was preventing his moustache from falling off. He seemed out of place, as though he was about to go for a job interview and catch a robber at the same time. The old couple and Cheran produced their tickets. He stamped them and ticked them off on his clipboard.

'Oye!' he called out to Karthi and Kalki. 'Do you two need a special invitation?'

Karthi began to fumble through his bag as everyone in the compartment waited for him to produce their tickets. He elbowed Kalki to join in the search. She shed her blanket and started to rifle through the bag. Everyone inhaled sharply as they saw Kalki's skin.

Kalki shot a disconcerted gaze at Cheran as though pleading for help. Cheran noticed that something was wrong. That they weren't supposed to be here on this train. He did not want to help them, but he wanted to find out how the boy knew about the chit fund owner, which he thought would make an exciting story to hear on their journey.

'I don't have time to wait,' the ticket inspector said, tapping the clipboard with his pen. 'Hurry up! Otherwise, I will throw you out of the train.'

'Don't you know, children?' Cheran spoke as an uncle would to a niece and nephew. 'The tickets are with your mother. She is in the other compartment. Sir, you better go to the next compartment. Their mother has their tickets. I am their uncle, and they wanted to be with me.' Cheran said to the inspector.

'Why couldn't you have told me earlier?' the inspector

clicked his tongue in annoyance. He walked down the aisle, calling out, 'Ticket, ticket, ticket.'

'Now that I have helped you two, I think you owe me a story,' Cheran said.

'We don't have a story,' Karthi said, covering his sister with the blanket.

'Everyone has a story. Especially the two of you. What is it? Running away from home? Drunk father? Did your mother abandon you? How do you know about the chit fund?'

An announcement trilled through the platform in staccato sentences. People scrambled. The train whistled its departure and started to leave the station.

Karthi spoke at length and told him all that had happened to him and his sister. How his sister wanted to lighten her skin so that people would stop teasing her and thinking of her as a bad omen. About the thrill of meeting *Talaivar* when he came to their village. The anticipation of asking white tourists the secret of their fair skin, the mad priest who told her to eat mangoes to lighten her hue, the exhilaration of raiding the mango orchard and eating the mangoes, about their mother saving up money to take Kalki to a good doctor in the city. The anxiety of being summoned to Subramaniam's house to pay for damaging his mango saplings. The unexpected, expected death of their neighbour Priya after she was rejected as a prospective bride for the third time because she wasn't fair enough. About stealing their mother's money and giving it to the chit fund man who had promised to double it. The sense of dread when they saw the chit fund man run away with their money and how they ended up on this train. How they planned to go to the main office in Chennai to get their money back. Karthi selectively left out the reason he believed that he was the cause of his sister's dark skin. As he ended his story, the flashback of events drained the energy out of Karthi. A numbing lethargy settled on him.

'Serve you both right for stealing money from your mother,' the old woman said. She pulled her bag closer to her leg. She directed her husband to do the same.

'But we need to get the money back,' Karthi said.

'The money is gone, you foolish boy,' the old man said, adding under his breath how these villagers get fooled so easily.

Karthi looked at Cheran to gauge his thoughts.

'Your mother must be so worried,' Cheran said. 'Here, keep these,' he added, hand over a packet of biscuits. 'After eating, sleep for a while. This train won't stop for another five hours. At the next station, I will make sure you get on the right train back home.'

Karthi and Kalki sat back on their seat, quietly munching the dry biscuits. Wind blew in through the grilled windows, sweeping crumbly bits of biscuits off their mouth. Karthi wanted to cry and the wind stung his eyes. The sky was darkening outside. Orphaned trains ruminated on abandoned rail tracks. Dogs barked at the train for disturbing their slumber. Dishevelled and crumbling buildings scattered the landscape. The train passed through a small town with lights flickering in the windows of the houses. Vehicles waited impatiently at a railway crossing along with a patient cow. Then followed verdant rice fields punctuated with mud huts.

Kalki's eyes were fixed on the horizon as the sun dropped out of the sky and a sheet of darkness fell over the landscape. Kalki pictured herself running towards the horizon, through green fields and shoddy roads, to fish the sun out of his hiding place. She managed to reach the precipice where the sun was getting ready for slumber. She asked the sun to hear her out before retiring for the day, that she had an idea that would allow the sun to be always up and never set into darkness. The sun sniggered at the absurdity of the idea but asked her to explain. 'What if you come to live on my skin? I hate how dark my skin is. It is like the night. If you do, you can be up all the time and chase away the night from my skin.' The sun thought for a while and said, 'Child, are you sure that is what you want? Once I get under your skin, there is no going back. There might be consequences.' Kalki nodded her head vehemently. 'I don't want to be dark anymore.'

The sun slowly crept into her feet first. The sunbeam spread like yellow liquid all over her legs. The dark skin was incinerated, flaking off like cinders. As she jumped around in happiness, Aaya's words came to her mind, 'Beware of the sun. It turns your skin dark.' She stopped dancing and pleaded for the sun to stop entering her body. 'I made a grave mistake,' she said. 'Too late. I warned you of consequences,' the sun said with a laugh and advanced further on Kalki's skin. Kalki started to kick her legs in hopes of shedding the approaching sun. She kicked and kicked, but it was all in vain.

'Oye, little girl,' Cheran said as he woke up to Kalki kicking him. His groggy voice was replete with sleep. 'You are having a nightmare. Wake up!'

Kalki rubbed her eyes as she woke up. The compartment was drenched in an inky hue, a dying light illuminating the cabin. Karthi was sound asleep with his mouth wide open. The old woman was asleep on the lower berth, clutching her handbag and using another bag as a pillow. The old man on the berth above her was asleep, his arm over his face. Cheran sat next to Kalki, wearing a cotton vest that fit his body like a glove and a lungi.

'What were you dreaming?' he asked Kalki, handing her a bottle of water.

'Of becoming fair,' she said, taking a sip of the water.

'Now that you have woken me up and disturbed my sleep, I think you owe me something,' Cheran said with a devilish smile. The pale blue light from the ceiling accentuated the sharpness of his nose, the archness of his eyebrows and the twist at the end of his smile, and the pointiness of his five o'clock shadow.

Kalki looked at Karthi.

'Let him be. He is sleeping. You said you wanted to be fair. I can help you with that. I can produce whitening cream for you.'

'I don't want it,' Kalki said. 'We will get our own cream.'

'I am sure you will, but you don't know what you are missing out on. What I have is the purest white cream you will ever see,' Cheran said, laying his nasty trap. 'It will turn your skin instantly white, just like that.' Cheran snapped his fingers and realised he had made a mistake. The rattle of the train swallowed the snap. Nobody stirred.

Kalki extended her hand to receive the cream.

'Not here,' Cheran whispered. 'If anyone sees it, they will also ask for it. Come to the toilet. First, I will go. Then you come after two minutes.'

Cheran stood up and pressed his index finger to his mouth to tell her to be quiet, and disappeared down the aisle.

Kalki waited for a while in the darkness, listening to the snores of the passengers. Then she walked towards the toilet. Passengers swayed in their berths as the train cradled them in their sleep. There were brisk movements on the floor. Kalki spotted a big, thick, hairy shadow scurrying around, followed by small, thin, smooth shadows.

She knocked on the toilet door. It jerked open sending out a stench that almost gagged her.

'Good. You have come,' a voice spoke in the darkness.

'I can't see anything,' Kalki said.

'We don't need lights,' Cheran said. 'Come inside first.'

As the train hurtled on, fingers of orange light lit up the toilet. It also lighted up Cheran's silhouette. His eyes glowed amber. His face was pale. The chortling wind rushing through the toilet windows ruffled his hair. It spread in all directions like writhing snakes. He smiled, revealing an inky blue smile. Kalki trembled.

'What are you waiting for?' Cheran asked. 'Here, I have chocolates.' He reached for his pouch and unzipped it. He took out something that crinkled. 'Take this,' he said.

He carries a bag on his side, filled with ashes and bones of the children he has consumed. Kalki remembered her mother's words on Poochandi.

'Those are not chocolates,' Kalki said in a nervous voice.

'What are you saying?'

'You are the Poochandi. The pouch is where you keep the children's bones,' Kalki said, pointing at his fanny purse.

'Foolish girl. Poochandi doesn't exist.'

'My mother told me about you. But why do you want me? Mother said you don't steal dark-skinned girls like me. So does that mean I am not dark enough,' Kalki said, a nervous smile quivering on her lips.

Cheran put the chocolate back in the pouch and zipped it up. 'Stupid girl. Spoilt my mood.' Kalki heard another zipping sound.

'So, you think I am not dark? Because Poochandi doesn't kidnap dark-skinned children.' Kalki asked Cheran politely.

Before Cheran could say anything, Kalki heard

someone approaching.

The man rapped at the door. 'How long will you take? I can't hold it any longer.'

Cheran flicked the light switch, and the muddy yellow light made Kalki's eyes squint.

'Come out quick,' the man outside snapped.

'Can't you wait a minute? Were you born in London, that you have to use the toilet? Can't you piss out the door?' Cheran snapped back.

The man rushed into the toilet. A steady clatter brimmed from inside.

'See, I am not the Poochandi.' Cheran declared to Kalki. 'Besides, why the hell would anyone want to steal a filthy darkie like yourself? Maybe your mother was right about that.'

Kalki remained silent.

'Get out of the way,' Cheran said.

'What about the cream?'

'Not only have you disturbed my sleep and spoilt my mood, now you are demanding things from me?' Cheran snarled.

As Kalki made her way back to her seat, Cheran rushed past her, deliberately bumping into her.

'I should not have lied to the ticket inspector to protect low-caste children like you. You deserve to be thrown out. You wait and watch,' he muttered to himself. Cheran sat upright and began munching on groundnuts greedily as though someone had sucked the energy out of his body.

'What are you staring at?' Cheran barked. 'Go to sleep.'

Suddenly the whole train cabin lit up. Passengers were jolted awake.

'Did I miss my station?' someone screamed.

'What is happening? Are we being attacked by bandits?' another cried.

The ticket inspector marched with long strides towards Kalki and grabbed her by her ponytail.

'You lying little rat. How dare you say your mother is on the train? Making me search up and down the train, and I missed my dinner because of you," he said.

Kalki stared at Cheran, provoking him to speak up, but he remained silent, popping groundnuts into his mouth like inside a cinema hall. A nutty dinner and a provocative show.

'Where is your brother?' the inspector dragged Kalki by her hair. She screamed. The old woman woke up and started wailing about her bags. 'They have stolen it. Those kids have robbed us blind.' She fumbled for her glasses. Her husband calmed her down and pointed at the bags. She counted them and counted them again to be sure. She thanked god that she had not lost them.

The inspector kicked Karthi. 'Get up, you wretched thing. Look at the way he is sleeping. As though he has bought a first-class ticket.' He yanked the chain above him, and the train came to a screeching halt. The old woman's bag was thrown to the ground. Groundnuts spilled out of it.

As the ticket inspector walked down the aisle pulling Kalki and Karthi, curious necks poked out, asking what was happening.

'Now go find your way home,' The inspector threw the children out into the night. They landed on a thorny bush. 'Next time, buy tickets or don't get on a train.' He spat at them. Twice. He missed the mark. A few passengers gathered at the doorway.

The ticket inspector calmed the passengers and ushered them back to their seats and sounded his whistle. The train jerked back into motion. As the train moved, Karthi remembered the bag that was still on the train.

'My bag, my bag, my bag,' he yelled, running by the side of the train. He reached the compartment he was sleeping in and shouted at the old woman and Cheran to throw his bag out. The woman didn't do anything. Cheran pretended not to hear him and went back to crunching his peanuts.

Tired, Karthi eventually stopped. Kalki came up behind him. The train was picking up speed, and as they watched, something came flying out from the window and landed in the thick forest ahead.

Aa sudden cloudburst drenched the children. A terrifying deafening thunder reverberated through the land, shaking trees, rattling train tracks, and bending power lines. The rain came down in sheets, washing off the acrid filth from their bodies.

Karthi and Kalki dashed into the forest for cover, but nature was too eager with her bountiful offerings.

Karthi's shorts kept slipping as they became heavy with water. Kalki could hardly walk in her wet skirt. She looked like an oil spill in the ocean as thick water trickled down her skin. They reached the edge of the forest and slunk into the dark hollows created by the thick roots of a banyan tree. Thick and twisted. A patch of banana plants moaned next to it, their tattered yellowing leaves looking like the sails of abandoned ships on rough seas. The children could feel things slinking beside behind them. Something hissed and something gnarled. They sat motionless, apart from shivering from the cold. Nestled among the roots like mythical creatures from tales told to scare naughty children, the children waited for the rains to cease, hugging each other for warmth.

A soft hooting woke them. It was still dark outside with clear skies and a full moon. The silvery moonlight cast a ghostly glow on the forest, bouncing off the trees. They wrung out their clothes. An upside-down yawning snake looked at them with glinting eyes as it disappeared into the dark roots. They let out a brief scream.

Karthi and Kalki picked their path through the squelching mud of the forest and headed in the general direction to where their duffel bag could have landed. Their hearts beat rapidly as they walked through the forest. Glowing fireflies lit their way. They carefully lifted their naked feet and stuck them carefully away from the tall pointy grass. And swollen fallen logs. And crumbling insects. And gaping burrows. Their clothes got snagged by straggling branches. Sharp twigs pricked their soles leaving a trail of blood on the forest floor. Leeches moved towards their meal before the rain washed it away.

The forest was watching with many eyes. A parliament of owls erupted into loud hoots as though the new immigrants had broken the law. A three-striped palm squirrel observed them. A grass owl with its cranking neck leered at the intruders. An egret spread its wings atop a tree branch, deflecting moonlight towards the unsuspecting prey. The owl shook. The squirrel scrambled. A chital with its many white spots peeked and vanished inside a bush. The yellow glow of a furtive leopard's eye narrowed on the disjointed walking silhouettes of the children. Kalki held on to Karthi. The leopard purred and gave up, thinking the shadow belonged to an ambling elephant searching for a late-night snack.

Soon the morning light seeped into the forest. A black stream of fruit bats flew with the night into the forest. Earthworms frolicked. Early birds twittered sporadically, lighting a singing beacon with every tweet. Woodpeckers banged their beaks on sturdy trunks in response. Peacocks crooned and unfurled their tail, dancing to honour last night's rain. A curious chameleon balanced itself on a swinging branch, dislodging old cobwebs.

The fireflies were replaced by floating iridescent dragonflies and butterflies that burned deep orange in the dawn light. The orange reflected off its wings and landed on something golden that hung low on a young tree like an anorexic boa constrictor.

Karthi clambered up the tree like a monkey and

dislodged the bag. The card was still intact, albeit damp.

'Where do we go now?' Kalki asked.

Karthi placed his ears on the cold rail track and listened. He discerned a vibration. 'I think we should go that way,' he said pointing ahead. He raised the business card to catch the sunlight to dry it off.

They walked, balancing themselves on the train tracks flanked by dense foliage on their sides. Their balancing act came to a halt when they spotted a house swaddled by trees inside the forest.

It was as though the trees had adopted the once-white house to live with them. Like strict orthodox parents, they suffocated and broke off its walls and shaped it in their image and forest colours. It had a pale blue almost green door in front. The walls were moss green. The slipping asbestos roof drooped on one side as a nearby tree extended its foliage over it like a nosy relative gathering secrets. The glass window on the side was bent under the pressure of the foliage. At a glance, it looked like an inebriated house because it couldn't become the house it wanted to be.

'I don't think we should go in,' Kalki whispered to Karthi. 'This is where he lives. Poochandi.'

Karthi remembered the words of his mother: Red glowering eyes and a ghostly white face. A head full of matted hair. Karthi shook off his fear as he heard a series of jingles coming from the glass window.

'What if it is not Poochandi?' Karthi was curious. The jingling stopped, and the front door creaked as a latch was undone. It flew open, scraping noisily against the hard floor.

'Finally, some visitors,' a hoarse voice said from inside.

Chapter 10

It was like entering another sub-world, disconnected and distanced. The inside of the dilapidated house didn't match the jaded exterior. They expected it to be entrenched in darkness with scampering rats in the corners. With nature reclaiming the walls from within, they expected a raving lunatic with dreadlocks to be living among the forgotten furniture, accompanied by wandering ghosts. But the room was quite bright with the morning light. An orange, fluorescent bulb hung like a forgotten pail in a well, but it was clean and made the room cosy dispelling the coldness from yesterday's rain. A faded sewing table, a flaking Godrej steel blue almirah with a large mirror on one side, and a mouldy wicker reclining chair furnished the room. Shiny fabric draped over the furniture hid many flaws. A string ran across one side of the wall, on which hung lungies and shirts, sarees and blouses. Two women's wigs hung on two hooks. One had short hair and was dull. The other was long with thick plaits with colourful ribbons running through it like vibrant comets streaking through the universe. Blue. Red. Yellow and pink.

One single bed stood against one wall. Dry clothes, neatly folded, rested on it. There was a kitchen with a clay stove and stainless-steel vessels in one corner. A backdoor led out to a yard where a lone tap sputtered water into a red bucket. Bits of crumbly blue soap floated on the pool of white foam rising in the bucket.

The walls were painted sky blue, and the ceiling had dark patches and rotting beams. Karthi and Kalki's eyes were on the resident of the house who was trying to light the stove by blowing air through a wooden pipe to coax the firewood to burn.

He squatted, gathering his legs inwards as he tended the flame. The cotton shirt undulated as he breathed, and his sharp bones shifted on his back. He coughed as the smoke billowed out. A double cough. His thick hair was slicked back with coconut oil.

'I think he is going to eat us,' Kalki whispered to Karthi. 'He is Poochandi, who mother warned us about. We should have listened to her and just stayed at home.'

'I don't think it's Poochandi,' Karthi said. 'He looks as though he is hiding from someone.'

'Hot milk will be ready soon,' the person said in a raspy voice. It sounded neither like a man's nor a woman's. Male and female qualities seemed to be competing for vocal dominance. 'Look at you two poor things. All wet and lost.'

The person walked towards them with two tumblers of milk on a tray. Grabbing the lungi with one other hand that revealed a pair of feet that took small steps, one foot in front of the other, the person walked towards them and squatted in front of Karthi and Kalki. They clasped their hands tightly, feeling each other's racing heartbeat.

'Drink up, drink up, kids,' the person said with a dimpled smile. They sipped the frothy warm milk, trembling with fear and anxiety.

Glass bangles clinked as the person's hands moved. The nose ring jingled and glinted. The children looked at the face with high cheekbones and a jawline that was sharp enough to cut through butter. The face was caked with white powder. The pencil-thin eyebrows looked like they had been drawn on while the dry lips were of an unnatural red hue. The eyes, however, smiled with longing intensity. The red nail polish on the hand that was extended to them was peeling. On the bangled arms were streaks of healed wounds in the shape of sickles.

'Are you Poochandi?' Kalki whispered through white moustachioed lips as she held tightly to the half-empty glass.

'What did you say? Speak up, dear.'

'My mother told us a story about someone who steals children. His name is Poochandi. Are you Poochandi?'

'Oh my, is that the story they have spun to scare people away? Tell me more.' A gleeful laugh was accompanied by a loud clap. It was clap different from the usual with the fingers on both hands spread out so that the palms struck with the same intensity and sounded off like a whiplash on an ox's skin.

'Amma said Poochandi has a white face,' Kalki said. The person wiped a palm across the cheek to reveal the actual colour – brown, the colour of strong tea. 'What else did they say?' The slapped one cheek with a hand and the bangles slid down, revealing bony hairless arms.

'That he has matted hair like snakes.'

'My hair sure is curly like a snake, but it is not matted, is it?' A shake of the head dispersed a coconutty smell. 'What else do they say?'

'That...that...,' Kalki struggled to recollect what Amma had said. 'Ah, that you have a pouch in which you carry powdered children's bones.'

The person stood up, towering over them. Lifting the lungi a little bit till the ankles could be seen, the person spun around gracefully on tiptoes. 'Do you see any pouches filled with powdered children's bones?'

The shook their heads.

'The only powder I have is this.' From a small container came puffs of talcum powder when pressed.

Something stirred within Kalki. Her body tensed, as if bracing for impact. She was waiting for a comment on her dark skin, the usual mocking and name-calling. But it didn't come. It felt strange. She wondered if there was a problem with his eyes. To test his vision, she asked why the walls were painted black. She deliberately chose the colour black to provoke him to comment on her dark skin.

'Black? Are you blind, my child? I painted it blue to bring the sky inside because I don't have the luxury of staying out for long to enjoy staring into the sky.'

Kalki felt her body relax. A pulse radiated from inside and washed all over and evicted her out of a dingy place where she was at constant skirmish with herself and her skin. She began to experience a strange new feeling, something she had never felt before. The pleasure of being talked to, smiled at, being cared for by a stranger who didn't condemn her for the colour of her skin. She had only got it from her mother before.

Even Karthi noticed that the man didn't comment on his sister's skin. The worms of guilt in his head shrank and shrivelled up in confusion.

'You are just too tired. Now tell me, what are you doing here in the middle of the forest and the middle of nowhere? Wait, before you tell me anything, both of you need a bath,' he said, wrinkling up his nose. 'And you need new clothes,' he said, fingering the holes on Karthi's grimy t-shirt and Kalki's top. 'I haven't even asked your names!'

'I am Karthi, and this is Kalki, my sister,' Karthi said.

'What is your name?' Kalki asked.

'You can call me Shreyas.'

'Does anybody else live with you?' Karthi asked, looking at the saree and the wigs.

'You will meet her soon,' Shreyas said, ushering them out through the back door.

'Close your eyes,' Karthi said, beginning to strip himself. Putting the business card for Shakti Investments into Shreyas' hand, he added, 'Please keep this safe. It is very important.'

Shreyas helped them bathe with closed eyes. Karthi and Kali scrubbed themselves thoroughly with pink Lifebuoy soap, passing the bar to each other as they cleaned themselves from top to bottom. Shreyas then poured cold water that felt needle sharp on their thin backs. With his back turned towards them, he looked at the black water that had puddled at his feet. Shreyas asked them to scrub themselves again. He poured water on them again, with his eyes tightly shut and confirming with Karthi whether he was holding the bucket over them right. This time the water was just white and foamy.

Maybe Shreyas would notice her black skin now, Kalki thought. 'Maybe he thinks that I am so dark because I was so dirty,' Kalki thought as they waited for Shreyas to bring them towels.

To their surprise, he dried them off, paying no attention to Kalki's skin. He seemed more worried about them catching a cold. He dried them off quickly and made them another glass of warm milk.

They sat in silence, wrapped in cotton plaid towels, sipping sugary milk. The children had stopped shivering as warmth spread through their bodies.

'What about our clothes?' Karthi asked.

'Forget about them. I will make new ones for you.' Shreyas dragged out the sewing machine and placed it in the centre of the room. The smell of coconut oil and machine rust pervaded the air. The sewing machine was black with a gold paisley pattern.

'I have old shirts and pants which I can turn into small shirts and shorts for you,' Shreyas said licking the end of the thread and threading the needle. Dragging a box from underneath the bed, Shreyas picked up a pair of large scissors and some fabric. The scissors sliced through the fabric like a bird skimming the sea surface for food. Shreyas lined up the cut fabric against the machine and began sewing. The treadles roared. The flywheels buzzed as the bands hummed to Shreyas' tune.

Kalki wondered if the scissors could slice off her skin. Perhaps Shreyas could stitch her a fairer skin.

'So, what brings you children to this place?' Shreyas said, feeding fabric through the machine as the hungry needle devoured it.

'We missed our train. Our mother asked us to buy some water from the station. So, we got out, and by the time we returned the train was gone. We jumped on the next train thinking that it would take us to Chennai, but it didn't, and the ticket inspector threw us out.'

'Oh, my poor dears. Your mother must be so worried, and she must be looking for you everywhere,' Shreyas said with an empathetic sigh.

Kalki looked at her brother quizzically. He returned a look of reassurance.

Spotting a gap of inattentiveness from Shreyas as he adjusted the position of the fabric, Karthi whispered to Kalki, 'We can't tell him the truth. Remember what happened when we told the truth to the man on the train. If we tell him what really happened, he might send us back home to our village. We need to go to the city to get out money back.'

'You don't have to be scared me,' Shreyas said. Obviously, his hearing was very good. 'You can tell me anything.'

'No, no. I was telling her about....'

'This house is a safe place. No one will hurt you or bother you,' Shreyas said. 'You can say anything here. Outside these walls, your secrets will hurt you. In here, those same secrets will comfort you if you spill them.'

'That's what really happened. We just missed our train.'

'Then why is the card so important?' Shreyas flashed the green business card at them.

'It is where our house is. Next to this address. It is a big company. My mother gave it to us, in case we got lost,' Kalki said, thinking fast.

'Well, then better keep this card safe,' Shreyas said, handing the card to Karthi. 'Your outfit is ready, dear boy.'

Karthi slipped into his shorts which were once full-length pants. It could only pass for shorts if he moved. When he stood still, it looked like a bulbous loose skirt. The shirt, which had blue checks on them, fit him perfectly. His face looked small behind the pointy adult size collars.

'It's your turn next, dear girl,' Shreyas said, taking another bag from underneath the bed. 'I will make something special for you.' Shreyas unfurled metres of shiny saree fabric. It was as though a mysterious cave was opened, and out of it, vibrant and colourful streams of fabric poured out, running in every direction, spreading brightness to every corner of the world. A purple saree had bronze leaves snaking all over it. A teal saree had light gold flowers. A bright yellow saree was covered with red stripes. A black saree was engraved with gold. Orange and pink. Pink and green. Mosaic patterned. Curlicue shapes. Shimmering with sequins. Radiant silk. Floral prints. They smelled of lost time and irrevocable misery.

'Kalki, which one do you like?' Shreyas asked, eyes shining with imagination. 'I will make a blouse and skirt for you.' Picking up a saree, Shreyas rubbed it on his face, and slipped into a fantasy where he could be free. Kalki saw that those sarees meant something to him.

'But they are all beautiful,' Kalki said.

'It will look more beautiful on you,' Shreyas said.

'But don't they belong to your wife or your mother? Won't they be angry?' asked Kalki.

'Can I tell you something?' Shreyas said.

'You are the one who said one could say anything inside these walls,' Karthi said.

'Yes, I did.' Shreyas laughed. 'Some secrets still hurt, even in a safe space. The dangerous ones that bloom in solitary disposition make one doubt and hurt oneself, and hate oneself. Love oneself a little less every day, leading to a perpetual war within. It has no peace treaty for either the aggressor or the defender. They are like two sides of the same coin, bound to each other but never to see, meet and reconcile. The sarees belong to me.'

'But you are not a woman,' Kalki said.

'I am, on the inside,' Shreyas said.

'Then am I a boy on the inside?' Kalki asked curiously. 'And my brother is a girl on the inside?'

'You would know it if you have someone else living inside you,' Shreyas said.

'Do you wish you were born a girl?' Karthi asked.

'No, I like being a boy, but I enjoy wearing girl's clothes,' Shreyas replied.

'Why? Didn't your parents buy you boy's clothes?' Kalki asked.

'They did, but I wore my sister's clothes most of the time,' Shreyas said.

Kalki giggled, which made Karthi giggle.

'Anyway, which one is your favourite colour?' Shreyas draped a saree and swayed his shoulders.

'I don't think I can allow you to destroy them,' Kalki said. 'Why don't you make me a set like my brother's?'

Shreyas made another pair of shorts and a shirt for Kalki. As the children stood together, they looked like skinny puppets covered in excess clothing to cover their spindly wooden frame. Like children of stingy parents who buy oversized sized clothes so they can grow into them.

'Just too cute,' Shreyas said. He caressed their faces

with his hands and cracked his knuckles on his head in appreciation and blessing.

'What about you?' Kalki asked.

'I bought a saree yesterday, but someone tore it,' Shreyas said, sucking in his breath in regret. Karthi and Kalki did the same. 'Maybe the two of you can help me fix it.'

A perfectly measured rip ran through the middle of the red saree with gold embroidery. Shreyas remembered the shopkeeper spreading the saree on the table in the shop. It rested on layers of rejected choices. Shreyas jumped at the sight of the saree and clapped. He usually tried to hide his excitement, but it had slipped out like a secret fish escaping the net. But the shopkeeper caught the secret fish with a shudder and jerked the saree away from the table. He said he couldn't sell feminine things to broken men. Shreyas protested and said that it wasn't for him to decide. He still refused and said, 'You can buy it if you are buying it for your sister, your wife or your mother or leave.'

Furious, Shreyas inched forward and questioned if he was aware of the implications of a curse inflicted by a transgender. Shreyas had to take back the secret fish from him. He performed the spread-finger clap not because he wanted to do it but because the shopkeeper expected it. The customers around looked up at the sound. Shreyas was about to press his palm on the shopkeeper's forehead to impart the curse when he changed his mind and said he would pack the saree for him. It was only when Shreyas reached home that he found out that the shopkeeper had torn the saree before packing it up.

Karthi and Kalki took one piece each and held it straight while Shreyas slowly stitched it on the sewing machine. Shreyas guided the two pieces to make it whole. If only it were that easy to fuse the two fractured, dissimilar and conflicting halves within him and make himself whole again. But just like the saree, a fusion of broken pieces makes it complete only for so long. The seams, cracks, and fissures eventually become undone over time.

'Look at the wall while I get ready,' Shreyas said.

One boy and one girl in boy's clothes studied the uneven blue wall while Shreyas changed. There was a large wave suspended in motion, just a few feet from hitting a cliffside. A butterfly with broken wings floated up. A fat man with thin legs walked on clouds. A lonely dog sat, waiting for someone. At the bottom a half-horse, half-man being or a man sitting on a horse sent boat balloons up to the sky. The fantasy pictures were enhanced by a series of jingles and jangles coming from behind them.

'You can turn around now,' Shreyas said.

They saw someone who looked like Shreyas, but it wasn't him, not entirely. Like a disgruntled homeowner clearing out any sign of the previous tenant, like a high tide cleaning up the beach, Shreyas was evicted and cleared out. In his place was a woman who shimmered in a resplendent red sari with a gold border and dots. Her face was dusted with white talcum powder, like it could drown the luminosity of a thousand flaming candles. Her thick plaited hair hung on both sides of her face, like a black waterfall. The colourful ribbons weaved in and out like slippery vivid fishes. Gold necklaces adorned her neck as though they belonged there, accentuated by the Adam's apple. A pointy cliff with treasures below. Earrings swung around like rambunctious church bells.

'You asked whom the sarees belonged to. They belong to Shreya. Not Shreyas.' Shreya pressed a button on a small radio. The strains of a song floated out. She began to dance. She caught the beat of the music with her toes, spinning around gracefully, her hands twirling above her head, the saree fanning out like a red hibiscus with the gold dots shining like spots of sunlight. Her feet tapped in tune and her shoulders wiggled in perfect harmony with the song.

The children realised why Shreyas/Shreya had to live in the forest inside a broken building, away from everyone. Because Shreyas couldn't be himself by becoming Shreya whenever he wanted. The ravenous society would have stripped Shreyas of every bit of Shreya rendering him bareboned like a carcass.

Just like the house she inhabited, Shreya was someone else on the outside and someone else on the inside. You expect something, but you are pleasantly surprised, a feeling only reserved for those who have not been sickened by the epidemic of tenets. Tenets that dictate who deserved to live among others and consign the underserving to living death till they can't live anymore.

'Super,' both Karthi and Kalki cheered Shreya. Jumping, whistling and clapping, they joined in and danced with her. Unseen, unheard, tucked in the bosom of nature, they danced in the dark. Unrestrained, Kalki leapt out of her skin, and Karthi's head felt light, rid of worms of guilt.

'Tomorrow, we will go to the bus station, and you can catch the correct bus to Chennai,' Shreyas said as he tucked them into the bed. He still wore his sari, but he had removed his wig. 'I wish I could come with you, but I am going to a festival.'

'What festival is it?' Kalki asked.

'Can we come?' Karthi said.

'No. It is not a place for children. You two need to go home first. Your mother is waiting for you,' Shreyas said, switching on the table-fan next to them.

'Sleep well,' he whispered. The agile blades of the fan whipped up cool air that floated over them.

'Maybe I will sing you a song,' Shreyas said as he noticed the fan's whining rotation was stealing their sleep. He cleared his throat to suppress his manly voice. In a mellifluous female voice, Shreya sang a lullaby. As Shreya sang, Shreyas' manly voice interfered but was quickly turned away.

Aararo Aareraro
Uprooted flowers floating in the wind
Don't you fret. It is just a soft breeze
Carrying you to a place where one is kind
Oh Lord, watch over them, won't you please
Aararo Aareraro
You are almost there a little while more,

My tender flowers, and my little fawns.
You will be brave, strong and be adored
Grow in the world with promising dawns

Aararo Aareraro

No predatory nightmares disturbed their sleep. They slept like moonlight on calm ocean waters.

First, it was a smattering of sobs, then a series of uncontrolled laughter and then a deep howling and crying. Kalki woke up and saw Shreyas writhing on his bedspread. His silhouette was in the shape of a foetus. Refusing to be born into the world.

She extended her hand and wanted to comfort him, but she chose just to let him be. She watched him like one would watch an animal hit by a car. Unable to help. With utmost pity and wishing it would stop breathing soon so the suffering could end. The same thought she usually had for herself when she realised that the dark skin was here to stay. She wished she could cry all the darkness out of her skin through tears as Shreyas did with his internal pain.

Soon, the hysterical laughing and crying ended, and Shreyas lay still under the blanket. He slept peacefully. It seemed like an exorcism of oneself, like emptying one's bladder before bed.

Two tortured souls with irreconcilable polarities slept, preparing for another day.

There was no sign of tiredness on Shreyas' face despite last night's restless sleep. His eyes were bright and he looked rested. It was as though it was his nightly routine, to cry himself to sleep.

The three of them reached the bus station. Kalki wore a cap to tuck her hair in. She looked like a boy in her new clothes. A black sheep in boy's clothing with an imposter man and a boy years away from growing into his voluminous shorts.

It was seven in the morning. The bus station looked like it never slept. Never had a good night's rest. The walls that encircled the station looked at them with dried crusty yellow tears. Men stood in front of the wall, furiously urinating before rushing to catch their bus. The wind carried the smell to all corners of the bus station. A cleaner in an untidy oversized blue overcoat with orange trim and old slippers waited patiently for someone to use the public toilet so that he could use his new broom.

Dull government buses entered and left in quick succession. Private buses were given superfluous hyperbolic names and had exquisite designs. Flaming Flower didn't have one flower on its chassis. Spaced Blaster mirrored the driver's erratic turns and mad honking. Viper Boys was far from being vicious and had a resplendent peacock painted on its side. Like a peacock, it wooed its passengers with in-house entertainment, TV and hi-fi stereo, and cushioned seating rather than plastic seats.

The bus conductor hung out of the door and yodelled the destination of Viper Boys. 'Chennai! Chennai! Chennai!'

'When is it going to depart?' Shreyas asked.

'Soon,' the conductor answered flatly, beginning his yodelling again.

'Soon when?'

'It is early morning, and you are eating my head already.'

'So, look at me and answer properly,' Shreyas said sternly.

'7.30,' he snapped, giving Shreyas a dirty look. 'Now get lost.'

'That gives us half an hour, children,' Shreyas said, looking at his thin gold watch. 'Maybe we should eat something.'

Passengers stood in groups around the teashops sipping tea and filter coffee. Some slept soundly on the floor using their footwear as pillows. Soggy, oily dosas and steamy hard idlis were being served to hungry customers on foil paper plates.

Karthi and Kalki finished their meal and sipped the cold drinks. They started to blow bubbles. Kalki's bottle fizzed up and bubbled out. Someone belched. The aftertaste of digested rice and chutney hung in the air.

Kalki noticed that no one took notice of her dark skin. She looked around to see if anyone was staring at her. Everyone appeared busy with their own business, fervently looking at their watches and wiping their foreheads with their handkerchiefs. A man walked up and down in equal paces, like a soldier practising his march, his eyes fixed on the ground. A few men ogled at Shreyas, air-kissing and whistling, teasing him. Was it because of him that nobody paid any heed to Kalki's dark complexion? Shreyas was the black hole in her dark universe. He sucked all the attention away from her. His circus show was far more entertaining and scandalous than Kalki's could ever be. Greedy eyes devoured Shreyas as he showcased his eccentricities with his gender morphing ability to turn into a woman as he pleased. The crowd laughed, mocked, spat, and hurled insults. Shreyas kept performing despite all the blows. They used his pain, siphoned it, and clothed themselves in a fabric of smuggled happiness.

Just then, Kalki saw a man looking at her, while sipping his tea. He blew on the tea, took a sip, and eyed her up and down. Maybe he saw through her disguise. She thought it strange that she actually wished he would comment on her dark skin. After years of insults, a day without one felt as strange as waterless oceans and sandless deserts.

'Do my eyes betray me or are you the reincarnation of Lord Krishna?' he said, prostrating himself in front of her. Confused, all three of them shuffled backwards.

'Please bless me, oh Lord!' The man continued to crawl towards them on his knees. 'My wife and I have been trying to have kids for so long, but there is no luck. Maybe this was destined to happen. For me to come here and meet Lord Krishna in your form.'

Kalki realised that as long as you are a boy, dark skin didn't matter. The remedy for her dark skin was for her to turn into a boy. Maybe Shreyas had the right idea, to wander between two genders, where one gender's imperfections were exalted in the other.

Shreyas whispered something in Kalki's ear. She went towards the man, and he began to prostrate himself again. Kalki hovered her hand over him, touched the back of his head, and blessed him by mumbling something. The man began to sob. The three of them giggled as they made their way to the bus. Karthi felt almost lightheaded. He could actually look forward to a bright and lightheaded future, free of guilt. It felt good.

The bus smelled of fake leather. Music played from a TV locked behind a glass cabinet. The passengers pushed through the narrow aisle to their seats. Some passengers slipped a piece of their belongings through windows to reserve their seats – newspapers, shoes or handkerchiefs. Shreyas didn't even have to try. His presence made the passengers cringe, and they moved out of the way so that they didn't have to touch Shreyas.

'Do you have the business card?' Shreyas asked, seating them near the window. 'Will you get home safely?'

Karthi flashed the card. Kalki nodded her head.

'Oye, conductor!' Shreyas called out to the conductor who was at the other end of the bus. 'Look after the kids, will you?'

Shreyas' eyes began to well up as he looked at the children. Their unsure eyes, their trembling lips, their colourless faces. He knew this expression. It was the same look that his mother and sister would have seen as his father threw him out of the house.

Chapter 11

Shreyas stayed inside his mother for another 15 days, way past the due date. The doctors tried every conceivable method. They fed her pills till she was constipated. She was injected with relaxants every day past the due date. She walked the length of the hospital corridor till her knees grew weaker. But he didn't budge. When science didn't work, they turned to the spiritual. His parents hired a sadhu, a holy man. He mumbled incantations with eyes rolled up so far till only the whites of the eye could be seen. He burnt incense inside the ward to smoke him out of the womb. Even that didn't work.

His parents gave up and decided to wait it out. His sister would sing him songs and tell him stories every night, urging him to come out so that they could play together. She was looking forward to having a brother, a boy so her father could stop worrying about who would carry their family name forward. An invisible, ancient burden placed on the shoulders of men and women who start a family that they carried like a ticking time bomb until a male child was born to diffuse it.

Despite the annoyance of the wait, his father consoled himself that it would be worth the wait because it would be a boy. Sometimes he'd worry about the protracted gestation period. A terror would pass through him thinking about the prospect of a stillborn baby. Whenever that happened, he put his hand over his wife's distended belly to feel his son moving. Sometimes it was a soft kick. Most of the time, it was just a gurgle. The faint sound would calm his heart.

'Maybe it is a good thing that he is still in there,' a relative speculated. 'With all the time he is spending inside the womb, he is going to be the manliest man.' The father's eyes sparkled as it was an indirect compliment to his manhood and the quality of his sperms. The father interpreted this as a sign of radical redemption as a girl was his firstborn.

'Let him come out when he is ready. The world can wait. For a boy, it can,' another said.

Fifteen days later, he was born. He slid out like he had had enough of staying inside and didn't cause any pain to his mother, which was surprising. She was expecting an excruciating labour. Even the raucous crying didn't persuade the curious father to look at his baby's face. He was busy checking the baby's genitals. Once he saw a penis, the delirious father's chest expanded, making him look more prominent.

They named him Shreyas. An niggling doubt subverted their happiness even though their son appeared healthy. That he might have some issues because of the extra time he had spent in the womb. His parents pored over him to look for any signs of deformities or waywardness. In his toothless yawn. In his bundled toes. The bulge of his belly. The way his hair stubbornly swept to one side. The bent in his hand when he slept flat. The inordinate length of time he could go without crying.

'When you were a baby, you were the exact opposite,' the father said to his daughter, Rukmani. 'All you did was cry and give us sleepless nights. Look at my son, my boy. It is true what they say. Only a male child will carry our name forward.'

Rukmani was too ecstatic about the new addition to the family to notice the generous amount of insidiousness that saturated her father's words. As days passed, her father's words got harsher and more potent. Her mother consoled her by saying that he was still excited about the birth of a boy, and that one day he will be over it. Rukmani ignored her father's demeaning words and regaled her brother with stories and songs.

As her mother predicted, the father stopped ridiculing Rukmani altogether, but it was replaced by negligence. He would go out of his way to prove his intent. Once Rukmani fell while playing with Shreyas and bruised her knees. Her legs were all bloody. She cried from the searing pain. Her father rushed towards her only to walk past her and pick up Shreyas. He scanned every inch of his body for any bruise and made sure he was safe. Then he turned towards his sobbing daughter. She looked at him through watery eyes, seeking comfort. But all she got was a scolding.

'Thank god you fell instead of my baby boy,' he said, finishing his tirade. 'Just imagine what would have happened to my boy. Next time, be careful while playing with him. If anything were to happen to him because of you, I don't know what I will do.' He left her mother to tend to her wounds.

Since that day, her love for her brother morphed into something else. It was a cautionary love. A love where she had to be on guard constantly. A love where she began to hate herself, a little bit every day, to love him.

As Shreyas grew and attained puberty, he started to develop some quirks. A swing in his step. A sway in his hips. He would gesticulate with his hands as he talked using them like exclamatory rhetorical devices. He would sweep his hair to the side. Most of the time, it was just phantom hair as his hair was well set with coconut oil.

'It is just how boys are,' his father said, brushing off any concerns. 'He is still growing. These things he does will fall off like old leaves. Before you know it, he will become a strong man. You wait and watch.'

But Rukmani knew that these oddities would not disappear over time. They were here to stay, attached to her brother like the earth's orbit around the sun. She knew this because she caught Shreyas in her room doing womanly things. Her father did not know this because he didn't like to go inside an adolescent girl's room. She saw her brother through a gap in the door. Using her talcum powder. Using her eyeliner. Dabbing his lips with her lipstick. Swaying an imaginary braid of hair from side to side while lip-syncing to a song. He wore her bangles and donned her chains. She never disturbed him. She watched her brother with the same wonder an entomologist had when watching an unidentified caterpillar morph. Through the gap in the door, she observed the unbecoming of her brother. He shed himself bit by bit till he wasn't the brother she knew outside the room.

Soon, it was hard for his father to ignore Shreyas' feminine traits. When he couldn't justify his son's flamboyance as the follies of puberty, he turned to the mother. He blamed her for deliberately holding his boy inside her womb beyond the due date. As if the nine months didn't count, only the extra 15 days. As though something unusual accounted for Shreyas being this way.

'I am sure you made him this way. He is broken because of your cursed womb. You wanted to shame me, so you kept him inside you,' he chided his wife as though Shreyas was an overcooked meal left too long on the fire. Burnt. Flavourless. Not good enough to be even rat food.

He would beat his wife, and once she became a blubbering mess on the floor, he would turn towards his daughter. He faulted her for spending too much time with her brother.

'All the stories you used to tell and the songs you sang when he was inside your mother, I think that's what made him this way. Like you. An abomination. What else can one expect if a lake is fed with sewage?' her father said. In his world, it made sense to blame it on the females in the family. After all, they were the ones who spent the most time with Shreyas.

So, the father took matters into his own hands. He decided to undo his son's morphing. He didn't want to be stern at first because he didn't want his only son to despise him as who else would look after him in his ripe old age? The son, of course. But he needed to extract the male out of his son. He would casually remark to him about how he walked and show him how to walk with longer strides, with his chest thrust forward and head held up high. He encouraged Shreyas to play cricket to widen his contained hand gestures. He even sent him to an all-boys private school to minimise contact with girls. Under the pretence of teaching him singing, he engaged a vocal coach to make Shreyas sound less shrill. He ordered his wife to serve him meat to make him taller and bigger.

As days passed, the father couldn't notice any change in his son's behaviour. His voice was still shrill. His gait was quick and short. His gestures were even more dramatic. So, he resorted to harsher methods despite pleas from the mother to not subject her son to cruelty. He would cane Shreyas when he didn't walk straight. He forced him to do laps around the school sports ground till he was satisfied. A flick from his father's fingers would land on his lips if his voice didn't sound low-pitched. He made Shreyas eat till he vomited and then force-fed him again.

It was becoming increasingly evident that Shreyas was not going to become the son his father had envisioned. He gave up his crusade with his son's biology and resigned himself though he felt deeply dishonoured and ashamed. He retreated from the embattled field of Shreyas' body. The field healed.

The family learnt to live with Shreyas and the affliction he was to them. They tried to keep it a secret first, then a distant memory and finally a rumour that could be discredited. They restricted Shreyas from spending too much time outside. They had hoped that as time passed, people would forget or get used to the fact that a transgender lived with them. Before dawn's first light, the mother would dash to the bazaar to buy groceries to avoid awkward conversations with neighbours and relatives about her son. The father took shortcuts and long routes, depending on the destination and distribution of the crowd, to get where he needed to be. Rukmani didn't care that much about what others said. Because she became the normal one despite being the girl in the family. People were glad that she was born generally without any flaws to give the family a semblance of normality. Apart from being a girl, they would add, just so that she didn't get a bloated ego. She took what they gave and fished out the compliments.

Years passed. The family walked in shadows and kept to themselves. It was time to search for a groom for Rukmani. They searched in other towns and cities where the family's dirty little secret was not known. Doctors, engineers and lawyers came to see Rukmani. Shreyas was sent out of the house and asked not to return till the evening. As they talked, the father spoke of the dowry he was ready to give: a brand-new car, appliances for the home, and a sum of Rs 5 lakh. The prospective groom's family left with broad smiles and boisterous wobbling of the head, reassuring Rukmani's parents that the alliance was as welcome as it could be. But once they left, that was the last Rukmani saw of them. Somewhere on the way, a local would congratulate the prospective grooms and praise their bravery in marrying into a family that gave birth to broken male offspring. 'Who is to say that the girl is not all girl either?' they would say with a shrug of their shoulders, casting a spell of doubt in the minds of the grooms. Even the generous dowry offered couldn't stop them from running away. The money was tempting, but the threat of a life of shame scared them.

Rukmani was secretly happy that none of the grooms said yes to her. She was glad that her brother was the way he was, scaring away prospective grooms because she was in love with someone else, a man who wasn't her equal in caste. For this reason, Rukmani didn't divulge her romance to anyone but her mother. Her mother carried two burdens. The burden of her half-son that ate her from the inside and that of her daughter that consumed her from the outside. The former was impossible to change, but the latter could be processed to work in their favour for living with a daughter who no one wants to marry was a fate worse than anything.

So, they both did what they had to do. Rukmani devised the plan. Her mother was the catalyst. The mother asked Shreyas to take the dowry money and deposit it in a bank as fixed deposit to earn interest instead of being wrapped in an old saree. On his way to the bank, Rukmani's lover would confront Shreyas and steal the money and keep it safe with him. Because Shreyas didn't know what sister's lover looked like, he would believe he was getting robbed. Rukmani couldn't predict how her father would react, but she thought that the act of Shreyas losing her dowry money would send him over the edge. She hoped that this would make her father disown Shreyas and throw him out, making Rukmani the only child left in the house. Then, she would reveal about her lover to her father and convince him that he didn't want any dowry to marry her. Her father would reluctantly agree to salvage any honour his family still had.

As Shreyas carried the bag of cash to the bank, he was distracted by a large crowd watching a man as he spoke with grand gestures. After inquiring, he learnt that the man was part of an investment company that gave better interest rates than local banks. Shreyas asked for directions to their office and marched to it instead of the bank to take advantage of the investment scheme.

As he made his way to the office, Shreyas felt someone following him. He didn't turn around to check as that would be an acknowledgement of his fear. He picked up his pace and clutching the bag of money tightly. He tried to remain on the busy road, but the pursuer steered him into a quiet alley by pelting him with stones. He turned around to see a man with a wheat-coloured birthmark on his dark brown cheek, shaped like a plump kidney. It enlarged as he gave a derisive laugh. Shreyas bolted towards the end of the street and started to climb a low wall, only to be viciously dragged down. His shin and elbows were streaked with blood. Shreyas tried to block the punches with his arms, but in vain. Blows rained on his face. He was kicked in his body and legs. The man peppered his blows with insults about him being a transgender. He finished with one final kick in his groin, sending a searing flash of pain through his body. Shreyas let out a howling gasp. The man giggled. The mark on his cheek jiggled in joy. Shreyas saw the man leave with his sister's dowry money as he lay in a foetal position to allay the pain that seared through his body.

A bruised Shreyas with bloody lips and blue-black cheeks limped home. The pain in his body fizzled only to be replaced by the crushing pain of losing his sister's dowry money. Like a heavy anchor, it dropped and latched itself in the deepest abyss of the ocean, inhibiting Shreyas from moving and suffering the wrath of the treacherous sea. Not only had he brought eternal shame to his family, but he had also destroyed any chance of his sister being married. Now his sister would also be subject to the same humiliation he faced.

He reached home and vomited blood. His mother ran towards him and gathered him in her arms. His father watched from a distance and looked as though his son deserved the beating.

'Someone stole all the money from me.' Shreyas burst into a peal of mad laughter as though he was possessed. He laughed because he had no tears left in him.

'Not only have you shamed me with your presence, but you have also spoiled your sister's life,' his father said, trembling with rage. 'I have overlooked everything because you were born a boy, but I can't anymore, Ombothu.' It was the word for nine in Tamil used for transgenders. Just like number nine, which could be six when turned upside down. He had heard the insults from the public but hearing his father say it was so toxic that it turned his insides to water and he felt he was drowning from within.

Rukmani's cheek glistened with tears, but a playful smile played at the corner of her lips as she watched her plan unfold in front of her. All that was left was for her father to kick Shreyas out of the house. Then she could introduce her lover to her father.

'Get out of my house,' his father said as he caught Shreyas by the collar of his shirt and threw him out on the street. He landed on the rough ground, rolling before coming to a halt. A small crowd gathered around Shreyas, suffocating him. They joined in humiliating him by spitting at him and kicking dust in his face. They were like jackals, baying at a dying animal.

He ran to the front door begging to be let back in. His father bolted the door against him. He caught a glimpse of his mother and sister. 'If you open the door, I will kill you both,' his father threatened them.

Shreyas sat outside all night, pounding on the door, and begging his mother to let him in. 'Let me in, mother. Let me in. I have nowhere to go.' He could hear his mother muffling her cries into her saree.

'Please go, my son. Please. I will be forgiven eventually for giving birth to a girl by your father, but there is no forgiveness in this world for giving birth to you.' Her sobs became louder, and Shreyas could hear her hitting herself on the head.

'Leave now. Leave and never come back, son. Your sister needs to get married. No man will marry her if they know about you. Please do this for your mother and your sister. Leave!' She let out a scream that curdled his insides.

Shreyas stayed outside his house till nightfall. The crowds dispersed. He couldn't hear his mother behind the door anymore. All he could hear was the endless echo of vast emptiness interrupted by his heartbeat.

He took the first bus out of the city. He didn't know where it was headed. He just wanted to go as far away as possible to live a new life. Eight hours later, he was dropped off in a new town. He had hoped that distance from his hometown would make things easier and no one would pay attention to his feminine traits, but that was a pipedream. Jaded, he embraced his dual gender and stole a saree from a clothesline. He dressed as a woman.

People heard Shreyas before they saw Shreyas. His raspy voice floated like a rogue gust of wind. He would snap his fingers and do the popping spread-finger slap, entering stores to demand money. Most of the time, the shop-owners gave him money to ward off Shreyas' curses. Some didn't. He would hurl profanities and perform obscene gestures till they paid. With cash in hand, he would bless the store and its owner. Slowly but steadily, he set up his life, a bit away from the town, near a train track, inside an abandoned house because he knew no one would rent him a place to live.

One day he learnt from a stranger that there was a festival in a town not far away that is dedicated to transgender people, where they are deified. The stranger mentioned a *Jamaat* system where members of the transgender community could live together with a semblance of family life. He lived in the derelict house with a new purpose, begging during the day and stitching dresses at night to attend the transgender festival.

Karthi, Kalki and Shreyas were seated at the back of the packed bus. Their eyes were glued to the TV behind the glass cabinet playing a classic *Talaivar* movie. Rows of heads bobbed as the bus sped past paddy fields. In his crispy khaki uniform, the bus conductor glided like a flying squirrel from one row to another balancing his back against the metal poles.

'One adult and two children,' Shreyas said, giving him the money.

'Are they your kids?' he asked with a raised eyebrow as he stuffed the cash between his fingers which were burgeoning with notes.

'My sister's,' Shreyas said, snatching the tickets from him.

The bus conductor lingered for a while, studying the trio, perhaps checking the similarities between the kids and their uncle. Shreyas straightened himself, unbending his back, pushing his chest forward and spreading his legs.

As the eyes of the bus conductor fell on the children, Karthi called out, 'Uncle, I am starving.' He nudged Kalki. 'Yes, me too, Uncle,' Kalki said.

'Don't worry, children. The bus will stop somewhere soon,' Shreyas said, stroking their heads. Satisfied, the bus conductor walked away. Shreyas loosened his stiff body.

The bus journey was uneventful. Some passengers were glued to the movie. Most of them were sleeping. Kalki spotted a man looking at her, at them. He quickly pretended to yawn and go back to sleep. Throughout the journey, he tossed and turned his body deliberately so that he could open his eyes for a moment and catch a glimpse of Kalki. She shrank into a corner of the seat so that she was out of sight for him, but he wasn't from her. But he kept looking. Then she realised the man wasn't looking at her and her dark skin but at Shreyas. His lips curled, and his nose wrinkled as though he was going to vomit. Kalki wanted to tell him to look away, but she was scared that she might divert his attention towards her dark skin, making him shrivel up in disgust.

'Food stop,' the bus conductor called out as he clanged his keys against the metal railings to wake sleepy passengers. 'Do your business and be back in half an hour.' The driver honked the horn loudly for good measure.

The bus pulled into a rest stop with a roadside restaurant called Highway Hotel. As the engine sputtered to a halt, ambient noise took its place. The wind carried the songs from a lone radio and dispersed it into the air outside. A sweaty chef manned a rectangular hot plate. His once white vest was now brown. He produced loud successive chinks that sounded like gunshots as he diced the *parottas* into a million pieces using two metal spatulas. Sweat dripped from his forehead, salted the food, and sizzled.

The passengers trickled out of the bus, stretching and yawning. Men scrambled to the nearest wall to relieve themselves. The staring man from the bus continued to stare at them. As they made their way into the restaurant, Kalki saw him calling out to a few men and telling them something, which made them gasp loudly.

They stepped into the dining hall. It stank of oil and fried food. And satisfied burps. The low-hanging ceiling fans drowned any small talk. When they stepped inside the hall, the noises stopped for a moment because Shreyas didn't walk like a man. To avert their gaze, he pretended to fall, stood up and walked with big strides. The noises resumed.

Waiters went around dispensing sambar and chutney, refilling empty plates. They brought lunch for the trio on steel trays sectioned out for perfect portion sizes, like a paw print. The waiter loaded the children's tray with a spoonful of dal and said to Kalki, 'A growing boy needs more of this. Eat.'

What the waiter said shook her into the realisation that she was still dressed as a boy. She thought of abandoning her dream of becoming fairer because dressing as a boy was much more accessible. It was a matter of cutting the hair short and wearing shorts. It was as though every flaw was acceptable as long as you were a boy. She was thrilled to have finally found a permanent solution to her skin problem. If Shreyas could become a woman, why couldn't she become a man? What would happen when she grew up? She wouldn't be able to be a boy forever. She swirled the chutney on her plate, lost in thought.

'Don't you like it?' Shreyas asked, breaking the parotta into tiny pieces for Kalki.

Kalki swirled a bit slower.

'Eat soon. The driver is almost done with his meal,' Shreyas pointed to the bus driver, who cleaned his plates with furious palm swipes and licked his hands dry.

The Staring Man walked past them and signalled Kalki and Karthi to look up and mouthed, 'Are you ok?' They couldn't understand him, so they ignored him, which fuelled his suspicion even more. He showed his palms to them as if to say, don't worry.

As they were about to finish their meal, three bodies loomed over them.

'Bloody rascal. Isn't it enough that you are corrupted? Now you are kidnapping children to corrupt their minds too? Dirty rat.' Before they could turn around to see who spoke, a swift blow hit Shreyas at the back of his neck, making him splutter. He gasped for air, stroking his neck. His eyes rolled back, and he fell onto his plate, unconscious. Two pairs of hands grabbed Karthi and Kalki from behind and they were whisked away outside.

They didn't know who had lifted them from their chairs. Their eyes were fixed on Shreyas' limp body. They screamed for him. The waiters stopped in their tracks. The diners paused in their eating. The cook stopped dicing the parottas to watch. A fat police inspector whose pants were pulled up high on his body gestured to someone to pick Shreyas up. He looked as though he had stolen someone's uniform and was only pretending to be a police officer.

Two obedient constables picked Shreyas up. Shreyas hung between the policeman like a slaughtered animal and was thrown into the boot of the van. The children were loaded onto the back seat of a police jeep. The jeep drifted and stirred a mini dust storm which drizzled onto the parottas, dosas and rotis. The clangour of the cook's metal spatulas indicated that the show was over.

Chapter 12

The only time they had seen a police station was in the movies. In one of Talaivar's movies where he was a righteous police officer who rounded up all the robbers, miscreants, wife-beaters, hooch-makers, eve-teasers, tricky rabble-rousers, and threw them in jail. Talaivar's police station was busy. Constables, with stiff hats moved from table to table as though their shoes had wings. Paperwork, reports and ledgers were filled with due diligence. Talaivar, as the police officer, sat dreaming of a crime-free India where every citizen lived peacefully with one another.

The police station Karthi and Kalki were taken to was nothing like that. Hatless constables snoozed with their legs up on the tables. Reports and files were strewn across tables like yesterday's newspaper. A shelf was about to implode as it was full with paper. Portraits of Mahatma Gandhi and Jawaharlal Nehru hung on the wall, however. It was hot and stuffy.

They sat on a wooden bench, huddled together for comfort. Their mouths were parched. The gaping exit to their left tempted them to run away and escape. They inched towards the doorway slowly. Then a police officer would look at them, sending them closer to the wall. They looked like two baby monkeys lost in a scary alien forest.

Inspector Mani, his pants pulled up almost to his chest, walked towards them with two steel tumblers. He wobbled as he walked. Squinting through his spectacles in an effort to see more clearly, he blew on the milk to cool it. White foam floated up and landed on his moustache, which ran down either side of his mouth like rat's tails. His dark purple tongue darted out and licked the white bubbles off his moustache.

'Have some milk, kids,' he said, handing them the steel glasses. A blast of his metallic rancid breath hit them. 'Take it,' he said again. They shook their heads in refusal. 'You need your strength. Drink. Then you can tell me what happened. I will make sure that thing,' he looked back at the cells from where a soft moan could be heard. 'That thing gets what he deserves.'

The presence of a police officer just inches away from them filled the children with dread and their bodies shook. With shaky hands, they took the glasses and sipped.

'Don't be scared. I am not going to hurt you. I am your friend. Look at you two boys. All skin and bones. That wretched thing must have starved you,' the officer said, reaching out to caress them. He missed their heads twice before finally getting a grip. As he stroked Kalki's head, her cap fell off, and her hair came undone.

'What the ...?' he fell back in surprise, his stumpy legs sticking up in the air. 'I am starting to see things. Those bloody hooch-makers are going to get it from this time....'

'Are you ...,' he rubbed his eyes and slapped his face for good measure. He took off his glasses, wiped them and put them back on. 'Are you a girl?' he asked Kalki. She nodded, her head bent.

'Not only is he corrupted, he dares to corrupt children as well. Constable! Give him another round of beating,' he ordered.

A burst of pleas could be heard from one of the cells. It was Shreyas' voice. 'Please. Please, stop. It hurts. I was just trying to help the children. I didn't kidnap them. It hurts.' The inspector ordered that the intensity of the beatings be increased. As though someone turned a dial, Shreyas' screams became louder. They heard the sound of leather belt on naked skin. On kneecaps and the backbone. The soft thud of the wooden baton on the buttocks. The scraping of his knees on the stone floor. A consecutive hollow grunt as he was kicked in the stomach.

'Look what he has done to you, poor girl. Made you all ugly.' The inspector rubbed his hands all over Kalki's face to remove what he thought was black makeup. When he realised that it was the colour of her skin, he stopped and gasped. His hands, either involuntarily or consciously, retracted, like he had touched something infectious. He wiped them on his pants till they tingled with frictional heat.

Kalki didn't budge. She waited for the inspector to ridicule her dark skin or not at all. Because the police are supposed to protect the good people from bad people and she wasn't a criminal. She was a good person, so she assumed he wouldn't mock her. A shrill cry sounded from the jail cell. It was Shreyas calling for his mother. He wasn't a criminal either, but they were beating him. So, Kalki abandoned the idea of police officers being friendly to innocents and awaited insults from the inspector.

He didn't say anything, however. Instead, he laughed. In fact, he rolled with laughter. He got up to look at Kalki's face closely, only to laugh even harder.

Karthi's head started to throb. The worms of guilt returned and they wriggled as the inspector laughed. Like real worms. They had been asleep since they met Shreyas. Their short but profound absence had given Karthi a taste of what freedom from the shackles of guilt felt like. He had thought that would happen only when he had eventually found a way to turn his sister's skin fair for good. He covered his ears with his hands and bent forward, pleading with the worms of guilt to stop moving. The inspector's cackle only made it worse for Karthi.

'I thought that Ombothu smeared you with black paint,' the inspector said, ending his laughing fit. He wiped the tears of laughter from his eyes. 'God knows what witchcraft he was trying on you. Anyway," he shook his head in almost disbelief. 'Tell me what happened. No wait, before that, I will get you proper clothes.' He yelled out to a constable to bring them new clothes. One boy set and one girl set.

A constable with a hunched back brought their clothes in crinkly see-through plastic covers. He made sure the head inspector was watching him as he gave them the clothes. Judging from his deferent posture, he was a junior constable. Only years, experience and bribery would straighten the servile backbone until one day it would bend the other way to support a distended belly.

The children dressed themselves in the new clothes – Kalki in a skirt and blouse and Karthi in a T-shirt and shorts. They sat down across the table from the almost sober inspector. They had to peer through the gaps between the tower of files and reports to see the inspector. They liked it this way. Kalki leaned further into the chair so the inspector couldn't see her. Or her skin. Karthi hid behind a pile of books, so he didn't have to tell the truth of what had happened.

The inspector cleared the table. There was nowhere to hide now. He seemed like a precarious khaki-coloured mountain to the two little lost, weary travellers not knowing where the path may lead. The submissive constable brought a glass of something white and fizzy. The inspector downed it. Smacked his lips and let out a loud burp, making the ends of his moustache flutter.

Before he could ask a question, Karthi and Kalki started to cry. First was Kalki followed soon by Karthi. Their eyes just overflowed. The Inspector didn't know what to do. He begged them to calm down. He even drew their attention to their new clothes and said tears would spoil them. The servile constable rushed to the inspector's aid and fished out two Dairy Milk chocolates meant for his daughter and gave them to Karthi and Kalki. His eyes locked with the inspector's. The inspector looked mildly impressed. This opened a path for the junior constable to buy Dairy Milk chocolate for his daughter every day in the future.

Their crying stopped as they munched on the chocolates. 'I am like your father. You can trust me. I am not going to hurt you,' The inspector said. It was his way of classical conditioning. The same way he got his criminals and some unlucky innocents to confess to crimes with a promise of letting them go.

'Are you ready to speak?' the inspector asked them, slouching in his chair and peering at them through the glasses that had slipped to the tip of his nose.

Karthi and Kalki looked at each other, wondering if they should tell the truth or the same story they had told Shreyas – about them missing the train and losing their mother. The inspector warned them that it was better to tell the truth or he would not be responsible for whatever happened to them. Out of fear and not wanting to end in a jail cell, Karthi told the inspector the real story. As he narrated the story, the inspector's eyes narrowed, followed by a hearty giggle. Then he leaned forward to listen to Karthi's story. Fingers touched his parted lips with a tsk!tsk!tsk!tsk! Then his face reddened as Kathi mentioned Shreyas and how he was helping them get back their money.

'Don't be scared of that wastrel. If he touched you improperly or is asking you to lie for him, just tell me. I will take care of it.'

'It's the truth, sir,' Kalki added.

'Oh, the dark one can speak,' the inspector said in a sarcastic voice.

'What will happen to Shreyas? Karthi asked, in an attempt to distract the inspector.

'Are you the police here, or am I?' the inspector asked rhetorically, glaring at Karthi as he straightened his glasses. 'He will get what he deserves.'

Meanwhile, in Shreyas' cell, the crushing silence was briefly interrupted by the prison metal door swinging open. Its metallic groan ended as it crashed into the wall. The inspector stepped into the dark cell, feeling around for the light switch. He pulled a cord. The bulb lit up spilling its bouncy orange light into the cell. In the corner, Shreyas lay facing the wall coiled up like an aborted foetus. His clothes were wet with sweat and clung to his body. For a moment, the inspector thought he was dead, but he sighed in relief when he saw his slim hips rise a little bit.

'Get up, you fool,' the inspector shouted.

Shreyas didn't budge.

'Are you demanding more beatings?'

Shreyas stirred and sat up against the wall, snivelling. He rocked between dread and acquiescence. He believed he deserved this and had it coming for mishandling his sister's dowry money. By doing so, he had created a large void in his sister's and his parents' lives. He had hoped that his pain and suffering would fill that hole and clear his karma. So, he accepted whatever the policemen meted out.

'You have lied. The children are telling a different story.' the inspector grabbed a chair and sat down.

'If I were to kidnap them…,' he paused to wipe his nose. 'Why would I take them on a public bus where everyone can see me kidnapping them?'

'So, you have thought about this then?' The inspector spat at Shreyas, but it lacked momentum and it fell a few inches short. Shreyas turned his face away.

Ok, I believe you,' the inspector said. Shreyas couldn't believe his ears. Just as he had accepted that his suffering had some meaning to it and was ready to receive move. Shreyas was about to peel himself from the wall and stand up.

'"But I want you to do something before I let you go,' the inspector said.

The inspector's toilet was filthy. Everything Shreyas touched had a viscous coating. The handles, the flush, the taps. Even after washing his hands, the slimy coating couldn't be got rid of and so he had to wipe his hands on his shirt. The mirror above the basin had mouldy spots. Or that's what he thought. Between that or the poor lighting of the toilet, he wished that that blurred thing in the mirror was not because of his bloodshot eyes trying hard to form a picture.

The sink was blue and mottled. Shreyas removed his shirt and wet it with running water. After squeezing it, he wiped the red grime off his face. He washed his shirt. Red water came out as he rinsed it. He concentrated hard with his eyes closed and listened to his body. To find out which part of himself ailed the most. He dabbed the cold, wet shirt all over his body wherever the pain was more acute. It gave him some temporary relief. He could hear the inspector getting impatient. His boot tapped frantically outside. He quickly dabbed his wet shirt around his body and got dressed.

Shreyas stepped into the room with the impatient inspector who sat on his table swinging his legs. He looked up when Shreyas entered. Shreyas could feel the prickly lecherous gaze on him. The inspector grabbed his glasses because he couldn't believe the transformation. Shreya had entered the room. The sheen from her yellow saree created a glow around her, masking the wounds on her arms. The hair from the wig was loose, curtaining the black eyes melded together by eyeliner. Nobody would have guessed that Shreya was hurting behind her outfit.

'Are you really a man?' the inspector asked.

'Shall I lift my sari and prove it?' Shreya said bitterly. 'Must be bigger than yours,' Shreyas said, suddenly becoming brave.

The inspector heaved himself off the table and ran towards Shreyas. He pressed his face against Shreya's powdered cheek and rubbed his fingers over her red lips. Alcohol stirred around him like a stinking armour. He swept his eyes all over Shreya. Her tense face. Her quivering neck. Her panting chest exaggerated by an uneven distribution of cotton balls. Her tender hips and her restless legs. 'Don't you dare question my masculinity!'

The inspector grabbed Shreya and thrust her against the wall on the other side. Frightened cries escaped from Shreya's mouth.

'There must be another way,' she said. She could feel the bulge of his tummy pushing into her back.

'I can incriminate you in all my pending cases. You would be behind bars for the rest of your life. Imagine all the sex-starved men inside the prison. Imagine what they would do to someone like you. You will be the whore for all. You will die all alone. Loveless. Without someone to even pity you. You will be tossed aside like a used banana leaf when every man has had his way with you. Unless you want that to be your future, you better shut up and let me do what I want to do to you right now.'

With a whimper, she acquiesced. First, he put a hand over Shreya's mouth because it made the situation more rousing. The more she felt uncomfortable, the more he felt comfortable. He spread her legs and slid his baton, and started to lift her sari. It slipped. He clicked his tongue, throwing the baton away and started again. Shreya heard a wooden rumble moving away from her. He pressed her against the wall. Covered her mouth. He pressed his nose against her back and smelt her skin vertically. Used his hand to lift the sari this time and undid his belt. Shreya tried to wriggle like a caught fish. Her heart jumped out of her body.

Maybe this is the final punishment, Shreyas thought, for what he did to his family. The final hurdle of unfiltered pain. All those years of heartache he had caused them will be forgiven once the inspector had destroyed him from within. She relaxed to let the pain in. Suddenly there was a scream. It wasn't her. The weight of the inspector squashing her against the wall disappeared. She was free.

It was already nightfall. Drunk criminals danced their way into the police station with their accompanying officers. An eerie atmosphere blanketed the police station. The sounds of crickets singing could be heard. Karthi and Kalki sat on the wooden bench where they had been asked to wait. The inspector told them that what had happened should not have happened and that they would be sent back to their village on an overnight bus.

The thought of being sent back devastated Karthi. They had been so close to getting their money back. Turning his sister's skin lighter was another thing altogether. Waiting was pointless. Something had to be done. So, he told his sister to wait while he went in search of Shreyas. Kalki waited for two things. Her brother. And time to pass.

The constable who had given them chocolates was pacing round the reception area, looking at the files. Karthi dashed to the holding area when the constable had his back turned. All the cells on either side were unlit and empty. Only the occasional burp or a drunkard's offkey singing pierced the dizzying darkness.

It was the wobbling yellow light. The strained panting. The smell of something caught but alive and writhing led Karthi to the inspector's office, where he found the inspector pressed against a woman. It was Shreya. The flouncy yellow saree gave it away. The muffled sobs. Her strained fingers were boring into the wall. Her rigid pose suggested to Karthi that whatever the inspector was doing was hurting Shreya and making her unconformable. His head began to throb as the worms of guilt were joined by something else as debilitating. In addition to mocking him for causing his sister's skin to turn dark, it blamed him for putting Shreya in such a terrible situation because of his actions or lack thereof.

The baton on the floor glistened as it caught the yellow light from the ceiling. It called out to Karthi. It was cold and firm. He knew what he had to do. This could be his only chance to set things right. He steadied his feet and gripped the baton firmly. He had seen how cricketers hit a sixer. They would swing the bat so that it could make the biggest arch, sending the ball up high. He did the same thing with all his strength. It struck the inspector right in the middle of the groin.

The pain from the hit shot up to the inspector's head like a searing bolt of lightning. His face shrivelled up in pain. He grabbed his groin and collapsed. Shreya turned around to see Karthi with the baton and the inspector on the floor. Urine and possibly blood stained the inspector's khaki pants dark brown. He tried to say something, but only strained gasps escaped from his mouth.

Shreya couldn't believe a little boy like Karthi had so much courage and strength to bring down a government employee. In doing so, he prevented a sour experience that would have seared into the back of her mind. Shreya grabbed hold of Karthi's hand and ran out of the office with her bag. They ran past the dingy cells. A hand shot out from the dark jail cell and grabbed Shreya.

'It's been so long since I saw a woman here,' a voice spoke in the darkness. Shreya's arms were squeezed so tight that they burnt her skin. Karthi quickly bit the hand, and the hand disappeared back into the darkness with a yell. They crouched in the reception area where the constable was now asleep in his chair, probably dreaming of sleeping in the inspector's chair and buying Dairy Milk chocolate every day for his daughter. Slowly they crawled to the waiting area where Kalki waited. The three of them ran out of the police station and fled into the thick, velvety darkness – the first non-criminal criminals to successfully escape the police station. The inspector managed to wobble to the front of the police station and vented his anger at his throbbing pain and the double humiliation of being bested by a transgender person and a little boy on the sleeping constable. The constable stood quietly, accepting the torrent of abuse. The dream of buying Dairy Milk daily for his daughter retreated further away.

Shreya and the children didn't stop running till they hit the highway. Shreya was in the middle and the children on either side. She lifted her saree and tied it around her waist. They ran past the crumbly dirt roads and climbed a jagged outcrop before sliding down the other side. They shuffled past the recently harvested paddy fields. The mud dried and clothed them in flaky brown socks. They ran past an unexpected establishment of a shantytown. Past the assembly of its residents gathered under the lone streetlight discussing something intently. The residents stopped their discussion to watch the three run past them. Karthi wondered why they were all gathered there in the middle of the night. His question was answered when he spotted someone lying on the ground lifeless, wrapped in leaves. In the distance, a howling of jackals could be heard. A chill crept into their skin and gave their feet a boost. They began to sense they were coming onto the highway as they heard honking as vehicles zipped past.

The moon lighted the highway as though searching for its missing portion. The headlights of the vehicles looked like luminous steadfast creatures at the bottom of the ocean. Buses ploughed through the darkness like beetles. As the three of them walked hand in hand, covered in car dust, the pain of running without pausing began to spread through their bodies like hot liquid.

'I can't walk anymore,' Kalki whimpered.

'Just a bit longer, dear. We will ask someone for a lift.'

'But I can't.'

'Neither can I,' Karthi said.

'Why didn't you tell me the real reason why you left home? Why did you lie to me?' Shreya asked.

'I thought if I told you the truth, you would send us back to our village,' Karthi said.

'I am sure you must have had a good reason to leave your home,' Shreya said.

Karthi stared at her blankly.

'I ran away from my home too,' Shreya said. 'I will tell you my reason if you tell me yours, and I won't send you back.'

'Promise?'

'Promise.' A glaring pair of headlights drenched them in white light just then.

'All this running around because you want to be fair?' Shreya exclaimed. She couldn't help but giggle at the innocence of their conviction.

'That is the only way to stop everyone from making fun of her,' Karthi said. He didn't disclose his own guilty secret, that he was responsible for Kalki's dark skin when he had forgotten her in the sun when she was a baby.

'It's not your skin that is dark. What is dark is the heart of those people who think you are cursed.'

'Look at me,' Kalki said, holding her arms up against the night sky. Her arms melted into the encompassing darkness. The dark sky shook with joy, appearing to alert the moon to someone reaching out to it. To return its missing piece that was lost on the earth down below. 'Look, I am as black as the night sky. I am so ugly. Kalki's eyes became moist.

'My dear,' Shreya clapped her spread-finger clap, which sounded like thunder and ricocheted up from the ground on the empty highway. It arrested Kalki's tears effectively. 'If there is one person in this world who should love herself it is you. Both of you, do you understand?'

Two heads nodded.

'It's funny that I should be the one who has to say this,' Shreya mumbled to herself. 'Ok, I promised to tell you my secret. Here it is. Once, a boy hated being in his body so much that he didn't feel like a boy and wanted to be a girl. He felt alive when he was dressed as a girl, combed her hair like a girl, and talked like one. When his parents found out about this, they were angry that he wanted to become a girl. They tried to talk to him about it. But nothing helped. The urge was still there. Soon, word got out about this secret, and the whole town laughed at the family for giving birth to such a boy. The secret broke the family from within, and they knew they had to get rid of him, but they didn't know how to. One day, because of the boy's foolishness, the opportunity presented itself, and the family got rid of him. He had to go through all of this because he hated himself so much. If the boy loved himself as a boy, none of this would have happened. He would be still with his family right now, having dinner and watching TV.'

'But the boy can change into a girl whenever he felt like it, and he would be happy. I can't do that with my skin,' Kalki said.

'And that is why we need to go and get the money back,' Karthi said.

'That's what you think, dear child. How can one find

happiness even when things change when they didn't know happiness in the first place?'

Karthi realised that the boy in Shreya's story was Shreyas. 'But is the boy happy now?' he asked.

'No, he is still looking for happiness.'

"When will he find it?" asked Karthi.

'That's where I was going to go. A place where all the unhappy people gather to find their happiness.'

'The festival?' Karthi said. Shreya nodded.

'Maybe I can find my happiness too there,' Kalki said.

'Let's find out. I will take you home.'

The children's eyes widened.

'I will take you home after we go to the festival and when we get back the money. How does that sound?'

The children, thrilled with joy, hugged Shreya tightly around the waist. Shreya smiled through the pain as the children's delight pressed on the fresh wounds gained at the police station.

The three of them walked further up the highway. Every time they heard a deep rumble, they turned around and waved frantically. The buses all ignored them as its passengers watched them with pity for a moment and later with a satisfied sigh that they weren't the ones stranded on the highway.

Moments later, something shaped like a large rectangular box with a sputtering engine came to a screaming halt behind them. It expelled hot air. Their necks stiffened. They turned around to see the front panel of a vibrating lorry with the words Ashok Leyland written on it. Behind it, the truck carried a massive hollow cylindrical structure. The almost full moon lit up as though it had found its missing piece.

The large door swung open. A sweaty smell of people having been sitting in one place for too long escaped the cabin. Rows of gods lined the dashboard. The decorative flashing lights around them cast a kaleidoscope of bright patterns around the dark interior. The driver wrestled with the gearbox and shut the engine at last. The truck was obviously his home. There was a rolled-up pillow and place to sleep behind the seat. Shirts hung on the bars, flapping like ghosts.

'What kind of idiots didn't stop to help a mother and her kids?' the driver asked, stretching and scratching his armpit. 'Where do you want to go, Amma?'

Shreyas named the town, Koovagam, where the festival was being held.

'Are you sick?' the driver asked, hearing the raspy voice. 'And why would you want to go to that kind of ....oh!' The driver realised he wasn't speaking to a woman and that the children weren't hers probably.

'You are that type of man,' he said, stressing the word. He gave a knowing smile and added, 'Are they your children?'

'Why don't you mind your own business?' Shreya said.

'Let's see if the police think that way too,' the driver said.

'What do you want?' Shreya asked, her arms folded

across her chest.

The driver stroked below his stomach. Shreya knew that the night wasn't going to let her escape her fate. It needed its sacrifice. She sealed her fate with a nod. The driver wet his hands with his mouth and straightened his hair and his moustache. Shreya ushered the children to the edge of the road and asked them to sit by the guardrails.

'Cover your ears,' she said. 'Karthi, I know you are a brave boy, but no matter what you hear, don't come near the lorry. Come when I call you. This time don't save me.' With that, she walked to the open door of the lorry's cabin. She walked in and it gulped her whole.

Chapter 13

After an hour of jiggling in the back seat in the lorry, the driver dropped them off at an intersection. They hopped down into a cloud of dust and staggered to the side of the road with numbed limbs.

'I will be coming back this way. Will you wait for me? And we can do it again.,' the driver blew her a kiss. Shreya slammed the door in his face. 'Get lost!' She spat at the lorry for good measure.

On the other side of the road, several streams of people, like tributaries joining the main river, walked into a narrow road leading to the town of Koovagam. There was a signboard in green and written in bold white was the name of the town. Curious and lecherous men, confused adolescent boys, women who were men inside, women who found an excuse to spend the day away from husbands – they filled the road.

The road was artificially lit with large rumbly

generator-powered lights that supplemented the dim streetlights. Along the side of the streets, vans had set up mobile shops. A mini lorry was loaded with water bottles. Two men sat idly staring at the ambling crowd while a deafening pre-recorded sales pitch blared out from a speaker. 'One bottle 5 rupees, but if you buy three, it is 15 rupees.' There was an ice cream freezer next to it. And a cart filled with earthen pots. Another one sold roasted corn. A spray of sparks drizzled onto the pedestrians. They flinched and giggled.

'Oye, darkie!' One of the water bottle sellers called to Kalki. 'I am talking to you, little girl!'

'Don't mind him,' Shreyas said.

'Are you both dark and deaf?' the seller yelled.

'You two wait here,' Shreya said, walking briskly towards the man, her right hand rolled into a fist. She funnelled years of rejection, the anguish of solitary living, the searing agony of the bruises from the police station – everything into the slap that landed on the water-seller's cheek like a clap of thunder. His cheek turned red, the imprint of her hand standing out like a white branding mark. He fell off the back of the truck and took with him the tape recorder. It still spoke though to the sky now, offering the deceptively priced water bottles. The pedestrians stopped for a moment, waiting for more action but seeing no retaliation from the man, they walked away.

'She is a just a child,' Shreya said, shoving her palm at his forehead.

'No, no, no. Please don't curse me,' the man begged. 'My business is already suffering as it is.'

'Do you know what happens when you tease them at such an early age?' Shreyas asked. 'The ugly words you feed them plants a hateful seed in them. Eating them alive from within, one bite at a time until they become living ghosts. Unable to give or receive love.'

The man promised never to make fun of anyone for as long as he lived. He just wanted to live.

'What did he see in your palm?' Kalki asked. 'He looks so scared.'

'I showed how he would look if he were a woman.'

'He must have seen himself as a very ugly woman to be so scared,' Karthi said.

'Very,' Shreya said with a giggle.

Kalki yanked Shreya's hands and stared into her palms. 'Can you show me how I would look if I became fair?'

'My dear,' Shreyas said. 'It only works for ugly people.'

'Am I beautiful?'

'More than beautiful. You are one of a kind.'

A makeshift shop fashioned out of a yellow autorickshaw was swarming with people, like a busy beehive. Columns of transparent sachets housing combs, hairpins, hairclips and hairbands dangled from it. Rows of rectangular boxes containing plastic and glass bangles beckoned enthralled customers, men and women alike. They tried on the bangles and shook their hands to check if they were noisy enough. The jingling and colours of the bangles flirted with the vivid and dizzying colours of the sarees many of them wore, shot through with gold patterns. Flowers. Paisley. Baroque. Fleur-de-lis. Jasmine (white and orange). Marigold. Roses adorned their plaited wigs. Gold necklaces crisscrossed their ebony chests which were browner than their powdered faces. Gold studs and earrings adorned their ears. Men became women. Aravanis in Tamil. Hijra in Hindi. They belong in the insult section of every vernacular. At least they belonged here, somewhere in the real world.

'You are not the only one here,' Karthi said.

'They all look like women, but they also look like men. Like you,' Kalki said, looking at Shreya.

To be surrounded by people who dressed, looked and acted like him gave Shreyas a sense of belonging. He could be himself or herself without being judged.

As they approached the bustling shop, one of the Aravanis gasped and clapped the spread-finger clap in front of Shreya's face. 'Look here, sisters,' she called out to the other Aravanis who turned around. 'Someone is committing a crime here.' She sounded as though her throat was blocked by pebbles.

'Who, me?' Shreyas asked.

'Who else?' the Aravani said. 'First time?'

Shreyas nodded.

'You have come here without any makeup, jewellery or flair. This is one place where you can express yourself freely. Sisters, we have work to do. Don't you think, children?' She looked at Karthi and Kalki. 'Who are they?' she asked Shreyas.

'Sister's kids,' Shreyas said.

'Come on now. We need to make you look like a bride. Why else would an Aravani come here?'

The group of Aravanis absorbed Shreyas into their glistening cocoon, and after a while, he emerged like a bejewelled butterfly. With big red full lips. Powdered face with pink rouge. Neck, nose and ears, bedecked with jewellery. Sweeping eyelashes and an immaculately braided wig with a garland of the plumpest white jasmines. Shreya weaved her colourful ribbons into the wig. Purple, pink, yellow, blue and white.

'Doesn't she look fit for the fashion show?' the head Aravani said.

'Our Lord Aravan will be very happy to take you as a bride.'

'Fashion show?' Shreya exclaimed. 'Marriage?'

'Yes, marriage for all of us. But only one will be crowned of Miss Koovagam.'

'Miss Koovagam? You mean like Miss World?'

'Why? Aren't we allowed to participate in pageants?'

'What is a fashion show?' Kalki asked.

'You wear beautiful dresses, lots of makeup, and show off on a stage,' Karthi said.

'Smart boy,' the head Aravani said.

'I don't think I can do that,' Shreyas said.

'I don't think Brindha will take no for an answer. She is the mother of all,' another Aravani said, giggling, referring to the leader who had dressed up Shreya. 'Besides, what have you got to lose?' The truth in that statement struck everyone. Their faces elapsed into a moment of self-deprecation for the things they had voluntarily lost.

'Can I be a part of the fashion show?' Kalki asked, pronouncing fashion as *pashion*. 'I want to be fair like you.'

'Look at this girl. She is not even as high as my waist, and she wants to be in the show,' Brindha croaked, lightly pinching Kalki's cheeks.

'Then can you turn her fair with your powder?' Karthi asked.

'Why? She is beautiful as she is,' Brindha said. 'But I think I have a role for you. Not in the fashion show but in the play after that. Stick out your tongue, child.'

Kalki obediently put out her tongue.

The Aravanis took a step back and looked serious. They tapped their neck and uttered a small prayer. One of them dropped to the ground and touched Kalki's feet in reverence. 'She looks just like our goddess.'

'You will be Kali,' Brindha said. The other Aravanis agreed vehemently.

'Trust Brindha to make the right decision,' said one of them.

'But my name is Kalki,' the little girls said.

'Yes, but you will be Goddess Kali tonight, and you don't need any makeup for that.'

The fashion show was held inside an auditorium decorated with curtains of lights. A massive arch made of wood welcomed everyone. Banners, flags and posters featuring politicians festooned the place, promising the Aravanis equality in the next election.

Karthi and Kalki were made to sit at the front of the stage so that Shreya could keep an eye on them. Their clothes and skin spilled through the holes in the chair as they made themselves comfortable. Shreyas promised he would be back and asked them not to go anywhere. Behind them, the auditorium was abuzz with constant chatter. It smelled of coconut oil and excitement. Sweat and perfume commingled in the air. Plastic chairs were being pulled and pushed. The soundman checking the microphone brought intermittent pause to the commotion with loud screeches. The music started to play. First softly, then loudly. It signalled to the audience that the show was about to begin. Men on one side, women, including non-modelling transgender people, on the other. They twirled fanned themselves with their handkerchiefs.

Men watched, licking their lips and leering at everyone. Whistles erupted like hungry little chicks competing for food, as Aravani models walked down the ramp. They walked as they pleased because they could, drumming the hollow stage with their feet in rhythm. Random pauses with jerky movements kicking their sarees. Stiff poses. Big smiles. Only god could judge them today. Shreya walked out with small steps, evaluating the crowd's reaction. As the applause swelled, so did her confidence grow like a swollen river in the monsoons. She twirled and spun around, showing off her meticulously braided hair, laced through with colourful ribbons. She looked like a spinning star come down from the heavens. Karthi and Kalki clapped till their palms turned sore.

Finally, all the glamorous Aravanis with beaming smiles walked out onto the stage. Brindha stepped out with a card containing the name of the winner of the pageant. Her face was ghostly white with glitter. It wasn't Shreya who won the title. A slender Aravani started to cry and collapsed to the ground when she heard her name. With tears ruining the makeup, she accepted the gold-plated crown. Her golden ticket was accepted by society because a transgender person with a pageant title must be special. A shiny earthworm among regular worms. The other Aravanis looked happy. They clapped for the winner. For themselves. Waves of applause rose from the audience, a small but definitive act of acceptance from the community, even if short-lived. They might again face brazen prejudice once they walked out of the auditorium but at the festival the world was theirs.

The lights dimmed. The Aravanis cleared the stage, the winner still shedding tears over her trophy. A slightly bent, older man came onto the stage and started to sweep away the fallen sequins and glitter. Finite joys and compressed hopes.

Soft murmurs rose from the audience. Disbelief, shock, pleasant surprise mixed together.

'Can you believe it? They were all men. I could have sworn they were all girls.'

'If men can be made to look like women, can women be made to look like men?'

'Maybe. Maybe not.'

'I will be careful when I approach a woman in this town!'

'Look how fair they are. Like movie stars. Wish I could look like that!'

Kalki's heart sank when she heard the people behind her remarking on the Aravanis' fair skin. It could have been her with that fair skin. Only if Brindha had allowed her to use makeup. She could have seen how she would look with delicate, fair skin, and people would have marvelled at her glossy fairness instead of comparing her to a piece of coal. Sadness overtook her and her shoulders drooped. She stared at her dark-skinned arms.

'Do you know who Goddess Kali is?' said Karthi.

'No,' said Kalki.

'She is the one with many arms. She has a garland made of human skulls, not flowers. Her face is dark and sca...,' Karthi wanted to say scary but seeing Kalki's chin tremble, he corrected himself. 'I mean, she is dark and powerful. Even Lord Shiva to whom the whole universe bows, prostrates to Kali.'

'But I don't want to be dark and powerful. I just want to be fair.'

Karthi wanted to say something, but an Aravani came up to them and whisked Kalki backstage. She spotted Brindha in a heated argument with another man dressed as Kali, the Goddess of Destruction. Smeared in black paint, with a red tongue and papier-mâché arms attached to his back.

'You do this every year,' Brindha said. 'She is just a small child. You can do it again next year.'

'But she is a child. How can she be big and imposing? Goddess Kali needs to be huge and scary,' the man said.

'The portraits and statues of gods in our home are small as well. They do carry the same intensity and get the reverence as any big statue, however.'

The man tried to argue but Brindha quietened him with her index finger. 'There is something about her skin that just says she will be the best Kali we have ever had,' she said.

'Just listen,' the man persisted. 'I have an idea how we can both work together on stage.'

A great epic was about to retold. One that involved great wars. And fierce warriors. A mighty sacrifice. And gender fluidities. Transcendence. Becoming an undying legend. Every year, the epic was enacted. Nobody knew when the tradition began. Some said 5,000 years ago. Others said 10,000. The story couldn't be contained in words. It couldn't be dispersed orally with the same vigour, so it had to be presented as a play. Stories of gods re-created by god's creations so that they could be one with their creators. The story was as familiar as the earth. But everyone watched and listened like it was the first time because there was something indomitable about these tales. Something that time cannot unravel from the strands of its grand tapestry. Something that makes the faithless question their understanding. Something that spreads an ancient ache inside and makes man seek comfort in the vast pantheon of deities.

The story began as a love story. While bathing in the holy Ganga and performing a ritual, the mighty warrior Arjuna is suddenly pulled into the river by a fast-moving current. Arjuna watched the current unravel itself and a beautiful creature appeared in the river, a half-maiden, half-serpent called Ulupi. She revealed that she was smitten by Arjuna and wanted to marry him. Arjuna agreed. They married and had a son named Aravan, who is the titular character of this festival. Ulupi bestowed a boon on her son that no water creature would harm him, and he would be able to control them as he pleases.

In the land of Kuru, in ancient India, a great conflict arose between two sets of cousins, the Pandavas and Kauravas, for the throne of Hastinapur. The war last 18 days, from sunrise to sunset. It started with the blowing of the great conch by Lord Krishna, who drove Arjuna's chariot.

Arjuna requested his son, Aravan, to aid them in the war. With his army of Nagas, he went on to slay demons, valiant princes, and hordes of brave soldiers. Despite the heavy losses, the enemy kept advancing. Something had to be done, something drastic that could turn the tide in the favour of the Pandavas.

Lord Krishna, the eighth avatar of Vishnu, the compassionate one, the cheeky one who stole butter, the protector with blue face and body volunteered to sacrifice himself to Goddess Kali on the day of the new moon to ensure victory for the Pandavas. Aravan, the dauntless, objected and offered himself for the sacrifice. But he had one last dying wish – that he be married just for a day, experience a night of marital bliss with a woman before he departed the earth. No woman stepped forward as no one was ready to endure the curse of widowhood. All women dramatically turned away from Aravan despite the honour of marrying a brave warrior. A dejected Aravan fell to the ground, sobbing like the sound of a thousand galloping horses.

It was at this pivotal juncture that Krishna stepped in and agreed to marry Aravan. When a confused Aravan asked how this would be possible, Krishna merely gave a comforting smile. In front of Aravan's eyes, Krishna transformed himself. The blue skin fell off, his curly hair unravelled and flowed like a river. His bright yellow dhoti turned into a red sari with gold border. Bangles, necklaces, earrings, nose rings appeared and, in an instant, Krishna became Mohini. The transformation scene made all the Aravanis choke up because it was a representation of their reality, their acceptance, their voice. This was the only reason society tolerated them. They remembered the first time they wore their mother's saree, their sister's jewellery, and moving like an actress.

Aravan married Mohini. The marriage comprised only an exchange of arrows from both sides. Aravan spent his ephemeral day as a married man. And Mohini spent the night with her husband, like a mayfly wife.

The next day, Kali arrived on a thundering black cloud to accept her sacrifice. Kalki sat on the shoulders of the man who was originally supposed to be Kali. He was the cloud and Kalki was Kali. The papier-mâché hands attached to his back looked menacing. Kalki had her arms stretched out, holding a curved plastic blade and a bleeding head. The head bled red paint on the plate below. The man tapped Kalki and whispered, 'Do it.' Kalki put out her tongue to its maximum length. She raised her eyebrows and widened her eyes till it almost popped out. The background music rose to a crescendo of minor discordant chords, striking terror in people's hearts. The audience gasped. And her face collapsed as it usually did at people's reaction to her dark skin. She quickly remembered that they weren't looking at Kalki, the dark-skinned girl but at Kali, the dark-skinned goddess. She resumed her Kali pose and expression. Looking even more terrifying, she bewitched them. After enduring years of insults for her black skin, this was her moment – what she despised the most about herself was today holding everyone spellbound. It felt like the result of a once-in-a-lifetime planetary alignment. A feeling of power swelled inside Kalki like the cosmic energy that keeps stars afloat in the sky. She was blinding like the brightest day and abyssal as the deepest oceans.

When Karthi saw his sister as Kali appear on stage, the worms of guilt in his head were ready to rear their ugly heads. They waited to feed off the insults. the heckling, the taunts. To gather even more strength from this large audience. All they could hear, however, was silence. An audience in awe of Kalki. They tried to drill into him using flashes of older memories. Remember the time when the white tourist in the temple was disgusted by your sister. Remember how Priya died because of her dark skin. Nothing worked. They were losing their stranglehold over his mind. Some of them convulsed and shrank before becoming dust. Karthi felt the worms sliding out of his head, down his neck and disappearing. The tension eased and his head felt a little lighter.

Kali waited for the sacrifice on the battlefield. Aravan rode into battle, knowing that death would come swiftly at any moment. He fought valiantly. His imminent death fuelled his strength to slay more enemies on the battlefield. It was the last sound he would hear. The sharp blade whistled through the air and sliced his neck. Blood erupted from his neck in the form of twisted ribbons. His body convulsed in a pool of paper blood. Kali collected her offering and replaced one of the heads she held with Aravan's. His eyes bulged outwards as though even in his final moment, he wanted to scare death away. With his dripping head, Kali ascended to the heavens. The sky shook and the auditorium vibrated as she left. Kalki stretched her tongue out for one last time. Fear crept into people's hearts as they prayed in silence to Goddess Kali for forgiveness.

It was the last scene of the play. As promised, the war was won. The winning side celebrated as Mohini, the widow, grieved for her dead husband. Her wedding saree turned into a white one. She wailed as her bangles shattered and fell as bits of glass around her. She lamented as her *thali*, her nuptial gold chain, was forcefully yanked from her neck just like her husband's life was taken away. She cried as her *bindi* was wiped away from her forehead. They removed all marks of marriage from her body. Krishna leapt out of Mohini, resumed his true self, leaving Mohini behind like an empty cocoon, devoid of life. Forbidden to love and to be loved. Only sadness and despair left in her life.

There weren't any claps or ear-piercing whistles when the play ended. It was as though the joy was sucked out of the room. Despondence settled on the audience like a weight on their hearts. They ambled to the exit, thinking of other ways Aravan could have survived and Mohini could have been saved from such a miserable existence. The Aravanis found it especially poignant for they were all Mohini. In searching for an answer for Mohini, they were looking for solutions for themselves too.

The play was just a playbook for the events that were yet to transpire outside in the real world. The Koothandavar temple, which slumbers all year, is woken by the gunshot claps of the eager Aravani brides. The entrances to the temple were blocked with people like a vast, slow-moving river. Aravanis, with their bowl of offerings along with the *thalis*, laboured their way to the temple's inner sanctum. To the statue of Lord Aravan. He looked at his stream of brides with his pronounced eyes nestling under thick eyebrows, his moustache curved at the end like the prow of a boat. Two prominent fangs stuck out as he bared his teeth. A cobra hood, a reference to his serpentine roots, sheltered him.

The priest representing Lord Aravan, was smeared in thick sandalwood paste. He accepted the offerings of coconut, flowers and betel leaves. The *thali* would be tied by the priest around the Aravani's neck under the ubiquitous eyes of Lord Aravan. With their freshly minted smiles, the newlywed brides gathered outside in a night of dancing and merriment – the only night in the year when they could enjoy unfettered happiness.

Outside the temple, a boy diligently walked to and fro, selling unbroken coconuts and garlands to the latecomers. A small economy was thriving off the rushed madness and tardiness.

Festive lights draped the temple complex like cobwebs. Balloons bobbed gently among the heads of the people. Aravanis danced in circles with synchronised clapping. One to the ground and the next up to the sky. Bonfires peppered the temple grounds. Those who couldn't brave the crowds of worshippers thronging the temple wed outside near the bonfires. Men who have taken an oath to Lord Aravan agreed to marry Aravanis in exchange for a cure for their ailments. Their infertility. A mother's broken hip. Or a wife's torment.

Karthi, Kalki and Shreyas navigated through the frenzy like crabs, dodging mini dust clouds raised by the feet by the dizzy dancers. Here, Shreya didn't have to search for men. They sought her, begging to marry her. One fell to the ground. Another lay prostrate, refusing to budge. The crab crawled over his resolute body.

'Do you know why they are flocking to us?' Shreyas asked Kalki.

'No, I don't know.'

'It is because of you.'

It wasn't because of Shreya's looks. It wasn't because the place was running out of unwed Aravanis. It was because of Kalki as Kali. She terrified them. Not in a horrifying way but in a beautiful way. Like a sinner at church begging for forgiveness. They thought marrying Shreya, who was with Kali, would eradicate their misfortunes faster.

Shreya got married that night. A man in a white shirt and lungi with gold border approached her. Not fast or slow. He was different from the others because he prostrated in front of Kalki and asked for her blessing. Only then did he ask for Shreya's permission to marry her. There was no emotion involved in this transactional marriage. Shreya wasn't his wife. He wasn't her husband. Their eyes didn't lock with one another, trembling with everlasting love. No unbreakable vows were read. It was as plain as a sheet of paper and as emotional as daily routine. Shreya didn't feel any different inside. Nothing blossomed. Only a strange feeling of fleeting acceptance. And the weight of the *thali* around her neck.

The night was coming to an end. Fireworks shot up to the sky, fracturing the dark sky. Newly wed brides of Aravan danced and sang. The sound of urumi drums proliferated in the thick atmosphere. Men who just came to leer at the Aravanis watched with lust in their eyes and the same curiosity as at the zoo when watching a strange animal.

By midnight, everyone retired to their makeshift tents that lined the road, lighting it up like an airport runway. No planes would land here, however. There were enough souls on the ground ready to take off.

Shreya, Karthi and Kalki were invited to Brindha's tent with two other Aravanis. Their wigs were ruffled and wonky. Sweat blotted their makeup. They had big nose rings connected to the ear lobes with a gold chain passing over their glistening cheekbones. Earrings like suspended umbrellas dangled from their ears. Brindha introduced them as her two adopted daughters. She told Shreya about the *Jamaat* system.

'You can be adopted, you know,' she explained, in her raspy voice. 'You will have a semblance of family. A mother. A father. A brother and a sister. But not the normal kind. Our kind. This is as close as it gets for us to be normal and live with people other than staring at four walls.'

Brindha pulled a pen from under the blouse and wrote an address for Shreya.

'You will find someone there,' she said, putting back the pen into her blouse. She spotted the terror on Shreyas face. 'Don't worry. They will look after you.' The address written on the paper was the city Shreyas had fled from.

'And you, my black beauty,' Brindha said, turning to Kalki. 'The play is over. You can remove your costume!'

'I don't think she will ever remove it,' Shreyas said.

'I don't want her to,' Karthi said.

'Me too,' Kalki said.

'Rest up,' Brindha said. 'Tomorrow is going to be ...' She sighed. 'You will see,' she said in a choked voice.

The morning sky looked ominous. Dense clouds swallowed the smaller clouds to grow bigger like white thrones for gods in the sky. Silence permeated in the air as though everyone had taken a collective vow of silence. It hung heavy in the air like the last breath of a dying patient. Like unsaid words of quarrelling lovers. Like an unresolved regret. Yesterday's merriment was expunged.

The newlywed brides marched towards the temple. They straightened their sarees and hopes. Reapplied their makeup and rekindled their dreams. Adjusted their wigs and desires. Rearranged their jewellery and expectations. Shreya, Karthi and Kalki spotted billowing smoke in the distance. The smell of camphor got stronger as they neared it. Long bent sticks held by women on either side stoked the flame as it intensified and reached for the sky, purifying the air, and symbolising the union with Lord Aravan.

The cheeks of the Aravanis were smeared with turmeric paste. Yellow thick finger-marks crusted in the sunlight. *Kollams,* huge intricate designs made on the ground with rice flour, sporadically dotted the road to welcome someone big. A hundred-and-eight coconuts were broken to summon Lord Ganesh's help to clear any obstacles and vanquish bad energy that might be blocking predestined destiny. Coconut shells bounced, and coconut water sprayed on the crowd like a broken irrigation system.

Once again, just like last night, the Aravanis gathered in circles and danced and sang a folk song. But this time, the movements were out of sync. The song was off tune.

'Come on, girls,' Brindha shouted, cupping her hands over her mouth. 'This is our last moment of happiness for a while. Dance and sing like you mean it.'

The conviviality picked up. Percussion instruments roared, imparting new life to the dancers. They revelled in the last minutes of their married life. A man streaked with white stripes over a yellow turmeric body walked through the crowd. A steel rod pierced his tongue vertically, and another went through his cheeks. As he passed, the celebrations stopped. An omen of things to come. Through the perforated holes in this face, he sucked the joy out of the camphor-perfumed air.

Deafening shots of firecrackers sounded and, in the distance, a towering effigy appeared, pulled by 30 men on each side with thick bamboo ropes. The moving tower was at least 10 metres tall. Garlands of flowers drenched the tower in yellow, white, red, and green hues. People threw petals and confetti made of shredded newspaper at the effigy, the severed head of Lord Aravan. His protruding eyes watched everything. A priest stood at his side. This was his last parade around the battlefield that would take his life.

As the towering effigy made its way through the streets, dousing the camphor flames, people began to crowd closer, sending their prayers and desires up to Aravan. Babies were hoisted to his face like dolls. The men in the tower passed the toddlers up to the top. With an ear full of blessings, they were returned to their parents down below. On their way down, they lost their clothes and gained a fear of heights. The Aravanis thronged the tower too, asking their only husband to hear their woes and bless them for the next 364 days till they would be married again. They caught every flower and paper clipping that came their way.

The tower was pulled to the centre of the temple ground. Out of garlands. Out of men. Out of blessings. Only the head of Aravan left. Streams of kerosene were poured on it before setting it on fire. Flames danced and wrapped around the tower and devoured Aravan's head. He gazed upon all his wives one last time before the fire scorched his eyes as he widowed them. He was no more. So, they couldn't be his wives anymore.

The one-day brides, now freshly widowed, including Shreyas, went around searching for men or anyone armed with a small sickle or knife. To break their bangles. To cut their nuptial chains. To wipe the *bindi* from their foreheads. To rip their flowers from their heads. Their ephemeral dignity, honour and societal acceptance gone. Intense moaning from the widowed Aravanis billowed in stark contrast to the songs that had engulfed the air moments ago. They went into a deep state of mourning like Mohini did for Lord Aravan.

Shreya, Karthi and Kalki walked over broken bits of

bangles, wilting flowers, and snipped *thalis* littering the ground.

'Do you want to become a widow?' a short man asked Shreya, brandishing his sharp knife at her.

'Why? This is the first time in my life that I was treated as a human. To live a normal life. Why would I give it all away?'

'You can't do that. Otherwise, bad luck will follow,' the man said. Karthi and Kalki on either side took Shreya's hand and gave a comforting squeeze. Shreya returned the squeeze. As if her life wasn't a string of bad luck anyway.

Then, she gave in and bent down to his level.

'You can become a bride again next year,' he said as he snipped her *thali*, rubbed off her *bindi*, and tore the flowers from her hair and broke her bangles. One by one, he stripped her. Layer by layer, like an onion, till there was nothing left to peel.

Shreya joined a wailing group of Aravanis huddled together, their heads resting against each other. They beat their chests to cry even more. They swung their loose hair like trees in caught in a storm. White sheets were passed around to cover their loud sarees. Some gathered around Kalki, who was still dressed like Kali, to forgive Lord Aravan, their husband and not behead him. They pleaded with her to allow them to live a normal life. There must be another way, they wailed.

Karthi and Kalki watched them lament even though they couldn't fathom the sadness. Kalki wondered what it would be like to be them, desperately trying to hold the broken pieces together. No matter how hard they tried to become a woman, they could never be fully one. Society wouldn't let them. They would be purged as freaks of nature, abnormal beings, things that should not have come to pass. What if she were to meet the same fate as them when she turned fair? Would everyone accept her as the fair one? Or the one who was dark before? Would she straddle two worlds forever? Light and dark. The mushrooming sadness from the Aravanis made her choke as she thought about her fate.

Spectators gathered on the periphery and watched the wailing Aravanis as one would watch a wounded animal lying on the road after being hit by a car. They wanted to know the reason for their intense, passionate crying. Maybe it was the death of their husband, Lord Aravan. Perhaps they cried for the years of rejection and abject humiliation. Or perhaps they mourned for the lost love that was never meant to be theirs. So, they went back to a familiar place they all knew, the world of pain. They clothed themselves in another layer of pain. The pain of a bride who had lost her husband.

Chapter 14

It had been three years since Shreyas had left this city he was born into. Flashes of the day he ran away appeared before his eyes. The city carried on with its life despite losing one of its own. It had swelled. Elevated bridges buzzed where narrow roads had been. Sounds from construction sites filled the air. Apartment complexes rose towered where humble one-storey houses had stood, only a few dotting the landscape now and counting their days. The population had swollen to ten times the number. It was as if the city was trying to say that it didn't mind losing Shreyas. In more than one way, the town was like an Aravani. Balancing the old and the new. Finding itself. Trying to impress and constantly vying for approval.

A 50-foot cardboard cut-out of Shakthivelu greeted the city. His palms were pressed together and a shining light radiated from his hands. His shirt wasn't buttoned up like on his business card. It was open, complementing his pearly white grin. Crows lined up on his shoulder, leaving dribbling white streaks on his dull orange shirt. The cut-out straddled a neem tree. One half of the tree was stripped of its branches. The other half was left as it was in case any environmental activist groups were offended.

The head office was a far cry from the small, cramped office Karthi, and Kalki had visited in their village. Instead of just one queue of people, multiple disorderly lines jostled to get ahead. Slender security guards in their oversized blue uniforms tried to impose order on the lines. People at the front of the queue deliberately pushed one another, hoping that the highly sought first position would be theirs. A sign over the entrance proclaimed: WELCOME TO ONE AND ALL. THIS IS THE GATEWAY TO CHANGE YOUR LIVES. INVEST TODAY. ENJOY TOMORROW.

Portable enterprises were set up outside. Dextrous typists pored over the documents, their fingers flying over the keys. A woman served idlis and dosas. Tea- and coffee-sellers carried large metal containers on a large bamboo stick suspended over their shoulders. Little boys went around with smaller denomination notes between their fingers and exchanged them at higher conversion rates for people who didn't have enough loose change to buy a steaming cup of tea or plate of dosas. A few beggars loitered and pestered the attendants who shooed them away like unwanted flies.

It was five minutes to nine. First, it was one man who stepped out of line. A woman followed. In an instant, the lines disbanded. The eager ones at the front had their faces squeezed against the iron grilles of the main gate. The security guards ran around, flourishing their sticks, trying to control the boisterous crowded.

'If you don't behave yourself, nobody will be able to come in today,' an announcement came from a speaker somewhere inside. 'Form a line, and you will be let in.'

Shreya, Kalki and Karthi joined the queue.

'It is going to take a long time,' Karthi said as he counted the number of people in front of them. '78, 79, 80…,' the rest he counted in his head. '101, 102, and we are 103!'

'We have all day to go inside,' Shreyas said.

'What if they don't have our money here?'

Before Shreyas could answer, the invisible loudspeaker blared again. 'Ladies first. If there are any ladies, come to the front of the line.'

'Go, Amma,' a man behind Shreya spoke. 'They are calling for you.' Shreyas thought the man was talking to someone else.

'I think he is talking to you,' Karthi said, tugging at Shreya's hand. 'Mother!'

'What did you call me?' Shreya asked, squishing her eyebrows.

'What else would a son call his mother?' the man said. 'Can't you hear the loudspeaker? They are calling for all women to the front. You have two kids as well. Go Fast!'

Seconds passed, and Shreya realised that the man believed that she was the children's mother. She quickly wrapped the saree around her face to hide her features.

'Thank you for reminding me,' Shreya said, clearing her throat. 'My brain is filled with things to do, so I wasn't listening.'

The man gestured to her to hurry up, adding, 'Wish I was a woman.' The other men around him sighed and agreed.

All other men shared the resentment in the queue as they watched Shreya, Karthi and Kalki walk past them. 'And they say we men suppress women. Look at how privileged they are. Getting called first at everything. Their own compartments in the train and when something goes wrong, ladies and children are the first to be rescued. What? Are we men supposed to perish when the building burns down?'

'If they saved men first, who will you sleep with at night? With men?' Shreya said through the translucent scarf she had fashioned out of the sari.

The men giggled. The complaining man looked away, rubbing the back of his neck.

Men yelled for their wives and sisters who were waiting under the shade of the tree. They waved at them vigorously. Economics and banking were taught rapidly to blinking housewives. They folded some concepts into their fingers. The index finger held information on interest rates. The middle finger, maturity. The ring finger, dividends. The little finger? It slipped their mind.

As they passed through the gates, Karthi was surprised to see the number of women inside. The queues outside comprised mainly men. For a moment, Karthi wondered if all the men had taken a leaf out of Shreya's book and worn a saree to pass off as a woman. Even if they did, they were all pretending. Shreyas wasn't.

An old, abandoned school building had been converted into the head office for the Shakthi Investments. More rooms meant more people to let in and sign up for the investment scheme. Inspirational songs of *Talaivar* played through the building. The smell of pencil shavings and chalkboard dust lingered in the rooms like stubborn memories. Karthi could feel his mother's savings moving somewhere inside the building. In the brisk footsteps of the peons. In the fluttering of the paper as it was stamped. In the water-heavy mop as it created wet swirls on the floor. In the door knocks. In the fatigued fans. And in the forgotten cobwebs in the corners of the ceilings.

The women hurried inside to find a seat. The grating sound of steel chairs were heard all around. A security guard warned them to behave, or they would be asked to leave. Did they think that the chair was their own property to be manhandled?

As the security guards and the restless women quarrelled, Karthi, Kalki, and Shreya sneaked past and into the corridor.

'Do you remember what the man looked like?' Shreya asked. 'The man who ran away with the money. Do you know what he looked like?'

Karthi spotted few men in black pants and white shirts, wearing the same black tie with blue swirls.

'They all look the same,' Kalki said.

'I can't remember his face,' Karthi said.

'That's alright,' Shreya said. 'He must be here somewhere. Let's just knock on every door till we find that fool.'

They went from room to room. They peered into every classroom, knocking on doors, and checking the inhabitants. Murmurs of remnant morning greetings from past students fluttered past their ears as the doors swung open. Men behind desks gave them a what-do-you-want look. Nothing, sorry, their shaking heads said, as they opened another door.

A high laugh came from a room in the distance. Karthi knew that laughter. The image of the Surya's long fingernail as he dragged their first income of five rupees towards him flashed before him.

'That's him,' Karthi said. 'His name is Surya.' He recollected the gold nameplate on the desk.

'Are you sure?'

'Yes, he has a weird laugh,' Kalki confirmed. 'He had the same laugh when we gave him all the money.' Kalki pitied the person in the room with Surya, whose money was about to be snatched away at any moment.

'Look what we have here. Didn't I tell you that today is a lucky day? Even Goddess Kali has come down to convince you to sign up for this exciting offer,' Surya said as soon as he spotted Kalki.

'But Kali Amma is not a good sign. It is like a warning,' an unconvinced woman who sat across the table from Surya said. She clutched her purse tighter.

'It depends on the perspective. Sometimes she is bad. Sometimes she is good,' Surya said, trying to smile sweetly, but only managing to give a sheepish grin. 'Just a minute, madame. Please take a look at this.' He handed a brochure stating the benefits of the investment to the woman. He marched to the door and almost slammed it on Shreya, Karthi and Kalki.

'Nobody hired a circus troupe for today. What the hell are you doing here? who are you, people?' Surya scowled.

'Don't you recognise us?' Kalki asked.

'You had come to our village,' Karthi said. 'You had an office there.' Karthi looked for the long nail of his index finger just to make sure if the man was Surya, but it was stuck inside his ear.

The man wrinkled his forehead. 'I don't know. Stop bothering us. Shall I call security?' He made a ball of his earwax and flung it at the wall. Missiles of gunky wax made a constellation. A spider in the ceiling scampered out of the way.

'How about now?' Kalki lifted her crown and let her hair down. She undid the straps holding the arms of Kali and let it fall. She tied her hair into a bun and tapped on her skin. 'Do you remember this?'

'Now I remember. You are the darkest person I had ever seen,' Surya said.

'It doesn't matter. You can be purple or yellow for all I care as long as you are giving me money,' Karthi and Kalki said in unison, recollecting Surya's words from that day.

'How did you …when did you…?' Questions sputtered out of Surya's mouth.

Before Surya could gather his thoughts, Shreya lunged at him, grabbed his neck, and pulled him out into the corridor. She could feel the sharp edge of Surya's Adam's apple wriggle in her grasp.

'Let go,' Surya cried.

'Listen, you bastard,' Shreya said, bringing her saree-covered face next to his. 'You tell them where their money is. Otherwise, the thing which is moving up and down inside your throat will be out on the floor.' Shreya squeezed a little harder.

Surya clawed at his neck. 'Let meeee gooooooo,' His voice struggled to come out.

'The next sentence that should come out of your mouth is you telling us where we can find their money,' Shreya said, letting Surya go. He fell like crumpled fabric.

'Your mother sure is strong. Like a man,' Surya said as he coughed and cleared his throat.

'Maybe I am a man,' Shreyas said, revealing himself.

Surya again choked though this time there was no hand at his throat. 'You are …you are...Ombothu!' He laughed his high laugh, which resonated throughout the corridor. Inquisitive necks craned.

Shreyas entered his office and began to admonish the

woman sitting inside. 'You better take your money and get out of here... these people are all frauds.'

'Yes, Akka,' Karthi said to the woman. 'This man took our money and…mmmhmmmmm.' Surya's hands clapped on Karthi's mouth and he pulled them outside. 'What are you doing? Are you trying to kill me?'

'We were just telling the truth,' Kalki proclaimed.

'Where is their money? Tell us quickly,' Shreyas demanded.

Surya knew he had to do something. Curious faces in the corridor were already showing apprehension. He could almost sense the woman inside his office doubting the wisdom of investing with him.

'I will show you where the money is but, please calm down,' Surya said. 'I will be right back.'

Shreyas could hear Surya calming the woman inside. 'They are my family. My wife and children. They are angry with me because I didn't fix the television as I said, and now my wife missed an episode of her favourite TV serial.'

The woman relaxed, loosened her grip on her purse and giggled. She even offered to fill in the story of whatever episode his wife had missed.

'No need, madam. All I am asking is for you to relax and read our booklet, and I will back in a minute, after I sort my family out.'

The woman nodded, her mind going back to events in yesterday's TV serial.

Karthi, Kalki, and Shreyas followed Surya who led

them down the long corridor. They went down the stairs at the end of the corridor to a pair of grilled doors.

'Your money is downstairs. Everyone's money is downstairs,' Surya said.

'So, you were not lying. The money is in the ground and is growing,' Kalki said happily.

'Growing or not growing. I am not sure,' Surya shrugged. 'But that is where the president of our company's office is. He is always there. Downstairs. Praying. The money is sealed inside a big safe as big as a room.'

'Are you playing with us?' Shreyas said with a quizzical look. 'This is a trap.'

Surya sighed and admitted that he felt guilty about fooling people, but he had no choice. 'I have two kids like you two. I will do anything for them. I was so poor once that we had to share one meal between the four of us and our boss came to us like a god. He gave me a job and saved us from starvation.'

Shreyas didn't know whether to believe him or not. But there was sincerity in his eyes.

'If this is some kind of joke, I will find you and your family like how we found you today and curse you. If we curse, your children, your children's children will be cursed, and I don't think you want that,' Shreyas warned.

Surya joined his palms together and bowed down to them. 'I know. I know. I am not playing with you.' He walked backwards, maintaining his genuflecting pose. 'Wait a minute,' he said, calling out to them. 'He is an extremely religious person.'

'What do you mean?' Shreyas asked.

'She can help,' he said, pointing at Kalki.

'Me?' Kalki said in surprise.

'Not you exactly. But your outfit. The boss is terrified of Kali,' he said before disappearing up the stairs.

It felt like the earth was swallowing them as the elevator carried them further down. Only a lone yellow light kept them company. The bladeless fan in the corner stared at them ominously. Even though it was one level down, they could feel the air pressure increasing. Kalki opened her mouth to suck in some air. The elevator grumbled to a halt. Three pairs of feet jumped. They pushed the grille door sideways and opened it.

They entered a narrow corridor. At the end of it was a green door with a rectangular glass panel. The glass shimmered with an orange glow that moved around. They walked towards it, holding on to each other.

'I am scared,' Kalki said.

'Don't worry, I am here,' Shreya said, bringing them closer to her.

They could feel life above them. Muffled footsteps were heard like squirrels in a tree, moving eagerly to give away their hard-earned money. A bus honked in the distance. A car's tire burst.

As they neared the door, delicate wisps of perfume danced out from the bottom. Fire? No, it was the treacly smell of incense and sandalwood. Then they heard the sound of bells. A man's voice was chanting and praying.

Shreyas pressed her face against the glass panel.

It was grey and smoky inside, with speckles of orange light caught in the haze. As the haze moved, it parted just enough for Shreyas to catch a glimpse of the man praying. It was Shakthivelu. President and founder of Shakthi Investments. They had reached the belly of the beast. The nucleus. The foundation stone. It looked like the boiler room of a massive passenger ship. Instead of coal and fire, prayers and swirling incense powered the entire vessel. The H.M.S Shakthi Investments.

Rows of portraits of garlanded gods and goddess adorned the wall in front of him. There was a small golden shrine with a statue of Goddess Lakshmi, the goddess of wealth. Seated on her lotus petal throne, she held an upturned pot of pouring gold coins. She looked at Shakthivelu with an eternal smile.

'What do you see?' Karthi whispered.

'I see him. The man on the business card. But I can't see the safe anywhere.'

'How are we going to take our money back if he is sitting inside?' Karthi asked.

Shreyas looked at the praying silhouette inside, then at Karthi. Then he looked at Kalki and then again at Shakthivelu. He looked at Kalki in her Kali costume and remembered what Surya had said about Shakthivelu's fear of Kali. 'I have an idea. Kalki, I think the thing you despise the most might save us all.'

Shakthivelu's future was to be a manual scavenger like his father. Like genes, one inherits the job of the family and ancestors, preordained by the rigid caste system. His father did not want his son to follow in his squelchy and unsanitary footsteps, however. From the day his son was born, he began to save money. He dipped himself into more sewers before the crack of dawn to clear yesterday's blockage. The following morning's call of nature flowing from every household stream like a smooth brown river out of town. It didn't bubble back into the households. Extremely satisfied with the sewage system, the people were happy to give him a rupee extra per household. They would place the coin outside their gates for him to collect. No touching was allowed. He added cleaning septic tanks to his occupation, bolstering his income by another rupee per week per household.

'By the time he is ready for school, I will have saved up enough money to pay for the admission fee. After all, everyone needs to shit.'

His father saved up enough for his son to be educated and more. When Shakthivelu turned five, he was sent to the neighbouring town to study. His father hoped that he would be the one to break the accursed caste system cycle. No one would know what caste his son belonged to in the new town. He could be whoever he wanted to be and not be constricted by the social laws.

The first few days of school were fine. The teachers and students didn't know any better. Shakthivelu looked like he belonged to the upper castes with his well-oiled hair that stuck to his head like a thick layer of black paint. Well-ironed uniforms and a nose held up high, he fit in well. 'Tilt your head back slightly and let your eyes fall.

That's how those brahmins look at us,' his father told him.

Nobody noticed that Shakthivelu reeked of sewage because, luckily for him, a dirty river ran next to the school. Its cleaning was constantly delayed by finger-pointing local politicians. The smell of the river masked the stench of his father's job. Years passed, and one fine day the river was clean. Ducks flocked to it to breed and fishes splashed. That was when Shakthivelu's truth was revealed.

It started with the teacher wrinkling his nose. Then the students pinched their noses tightly. 'What's that horrible smell? It can't be the river. It is all clean now.'

They closed the windows. But the smell lingered. Like hungry jackals, they lassoed the stench in the air with the nostrils and followed it. Their olfactory expedition led them straight to Shakthivelu. Watching the upper-class students walk towards him, he quickly rearranged his pose and held his nose in the air to blend in with them.

'It's him. It is him. He is the stinky one,' they cried. One Brahmin boy with a head full of thick, shiny black hair went closer to Shakthivelu and sniffed him. The smell of raw sewage hit his nostrils, making him throw up his mother's ghee dosa all over the classroom floor.

'Filthy untouchable! How dare you come to our side of town,' the teacher scolded him.

Shakthivelu lifted his arms to his nose. It smelled like his father. The chink in the armour of his father's plan escaped like a suppressed fart. The constructed scents of being Brahmin could only contain the smell of a lower caste for so long. Eventually, he was sent back to his town and warned not to return. Later that day, the whole classroom was cleaned thoroughly, and the children's uniforms were burnt to rid of any flakes of lower-caste cells on their upper-caste bodies.

On his way back to his town, Shakthivelu learned an invaluable lesson. The realisation that he was an untouchable was all over him, like a blanket. His father chided himself for not realising that the smell that his occupation had fused with the pores of his body. How could he be so stupid? The smell stubbornly clung onto his skin even after he scrubbed himself till it turned red.

When his father went to work the next day, the thought of his son being forced to join him weighed him down. Maybe choosing another school in another town would work? But this time he would make sure his son was washed twice daily with Lifebuoy soap. As he calculated the amount of money he would need to spend on the soap, he didn't feel the noose around his waist unfastening. It was soon going to be dawn. He was already running late. Soon, he heard an advancing rumble in the dark void of the sewer. It was too late. The sewer flooded with the runny sewage because of food poisoning from last night's wedding. As he drowned in the human waste, numbers swamped his mind. He had finally worked out how much he needed to spend monthly on antibacterial, rose-smelling soap to keep the sewer stench off his son.

They had to wait till midnight to take out his body. He lay there rotting for 18 hours. They cremated him when the upper castes were deep in sleep and couldn't smell the nasty fumes from an untouchable's body being burnt. All the untouchables of the town attended the funeral. Mourners with dirt in their fingernails, shit on their sleeve and dust coating their hair.

Shakthivelu watched his father's body burn aided by cow dung. The fire spread outward as though it was indoctrinated with the caste system, and it didn't want to touch him. Fumes billowed, making massive black and grey shapes in the air. His mother wailed and moved around like a wet housefly.

Then something peculiar happened. Shakthivelu saw a face appear among the fumes. It was the face of Lakshmi, the goddess of wealth, with coins of dancing gold light around her. He rubbed his eyes, but she was still hovering above his father's burning body. Nobody seemed to notice because they were either busy crying or looking sad.

Shakthivelu knelt down in front of the illusion. 'Oh, Goddess Lakshmi. Why have you taken my father away from me?' he cried. The mourning crowd stopped weeping and watched Shakthivelu converse with the smoke. Had he lost his mind? Or was this a divine moment? Maybe a bit of both. But the appearance of a goddess before an untouchable swayed them to the latter.

'My dear child, do not be heartbroken,' the goddess spoke to Shakthivelu. 'You will be coming into money soon.'

'Money? What money?' he said.

'I grant you the gift of multiplying wealth. Your hands will have the magic touch.'

'My hands can multiply money?' Shakthivelu said, looking at his dirty hands.

'Use it wisely,' the goddess said before disappearing behind the flames.

The gathering uttered a collective gasp. 'Look, everyone! This is our day of reckoning. The mighty Goddess Lakshmi gives an untouchable a gift. Our lives will be changed forever. He can make us all rich.' With that, the gathered people were gripped in hope as Shakthivelu's father was reduced to cinders. They tumbled at his feet like falling autumn leaves.

The brief dialogue with Goddess Lakshmi was a result of something that can be explained by science. Carbon monoxide from the cremation tickled his occipital lobe. It wasn't a divine intervention or kismet. The dancing coins around the head was simply the reflection of the dull streetlight in the smoke.

The very next day, all the untouchables lined outside Shakthivelu's house with their meagre savings. First, he tried to the divine way. He held his hand around the money, muttered a prayer with closed eyes, and expected a miracle. Nothing happened. An idea wandered into his head when he saw all the crumpled, soiled money piled in front of him. Since the untouchables couldn't open a bank account, he could become their bank. And that's how it all began. Shakthivelu Investments.

By applying the same principles and conditions of a

banking system, albeit smaller, he meted small interest on the deposits made by people for a nominal fee. This way, Guru received a portion of Bala's daughter's wedding money which could be deposited at the bank of Shakthivelu for longer than Guru's deposit for buying a new slipper for his calloused feet.

Word got out. It didn't matter he was an untouchable. Once money is involved, discrimination becomes a dirty mistress that everyone denies sleeping with. The notion that he was once an untouchable was dismissed as an unfortunate mistake on the part of the gods.

Untouchables became desirables. Shakthivelu's carefully crafted pyramid scheme grew. More and more people from all around the town, the neighbouring town, the haughty city decanted their money into the scheme.

Shakthivelu, in the process, became a deeply religious man. No more an untouchable, he had access to all the gods and goddesses in the pantheon. He never had any divine misfortune, which he took as a sign that he was doing the right thing. But a worry plagued his mind. Like a drop of blood polluting a tank, it spread. He was scared that the fetor of his father's job remained in his skin cells. To combat that fear, he always surrounded himself in a dense fog of sweet incense. For the sole purpose of dousing him in incense smell, two men were hired as he moved around carrying out his business.

He believed that his next divine visitation would be another encounter with Goddess Lakshmi to bestow him with more power. Goddess Kali was the last deity he expected to emerge through the door. The smoke from the incense escaped out of the room. Kali stepped in. Almost seven-foot tall. Her shiny obsidian skin, the terrifying eyes, and the ruby red tongue sent him into a frenzied prostration as though he was begging the ground to swallow him whole.

Kalki sitting on Shreya's shoulders. The red saree concealed Shreyas.

'You have strayed from your path,' Kali spoke in the high voice of Shreyas. 'I have come with the whole rage of the universe and the bursting anger of the sun.'

'I am sorry! I am sorry! Please forgive me!' Shakthivelu said as his body shivered as though the temperature had plummeted to below zero.

'Sorry is not enough. What has done has to be undone. What was woven must be unwoven. What was built must be destroyed. So, I am here. As the destroyer of all evil. The price is your life.' Kali stuck out her tongue and bared her teeth, miming Shreyas' words. Karthi, as a puppeteer, shook the papier-mâché arms of Kali to instil terror. The arm which had the cardboard scimitar wrapped in red foil swooshed towards Shakthivelu.

'No! No! No! Please, Kali Amma, please forgive me. I will do anything. Anything,' Shakthivelu begged.

'In exchange for your life, I need you to give back all the money you have taken from the people.'

'I will do it today,' Shakthivelu said. 'I promise I will go to the bank and retrieve all the money.'

'So, there is no money here? Behind that safe?' Shreyas

spoke in his normal voice letting his character slip.

A bewildered Shakthivelu was about to lift his head at the discrepancy in the voice.

'Bow down to me, fool,' Shreyas set off a series of spread-finger claps that left Shakthivelu gasping like a fish. 'I am going to give you an ultimatum. By the end of this month, you are to return all that you have taken from the innocent. If I hear from one among my faithful complaining about you, I will come swiftly like an earthquake and swallow you whole like the voracious sea,' Kali sent off an evil laugh that bounced around the hallway in a frenzy.

With that, Kali evanesced as the swirls of white smoke engulfed her. Shakthivelu crouched like a foetus. He waited for a while before he lifted himself from the ground. His head spun, and he lost his balance, crashing into the wall of portraits. The frame containing Kali looked down at him. She grimaced at him one more time. Shakthivelu felt something warm pooling near his thighs.

Chapter 15

Sounds of voracious crunching, chutney slurping, and half-full mouths sputtering emanated from around the pani puri stall.

'Give me fast. I have to be somewhere,' a customer demanded.

In his undersized shirt and pants, the North Indian operating the stall asked him to be patient in broken, highly accented Tamil interspersed with silky Hindi.

'Bastard! Useless fellow. Coming to my state and telling me how to act in my land,' the man said in Tamil, looking at the others gathered around for support. Subtle nods were seen among the customers.

The *pani puri* seller only understood the word bastard because it had a sting to it.

'He is doing the best he can with two hands. If you can't wait, why did you order in the first place?' Shreyas snapped. The seller could sense that Shreyas was defending him even though he couldn't understand him. He nodded his thanks.

'Look at what we have here,' the customer said. 'Another one who doesn't know where he belongs is giving me advice. What has happened to this world? It is because of people like you who can't stay in their place,' he looked at the *pani puri* seller. 'Or in their body,' he looked Shreyas. 'That is why the world is rotting from the inside.' He turned to Kalki and said, 'What about you, darkie? You have something to say?'

When the man called her darkie, she was surprised that a wave of humiliation didn't shroud her. There was prickly feeling like what tickles the body when one sees cockroaches scurrying by. She wondered if all the reverence she had received when she was dressed as Kali had something to do with it. She snatched the insult from his lips and passed it onto Kali. She imagined Kali destroying the spiteful word. Kali looked on with rage in her protruding eyes. Her scimitar dripping with blood danced with the abuses furiously till they were nothing more than shreds. Darkie screamed in intense pain as its body was sliced open. Blackie fainted before the sharp edge of the blade that ripped it apart. Cursed One shrivelled in terror as it was lacerated. The necklace of severed heads on her body ululated as the sliced pieces of insults fell to the ground as dust. The words tried to get back together, calling out to its broken parts to reform. Kali bellowed, and the heads on her necklace echoed her. In a final attempt to erase the insults, she stomped on them in uncontrollable blind fury with the force of millions stampeding bulls till they had no power to hurt Kalki anymore.

'Leave my sister alone,' Karthi growled at the man and stood in front of Kalki, stretching himself to his full height. He did it out of instinct. He noticed that there wasn't any pulsating pain in his head anymore. No worms of guilt burrowed through his mind. He felt like an ox that has freed itself of the heavy cart and the painful whipping by its master. The ox bolted away, enjoying its freedom.

'Little boys are threatening me now!' the man scoffed. He threw his empty plate and some crumpled money at the stall and left, grumbling about the state of affairs. The money danced their way down to the puddle on the ground.

Kalki picked up the soggy notes and handed them to the *pani puri* seller. He smiled at Kalki and gave her a plate of the crispiest *pani puri*. Dark green chutney jiggled in the crispy centre.

'*Ley lo, ley lo, beti, raat ka tukda* (Take it, take it, child, piece of night),' he said in Hindi. 'Money not necessary,' he added in Tamil.

'When will we get our money back?' Karthi asked Shreyas as he took a *pani puri* whole into his mouth and green chutney dribbled out.

'We have done everything we could,' Shreyas said. 'Maybe a week, maybe a month. If that guy is half as religious as he portrays himself to be, he will do the right thing. We just have to wait.'

'But we can't go home empty-handed,' Kalki said as she wiped her mouth. 'Amma will be very angry with us.'

'Trust me, your mother will be more worried about you two than the money.'

'Maybe you should come with us,' Karthi suggested.

'Yes, yes, you should come with us,' Kalki added with a smile. 'My mother makes the best chicken curry. She only makes it once a month. But I think we can ask her to make it specially for you. The chicken is a bit chewy, but it's the best.'

Shreyas smiled. 'I will come one day. Till then make sure you eat my share as well,' he said, flicking Kalki on the nose. 'Finish eating now. Your mother will be worried about you. But before you go, we still have one more thing to do.'

On the left side of the wall was painted various flowers with an empty circle in the middle. On the right was a tranquil forest next to a moonlit lake fed by a raging waterfall. A mural of a cityscape stretched horizontally in the centre. It had a disfigured Statue of Liberty. The Eiffel Tower stood next to two pyramids and a pawless sphinx. The Leaning Tower of Pisa threatened to crush a Taj Mahal. The Great Wall of China jostled with African wildlife.

Rows of photographs looked down at Kalki as she entered the room. Family portraits. Wedding pictures. Children's photographs. They all had one thing in common. Stoic faces with no smiles. They posed stiffly as though the flash from the camera robbed their very soul.

'Why are we here?' Kalki asked.

'You will see,' Shreyas said. 'Now go and stand there, in front of the camera. Remove your Kali costume.'

'Where should I stand?' asked Kalki.

'The flower wall is good, but it might be too much of a distraction since it is only you. You might be lost in the city mural. The dark forest is no good for your skin,' the photographer said in a small voice, as though he was being strangled. He was quite short.

'You stand wherever you like. Don't listen to him,' Shreyas said. He looked at the photographer and said, 'You fool, I didn't ask you to give specific comments. You are acting like you have photographed the queen.'

'Just because I am short doesn't mean you can talk to me that way. You are the one who gave me an impossible task. I will have to bring the sun to light up her face in the photograph.'

'She is just a little girl. I am sure you will find a way to do that,' Shreyas said. 'Instead of using just one light, use two or three. Do what you have to do.'

As Shreyas was lecturing the photographer, Karthi slipped out of the studio and went outside. Shreyas saw him leave and followed.

'What is the matter?' Shreya sat down next to Karthi who was sitting with his back to the wall and his legs pulled close to his chest.

'It is my fault that my sister is this way,' Karthi said, hiding his face in his knees. 'I am the reason her skin is so dark.' He explained what had happened when Kalki was a baby. 'I have never told this to anyone, including my mother.'

'Is that all?' Shreya said with a big sigh. 'First of all, there is no way you are responsible for that. There is no way something like that can happen.'

'How can you be so sure? She started to become dark only after I accidentally left her in the sun.'

'If the sun can do that so quickly, almost all of us will be the same colour as your sister. I used to play outside from dawn till dusk. Did I become dark?' Shreyas said, holding out his arms.

'What happened to your sister's skin was not your fault at all, dear boy.'

'I should have listened to my mother. I shouldn't have gone out to play... I shouldn't have....'

'If you think it is your fault, you are going to keep believing that there is a cure for her dark skin when there is none because it is not a disease or a problem to be solved. She was born this way.'

'I didn't think of it that way.'

'You better stop blaming yourself. Are you listening to me? These thoughts will eat you alive and make you crazy. Do you want that? Do you want your sister to keep thinking that she is worthless? There is nothing wrong with your sister. No, it wasn't your fault at all. Just stop it. Take in a deep breath and let it go.'

Karthi audibly sucked in air through his mouth, allowed it to build up inside him and forcibly exhaled.

With it, he let go of a large part of his shackling guilt. Some worms of guilt still remained, however.

The photographer stood on a stool to reach the camera. Hiding under a black hood, he gave directions to Kalki. It was as though the camera was alive and spoke with flashes. 'Look here, little girl. Straight at the camera. Not anywhere else. That's it. Hold it right there.'

Kalki sat on a high stool in front of a plain white wall. She looked at the camera as pieces of Kali's outfit watched her from the side. Her red and gold crown and her spectacular hands, like artefacts from a bloody war. Kalki tried to push her lips to the side as intermittent white flashes kissed her. She wanted to ask the white-hot flashes to take away her darkness, but Kali stepped in. With every flash, Kalki pictured Kali doing a sword dance and defeating the white flashes that dared to turn her into a pale white ghost. Kalki's lips finally spread in a wide smile, dimpling her cheeks. Black holes in the deep dark space. Comfortable in her skin, she smiled as Kali looked delighted with her victory. Her most cherished one.

The tickets were purchased. Two half-tickets. So, there was no chance of them getting kicked out of the train. Shreya went from compartment to compartment, asking everyone for their destination. Some thought she was begging and gave her loose change. Shreyas took the coins and blessed them.

In the last compartment, she found a young woman in her twenties peering, with forlorn eyes, through the window at the chaos on the platform as the train whistled its imminent departure. Shreyas sensed that the woman was running away from home. The train puffed and hissed steam that brushed against the hair that covered her face. A fresh white bandage briefly showed itself. It was covered with red dots.

As they entered the cabin, the woman looked at them.

'Is something wrong?' she asked. Shreyas took a chance and explained their situation to her.

'Leave them with me,' the woman said. 'My destination is after their village. I will see to it that they get off at the right station.' She patted the seat beside her. 'Come, sit here, kids.'

'Promise me you will come to visit us,' Karthi said through the window.

'I will. What is your address?' Shreyas asked.

'Well… When you get off the train, keep going straight. Then you will find a teashop. From there, take a right and go straight till you see a big house with many mango trees. Those mangoes are the juiciest you will ever taste. From there, take a left and keep going straight,' Karthi stopped, trying the remember the directions.

'Just ask for the house where the dark girl lives,' Kalki interrupted. 'Everybody knows me.'

'You are more famous than *Talaivar* in your village,' Shreyas said. Kalki giggled. 'Give me your hand.'

Kalki stuck out her arm through the gap between the window bars. The part of her arm outside the window felt hot and sticky. The half inside the train felt cold and dry. Shreyas took out one of her ribbons from her bag and tied it around Kalki's arm. A lovely yellow ribbon.

'What is this for? To show how dark I am?' Kalki said with a smile.

'No, it is to show you how your skin lights up all the other colours. Without darkness, there is no light.'

The train's whistling ripped across the station.

'See, even the train agrees,' Shreyas said.

Kalki smiled. A tranquil smile creased Karthi's face.

'And this is for you,' Shreyas said, handing Karthi a yellow envelope. 'Promise me you will only open this when you reach home.'

'What is this?'

'The answer to your guilt.'

The train jolted and hissed. People scattered like bees when a hive is poked. Some got on the train. Some jumped out. Shreyas held onto one of the bars. Karthi and Kalki clasped his hand. They could feel his heartbeat through his knuckles. He could feel their heartbeat against his fingers.

The train began to move. Shreyas walked along with it. First a saunter, then a brisk walk. Then a jog. The train jerked. Shreyas stumbled but held on tightly to the window bars and their arms. He negotiated stranded baggage and even a chicken coop. The hen clucked loudly, announcing Shreyas as the lone winner. The chassis of the train vibrated, trying to dislodge him.

'Take care of them,' Shreyas called out, a big lump choking his throat.

The woman with the scar nodded and asked him

not to worry. Karthi and Kalki intensified their grip on Shreyas.

'Goodbye, Shreya,' said Kalki.

'Goodbye, Shreyas,' said Karthi.

Shreyas' eyes met the children's wet eyes one last time. The quickening pace of the train ruptured the silent goodbyes. In an instant, his hands were empty, but he could feel their little fingers' phantom clutch. All he could see was their hands waving frantically as the train carried them away from him. The yellow ribbon tried to ride the train wind and go back to its owner. A pair of hands grabbed it before it could fly away. A dark hand. A piece of Shreya went with them. Shreyas stood on the station till the train disappeared down the narrowing rail tracks into the horizon.

The pavements glittered with the fallen sequins. Pieces of decorative garland foils moved in the wind on the pavement as Shreyas walked. Discarded floral garlands rotted on the side. Rigid condoms lay scattered like exoskeletons of insects. Broken mirrors, crumbled lipsticks and empty nail polish bottles were strewn on the path. Shreyas knew she was nearing the address that Brindha had given.

The mansion stuck out from the rest of the buildings in the area. Like a piece of history left to carry out its life sentence as modernity slowly encroached, choking its breath and dignity. New construction all around gorged on all the sunlight leaving only little puddles of sunshine to fall on the mansion. The residents hoped that in due time it would have to be demolished. But it remained like a dirty secret in every person's heart that they would carry to their grave.

Intricately designed balconies jutted out of the mansion like neatly stacked almirahs. Inside them, pensive Aravanis observed the hoi polloi that walked by. From a distance, it looked like little shrines with animate gods and goddesses. A massive red double-door guarded the mansion. A smaller door withing the larger gate opened and out of it came to a group of bickering Aravanis, their talk flush with invectives. As soon as they saw Shreyas, they arrested their venom as though someone had turned them off. They made way and urged him to go inside. Don't be afraid, you are home, they said. As soon as he set his foot inside, he could hear scintillating banter and twinkling sights – nose rings and earrings. He felt welcome. He had never felt this way before. As though the whole world had adjusted to accommodate the homeless inhabitant.

A large Aravani was lying on a bamboo cot, fanning herself and romancing the ceiling. A black cat was curled below the cot, being caressed by the sagging weight of the Aravani as she rocked her body to a tuneless song. As soon as she spotted Shreyas, she hoisted herself up from the cot. The cat sprang up too. With her saree *pallu* falling and her hands extended, she hurried towards Shreyas. She sported a wide grin and hugged Shreyas, welcoming him. Her calloused palms straightened Shreyas' unruly hair and wiped sweat and grime from his face. She introduced herself as Khushboo and said that she was mother to everyone here. The black cat weaved around Shreyas' legs in an infinity pattern.

'If you stand here any longer, Shivaji will make you his pet. Let's got inside,' Khushboo said in a voice that grated like an old unused autorickshaw horn.

Inside, the mansion was teeming with life. Four floors opened into a large open courtyard in the centre. Life paused for a moment as people stopped to check out the new arrival. Then it went on uninterrupted. Eyebrows were threaded. Lips became redder. Sarees flew around like ideas that never came to pass.

As Khushboo explained the inner workings and architecture of the mansion and where everything was, Shreyas' attention was on the shifty-eyed men loitering in the corner. They pointed at the Aravanis and giggled and made lewd gestures. An Aravani interrupted them and one of the men walked along with her, his hands on her shoulders, fondling whatever his fingers could grab. They both disappeared into a room. The latching of the door reverberated through the courtyard and ascended into the skies. The remaining men burst into laughter. One of them looked familiar to Shreyas with this kidney-shaped mark near his mouth. It danced as he laughed. A splintering pain travelled through the centre of his body, reminding him of the day he lost his sister's money and his place in his family.

'What are those men doing here?' Shreyas asked.

Khushboo chortled. 'You have just arrived, my

darling, and you want to play with fire? You want to leap before you learn how to fly?'

'That man with a birthmark near his lips. Does he come here often?'

Khushboo looked surprised. But it only took a moment's study of his face to realise that Shreyas had a reason for his questions. Anger stretched over his face like suffocating cellophane. His eyes flashed red. A lone tear bubbled from his eye and fell down his cheek before getting lost in his stubble.

'I am not going to ask you what he did to you,' Khushboo said, wiping the tear away. 'You have unfinished business with him. I can see that. Come on now. We need to get you dressed.'

Shreya entered the room, the ends of her saree covering her face. The room was stuffy and smelt of manufactured fantasies. The man who had forever changed his life and destroyed his sister's future sat on the bed with his legs crossed. He wagged his tongue like a tired dog and barked like one too.

'You don't want to reveal your face?' he said with a toothy grin.

Shreya shook his head. Her saree almost slipped off her head. Shreya spotted another saree on the ground, ripped off several long pieces from it, and threw the rest on the bed.

The ripping sound of the saree excited the man and he was down on all fours. 'You want me to cover my eyes too?' he asked.

Shreya nodded.

'I like this game,' the man said, tying the fabric around his eyes several times. 'I can't see anything, but I will catch you.' His hands flailed towards Shreya.

Shreya pushed him onto the bed and quickly tied his hands and feet to the bedposts. The man moaned in excitement and asked her to make the knots tighter. The kidney-shaped birthmark shook with lust. Finally, Shreya removed the fabric from his eyes.

'Oh! Am I allowed to look at you now?' he asked as he watched Shreya go around the bed, pull up a chair and stare at him. Minutes passed. The man wrestled with the knots, trying to untangle himself. He screamed for help, but no one came. 'I am not paying you good money to sit like a statue, you whore. Do something.'

'I should have done something that day, in the back alley when you followed me and stole all the money,' Shreya said.

'What the hell are you talking about, whore?' he barked. 'What money? What alley?'

Shreya took off her face covering and started to wipe off her makeup. 'Do you remember this face? This face. This face. This face. You son of a bitch!'

'"Oh, it's you. Shreyas!' the man said. His mouth fell open.

'How do you know my name?' Shreyas asked.

The man shrugged.

'Tell me,' Shreyas shouted. 'You destroyed my whole life. My parents kicked me out because of you. My sister's life is ruined, and if you don't answer me now,' he said, grabbing a steel rod from the corner. He started to swing it towards him. 'If you don't speak, I will end your life too.'

'Please, don't. I will tell everything,' the man said as he wriggled in the bed. 'It was all your sister's idea. She planned this.'

Shreyas stopped just as he was about to strike him in the crotch. 'What?'

'Yes, your sister wanted to get rid of you. I am the man she fell in love with. We were supposed to be married.' He narrated the plot in detail. As he did, Shreyas crashed onto the floor and sobbed uncontrollably.

Shreyas sat on the bed with mascara running down his cheeks like black rivulets. 'Are you happy now? You ran like a coward after stealing our money. My poor sister. She would have been waiting for you. And you call yourself a man?'

'You are a good one to talk about being a man,' he said. Shreyas reached for the iron rod again.

'Not everything is lost,' the man said. 'I deposited the money in a chit fund account.'

'Shakti Investments?'

'Yes.'

Shreyas laughed till tears poured from his eyes. 'Now, let us just hope Kalki did a great job at scaring him into developing a conscience,' he said.

'Who is Kalki now?' the man asked.

'Someone on whom your life depends,' Shreyas said,

untying him.

Twelve hours later, the train carrying Karthi and Kalki arrived at their station. It overshot the station by half its length. Passengers alighted onto open fields. Karthi and Kalki had returned. Without their money. With her dark skin. Wearing the costume of Goddess Kali. And with no one chasing them.

The station felt like a wet cloth. They looked around for signs that they had been missed. That someone was looking for them. They wondered if posters with their pictures had been stuck on the notice board. Whether the police were notified. There were none. The notice board was replete with exaggerated triumphs of political parties. A lone policeman draped himself on the station bench with his mouth wide open, loud snores bouncing off him.

Kalki clutched Karthi and Kali tightly. A familiar dread crept back and Kalki could taste a metallic sting. The fear that Kali had helped remove threatened to return.

'Maybe you should wear that,' Karthi suggested fearing that his headaches would return now that they were back. 'At least till we get back home.'

Hand in hand, they walked the familiar streets of their village as they made their way home. They braced for someone to point at Kalki and ridicule her even though she was dressed as Kali. But no one did. No one shamed her. Some dipped their heads a little and asked for Kali's blessings. No one called her a darkie.

The town was quieter than usual. A palpable silence

filled the air, drenching everyone in collective sorrow. Karthi noticed that people were bothered by something. He could see it in the bent necks as they walked. In the arduous drag of their feet. In their sweeping hand gestures as they talked to themselves and the sky, to a lamp post, to someone more significant than themselves.

They went to the tea-stall and tried to get the attention of the tea-master. The tea-master's eye juggled between two jugs as he shot tea through them.

'Why is that man talking to himself?' Karthi asked, pointing at a man on the other side of the road, who seemed involved in intense debate with the air around him.

'He is just one of the many fools who have lost all their money to the chit fund company,' the tea-master said, pouring the tea into glasses. 'Why do you want to know about matters that don't concern you?' The tea-master peeked from his tea-stall. A hand flew to his open mouth. 'Where did you children come from? The whole village thought you were dead. Hit by a train or something.'

'We are not dead. The train stole us,' Kalki said.

"Oh, it is you. The dark one," he said. Kalki didn't sense any malice in his words. He was merely describing her. 'You left this town as a little girl, and now you have come back as Kali. Hurry to your mother now. She hasn't eaten since the day you two went missing.'

As they approached their mud house, gasps erupted from the people like unused firecrackers relit by their presence. Sibilant murmurs went around like snakes twisting and making their way through a dense jungle.

'I thought they were dead!'

'Look at the girl. She has come back reincarnated as Kali.'

A boy wanted to call her blackie. His father slapped him on the head and said, 'You don't say such things to a goddess.'

'She looks exactly like Kali. Why didn't we know this before? Maybe I deserved to lose all my money for making fun of her.'

'Yashoda! Yashoda! Your children have come back,' someone shouted.

Yashoda thought she was dreaming and hearing what she wanted to hear. She continued to sit against the wall in the dark corner of the crumbling mud house. Her eyes stung because there wasn't any moisture left in them. She wiped her nose. Her stomach growled and contracted in pain as she thought of her children, lost, hungry and possibly dead. Grief began to sting her again. She sobbed without tears.

'Yashoda! Your children are here!' The voice called out again.

This time she knew she didn't hear things. She looked up and in the doorway two silhouettes advanced, a boy and a short figure with four arms and a big head.

'KARTHI! KALKI!' she screamed and lunged towards the doorway. She didn't need to see them. She could smell her blood. Her dry eyes were awash with tears like an overflowing dam. She let her river of tears run unchecked. Karthi and Kalki fell on their mother's shoulder like sunlight on breezy trees.

'Do you have a white receipt?'

'Without that, you won't be able to get back your money!'

'What made him change his mind?'

'Bastard. He thought he could easily fool us all and swindle us out of her hard-earned money. Hope he rots in hell!'

'We should perform a special puja to Goddess Kali because she woke his conscience.'

'I will fast for a week.'

'I will build a temple in her honour.'

'Do you think that any of this has got to do with the dark child who returned as Kali?'

'It has everything to do with it. That child wasn't cursed. Kali blessed her.'

'They weren't lost. They were taken to heaven by Kali, and they asked for her help because they had lost their mother's money to that fraud.'

'Maybe it was to teach us a lesson too for mocking her dark skin. We as adults should have known better.'

A week had passed. Kalki was yet to hear anyone address her by anything other than her real name. Sometimes they called her Kali Amma and asked for her blessing. The rumour that she was somehow connected to Shakthivelu's sudden change of heart helped immensely. No one stared at her. No one wrinkled their noses at her. Nobody tried to move away from her. To be an extraordinarily ordinary person among the villagers felt like a rebirth to Kalki. She wasn't Kalki the accursed. She was Kalki the blessed.

'It was your kind who tried to cheat us all,' Lakshmi scowled at Yashoda when she returned to work with her children. 'This is why pigs should stay in a pen and tigers in the jungle. When you mix things up, the world will fall apart.'

Yashoda stood silently.

Lakshmi was seething with frustration. Her plan of stripping everything from her husband had hit a dead end when the money from the chit fund investment was returned. The enormity of her terrible wheelchair-ridden, infertile, powerless power over her husband weighed on her like a wrecking ball. Her wheelchair felt like quicksand swallowing her. Her frustration fuelled her abuse of Yashoda.

'From now on, I will follow you around the house. God knows what people will think of next. How do I know that you are not planning to steal my house? Or my husband?'

Yashoda wanted to say something but knew that would only aggravate her further. Yashoda had only a few more days left before Lakshmi promised to let her go as soon as her debt was repaid for her children destroying her mango saplings. She grabbed her children's hands and squeezed them. Karthi and Kalki knew what it meant: don't say anything.

'Why are you standing there like a log?' Lakshmi

shouted. 'Go, do something. Start with the kitchen. I will follow you.'

As they entered the house, she stopped Kalki and said, 'Just because every fool out there believes you are special doesn't mean I think you are special. You will still be the rotten, dirty, gorilla-faced, dark girl to me. Now go inside and sit in one corner.'

When she heard those words, Yashoda's nose flared and her hands clenched, but she quelled her rising anger. She worried that the children, especially Karthi, might say something. But they merely gave Lakshmi a smile, not too wide to affect derision and not too small to show resentment. Just a subtle smile that disarmed Lakshmi.

'Get out of my sight!' Lakshmi said, flapping the air.

'They are all rotten,' Kalki said, gently squeezing a mango. They found a basket of mangoes alongside an open container of waste waiting to be picked up by the garbage collector. Fruit flies swarmed around as Karthi rummaged for a not-so-rotten one.

'There must be at least one,' Karthi said. 'Aha!' He plucked out a half-squished mango. 'One half is still good. Take it.'

Kalki bit into the good side. It smelt of vegetable offcuts but tasted like summer.

'Is it good?' Karthi asked.

'Yes. Have some,' Kalki said, mango juice dribbling from the side of her mouth.

Karthi took a bite. It reminded him of the first time they tasted a mango. 'You know you still haven't looked at your photo. The one Shreyas anna had taken. Don't you want to take a look?' He took the envelope out of his pocket and handed it to Kalki.

Kalki felt the photo inside the envelope. A gentle breeze rushed through the envelope, and it fluttered. Open me, it seemed to say. All that she ever wanted to be was waiting inside. Her heart was beating so fast with fear and anxiety that it hurt. As she stared into the cover, she saw a face come into view. A pale featureless form stared back at her. Doubts assailed her like swinging sickles in a rice field. What if her fair skin wasn't all that she thought it to be? What if she liked the fair-skinned Kalki? What would happen then? Would she be constantly on the hunt for a way to turn her skin fair? What if there was no way to become fairer? What would happen then? Would she allow the fair-skinned Kalki to haunt her for the rest of her life like an unfulfilled ghost? What was worse? To put up with name-calling or be crushed by fictitious possibility?

'Go on, open it,' Karthi said.

Kalki opened the sleeve of the envelope but quickly closed it. Within seconds, she ripped the envelope and tore it into smaller pieces. She had her eyes closed in case she caught sight of her fair-skinned self smiling at her. Within seconds, the envelope with the photo inside was reduced to strips. She dumped them in the garbage.

'I don't want to see it,' Kalki said, taking in a satisfied breath.

Kalki took her brother's sticky hands. He was her

friend, her ally in every way. They walked towards their waiting mother on the sunlit road. She tilted her face towards the sky, towards the sun and basked in it. She wasn't scared of getting darker. I can't get any darker than I am now, she thought. She was happy to be with her brother and eating rotten mangoes. Happiness washed over her dark, gorilla-black, coal-coloured, dirty face.

Karthi couldn't help it. He needed to know. He turned his head and looked at the garbage bin. Most of the torn pieces were upturned and bare. He spotted a small fragment with the left side of his sister's face looking at him. Her skin was as pale as a dried paddy root. The wan skin sent jolts through his body that shook him. It didn't look like Kalki. The fair girl looking back at him wasn't his sister. It was as though he had seen a spectre. *Why would I need a ghost lookalike when my sister already looks like the great Goddess Kali?* His fault or not, a bottomless feeling uplifted him for the tiny part he had played in turning his sister into a goddess. Karthi could feel something dislodging itself from his mind. It slithered out and fell off his shoulders. Karthi's head felt light, the lightest it had ever been.

EPILOGUE

'You are telling me that he could change completely into a woman?' Yashoda asked, pressing her palms to cheeks.

'Not completely, but she could dress like one,' Karthi said.

'And you wouldn't even know if she was a man inside. She looked beautiful as a woman and handsome as a man,' Kalki said.

'I can't believe it. It looks like you just fainted along the way and dreamt it all up,' Yashoda said. 'There is no way a man could look beautiful as a woman.'

'I promise,' Kalki and Karthi said together, touching their throats and swearing to it.

Yashoda curled her lips.

'Who do you think gave me this yellow ribbon?' Kalki said, pulling Shreya's ribbon out.

'Alright. Alright, I believe you,' Yashoda said. 'I am just happy that the two of you are with me.'

They saw Hari and Pandi walking towards them. Hari walked with long strides, swinging his hands furiously. Pandi copied him.

'Where were you, darkie?' Hari asked. 'My skin was itching for days because I couldn't make fun of you.'

'Mine too,' Pandi said, scratching his arms.

'Perhaps you should see a doctor for your itching,' Kalki said.

Karthi laughed. Yashoda tried to stifle her laughter, but she failed.

'Don't laugh,' Hari said, stomping his feet. 'Otherwise, I am going to sing the *darkie* song.'

'Sing,' Kalki commanded.

Hari and Pandi began to clap and sing.

'Darkie, darkie only wants one thing
That is to be as fair as London's king
But she is dark as the night,
And when she smiles, we are affright.'

As they sang, Yashoda studied her daughter's face. It was brimming with confidence and resilience. Kalki looked into the eyes of her hecklers with a steady gaze and an unwavering smile. Yashoda's eyes welled up. She cursed herself for even thinking that there was something wrong with her daughter's skin. She was never broken. She was only cursed because society said so. She quickly dabbed her eyes before her children could see her crying.

Hari and Pandi stopped singing when they realised they were not getting the desired results.

'Maybe I should sing a song for you,' Kalki said.

'Try, darkie,' Hari said, standing with his arms crossed and his head tilted back.

'Yes, try, darkie,' Pandi echoed, copying Hari's pose.

'Two dirty rats wander around the town,
One thinks he is a hero, and the other is a clown
Picking on a girl and laughing at her skin,
We wonder if they are boys within
To mock a girl, they come in pairs,
To make up for something in them that is bare.'

Pandi burst out laughing.

'You idiot, she insulted you as well,' Hari said.

'Did she?' Pandi stopped to gather his thoughts. 'No, I am pretty sure it was all for you.'

'Why do you think she said we come in pairs?' Hari said.

Kalki walked away with her brother and mother as Hari and Pandi dissected her impromptu song.

'Yashoda! Chinna Kali!" The betel-leaf-chewing old lady yelled at them. Chinna meant little. 'A stranger came around enquiring about you. I don't know if it was he or she. God knows who it was. He talked like a man but looked like a woman. I pointed him towards your house.' Her distended earlobes supporting an earring in the form of a snake hood swung violently.

'SHREYAS!' Karthi and Kalki screamed and taking their mother's hand, they hurried home.

Panting and puffing, they reached their mud house. There was no one there.

'Where did he go?'

Karthi and Kalki scanned the area. They could smell the jasmine from Shreya's hair. They could also smell her lipstick and nail polish. Something caught Kalki's eye. A large slab was leaning against their hut. It hadn't been there before. Behind it was a dusty brown bag. Karthi and Kalki pulled the bag out. It made scratching noises against the wall.

'See, Amma, we told you Shreyas is real,' Karthi said.

'How do you know it was Shreyas? The old lady's eyes are weak. It could have been anybody.'

'Look!' Kalki said, pointing at the colourful ribbons that swirled around the bag and its handles. 'These belong to Shreyas.'

They unzipped the bag and peered into it. Four thick bundles featuring the face of Gandhi beamed a radiant smile at the holographic thread next to him. Karthi fished out of the bundles and ran his fingers through the cash. A gentle breeze hit Kalki's face. She remembered the wind her mother had mentioned a few weeks ago.

'Amma, I don't think you need to work hard to create the wind for me anymore. But what was the wind for?'

'You don't need that anymore, dear,' Yashoda smiled at her confident dark-skinned daughter.